Double Justice

*To my wife Lydia, whose immeasurable help and
encouragement turned the dream into reality*

Double Justice

Maurice Fluxman

ROBERT HALE · LONDON

© Maurice Fluxman 2006
First published in Great Britain 2006

ISBN-10: 0-7090-8095-6
ISBN-13: 978-0-7090-8095-4

Robert Hale Limited
Clerkenwell House
Clerkenwell Green
London EC1R 0HT

The right of Maurice Fluxman to be identified as
author of this work has been asserted by him
in accordance with the Copyright, Designs and
Patents Act 1988.

2 4 6 8 10 9 7 5 3 1

Typeset in 11/13½ pt Baskerville
by Derek Doyle & Associates, Shaw Heath
Printed in Great Britain by St Edmundsbury Press
Bury St Edmunds, Suffolk
Bound by Woolnough Bookbinding Limited

The truth is rarely pure – and never simple.

Oscar Wilde

Author's Note

My many years in legal practice in several countries have convinced me of the utter gullibility of human beings.

Because we lack the inherent capability of distinguishing fact from illusion, we are forced to rely on what we are told about the truth. Almost everything in our lives is influenced: our religious beliefs, our views of what is right and wrong, what we wear, what we eat and drink, whom we associate with, and, above all, how we comprehend the things we see and hear.

Given the right circumstances, people – even judges and juries – can be persuaded of anything.

As the following story illustrates.

Maurice Fluxman

PROLOGUE

There was nothing exceptional about my 'Greenwood experience' – as my wife Marion would later refer to it – until the arrival at the flat of a letter from the fourth-largest law firm in England.

By then, my affair with Marion's friend Lucy was over and I had the flat entirely to myself. As it was, I'd been spending far more time there on my own than with Lucy – not only on the days we met, but whenever I felt like escaping there. I enjoyed the solitude – and being the carefree Geoffrey Greenwood instead of Charles Brook, the unhappy husband and disgruntled lawyer.

At that stage, only a handful of people had heard of Geoffrey Greenwood. To my secretary and the accounts staff at the office, he was just a client who'd rented a flat. To Lucy, he was the South African chap who put his apartment at my disposal during his frequent and lengthy absences abroad. To Mr Clarke, the caretaker-porter at Beverley Terrace, he was the polite, quiet gentleman in flat thirty-four. And to Lawtons, the letting agents, he was one of their numerous tenants – an overseas businessman who had been vouched for by a reputable firm of Brighton solicitors.

To me, he was supposed to have been a name, nothing else, but in the event he had become my other, untroubled self.

What I didn't know then was that he was destined to become considerably more than just that.

1

I could hardly have taken a flat anywhere in or around Brighton in my own name and kept it quiet. Ours was only a three-partner firm, but we had a fair share of the better legal work on offer locally and I was pretty well known in the community. So was Lucy's husband, Dr Malcolm Cole, consultant physician at Royal Sussex County Hospital and the Sussex Nuffield.

When our affair had started, Lucy and I had made a pact: we were to have a brief, utterly discreet, purely physical relationship. Two marriages and the interests of three children were at stake. The first time we'd had sex, in a hotel room, she'd said, 'Sneaking in here was awful. We need our own place, Charles. A flat would be nice. Somewhere out of the way.'

'You're not suggesting we rent one together, are you?'

'No, that would be madness. You're a popular lawyer, with lots of clients. I'm sure you can sort something out.'

It suited me to do just that. I'd been toying with the idea of finding a small flat for myself for some time. Marion's great, ongoing sulk was doing more to me than driving me into bed with Lucy. The kids apart, there wasn't much for me at home these days, and the office was getting me down too – partly because of the ripple effect of my private life, but also because I felt generally stale and in need of change. It wasn't a midlife crisis – I was only thirty-five – but having my very own home away from home had a lot of appeal. I wasn't sure where my marriage was going or which way I wanted it to, and I could do with a retreat, a secret place of my own where I could sustain my morale while I waited for my wife and my life to sort themselves out.

Lucy didn't have to know the place was mine. Better she didn't, I decided.

Beverley Terrace had been a lucky find. It was a large Regency block standing in its own grounds on the eastern edge of Kemp Town. I'd driven by the property after visiting a client in Rottingdean and noticed a large sign on the main gate reading:

Property acquired by South East Properties plc for redevelopment. Small number of furnished refurbished flats offered on short lets pending commencement. Viewing by appointment through letting agents, Lawtons. A London phone number followed.

The location was ideal and the circumstances suited me because with a demolition in prospect there was likely to be less fuss over references. So I rang Lawtons, giving my name as Geoffrey Greenwood – one I'd thought up which seemed to have the right blend of authenticity and anonymity – and was put through to Eleanor Downing, the letting manager for the property. Doing my best to revert to the South African accent I'd lost many years earlier, I told her I wanted a flat in the Brighton area on a short tenancy, say six months to a year, and was interested in Beverley Terrace.

'You'd be guaranteed at least a year's undisturbed occupation, Mr Greenwood.' She sounded young and had a pleasant, friendly voice. 'The owners plan to put up a new block of shops and offices, but they're nowhere near ready to begin demolishing the present building.'

'A year will suit me fine, Eleanor. But meanwhile, is everything there – I mean services and so on?'

'Yes, it's all laid on. Water, gas, electric power – you pay for the last two of course. The flats on offer are all refurbished and newly furnished. They're being let because there has to be a nominal income flow from the property for certain reasons.'

I was tempted to ask if the reasons were tax-related, but didn't. 'I'm a non-resident, Eleanor. Does that disqualify me in any way? I come here on business trips and I want a break from hotels. I feel at home by the sea.'

'You live in South Africa, Mr Greenwood, don't you?'

'Is my accent so obvious?'

'Not really. You sound more English than South African – like a Brit who's lived out there. One of my school-friends was from South Africa – that's how I can tell.'

'I went to school in England. I live in South Africa now.'

'You're very lucky then, from what I've heard. And no, you don't have to be a UK resident.'

She gave me a viewing appointment for the next morning. 'Please see Mr Clarke at the desk in the lobby, Mr Greenwood. He's the caretaker and he doubles as a porter to the tenants. Then come back to me if you want to take it further.'

Mr Clarke was a grey-haired, shrivelled-up little man who said, 'Ah, the lovely Eleanor,' when I mentioned her, then showed me two of the flats as well as a private rear entrance to the block which gave tenants direct access to their apartments from an adjacent covered car-park by means of a separate lift. The flats weren't luxurious, but they were clean and adequately appointed.

I rang Eleanor again after getting back to the office, told her I liked flat thirty-four on the third floor, and asked her a few more questions. Again, she was helpful and friendly – enough so for me to get stupidly personal. 'Eleanor,' I heard myself saying, 'I hear you look as good as you sound.'

Instead of taking exception, she chuckled charmingly. 'Flattery won't help you get the tenancy, Mr Greenwood. Who have you been talking to?'

'No one in particular,' I lied. 'And the name's Geoffrey.'

Again the chuckle. 'Very well. Do you want the flat then, Geoffrey?'

'Yes, I think I do, Eleanor.'

It was all tied up within days. Alone in my office, I filled in and signed the application form and tenancy agreement as Geoffrey, using a hand-writing technique I'd learned about from the evidence of an expert witness in a trial I'd once handled. I gave Geoffrey the middle name 'Robert' and his date of birth as my late mother's in the year of my own birth. The next day, the signed documents were on their way to Lawtons together with the firm's cheque for the first six months' rent and the deposit, as well as a letter from the firm, signed by me, attesting to Geoffrey's personal and financial integrity.

He was now officially a client of Brook, Amery and Phillips, the neces-sary verification of his identity having been vouched for by my tick in the *Yes* box against the question in the firm's *New Client Particulars* form, 'Have the procedures for verification of the client's identity and address been complied with?' as well as the note I had left in his file recording that certi-fied copies of the supporting documents were in my personal custody. My position in the firm and the insignificant nature of Geoffrey's 'business' would ensure that neither statement was ever challenged.

'It sounds perfect,' said Lucy, when I told her about my friend Geoffrey, his flat, where it was, and the access arrangements. She'd have her own set of keys, I said, and a parking card, so she could use the covered car-park and come straight up to the flat, bypassing the lobby, and with it the opportunity of finding out that at Beverley Terrace I was known as Geoffrey Greenwood.

'But what about this Greenwood fellow?' she asked. 'Won't he or his wife or partner come barging in on us one day?'

'Not a chance, Lucy. There are only two sets of keys and I've got both. So he has to let me know in advance when he's coming.'

'Well then, what are we waiting for?'

That was in November. Five months later, on a wet March afternoon, Lucy delivered her ultimatum.

'It's crunch time,' she said, sitting up in the bed and looking at me through the blonde strands that fell over her face. She'd just made love to me more affectionately and erotically than ever before, and I'd found it all a bit overwhelming.

'Meaning?' I braced myself. I had an idea where this was going.

'I love you, my darling Charles. More than I ever meant to – much more. I'm hooked, but I can still tear myself away if I have to. What I can't do is go on like this.'

She paused, as if expecting me to say something, and when I didn't went on: 'What I want – more than anything in the world – is to make this permanent. I mean you leave Marion and I leave Malcolm. And we live together. That's what I want.' She looked to one side. 'Oh, I'm hating this,' she said to the wall. Then she turned towards me again, her grey-green eyes staring into mine as if searching. 'If that's not what *you* want – if you don't want to live with me properly, I mean – you must tell me now and this must stop, right away. So I can save my marriage, or what's left of it.'

Now there was a deafening silence. I *had* to speak.

'Lucy, I love you too.' Her face lit up, but fell with my next words: 'I love you as my lover, but I can't think of leaving Marion – not now, and maybe never.' The 'never' part wasn't true any more, but it was kinder than telling her what *was* true – that I'd been tiring of the affair; it had run its course and I certainly didn't want to make a life with her. 'I don't want this to end,' I lied, 'but. . . .'

She held up her hand and started crying, softly. 'That's it then. I'm going now, Charles.'

'I'm sorry, Lucy. You must be angry with me.'

'Emotionally, yes, I am. But I've got no right to be. We had an agreement and I've just broken it.'

Emitting a loud sob, she picked up her things, went into the bathroom to dress, emerged about three minutes later, and left without another word.

2

Three weeks to the day after Lucy's tearful departure, I found the letter in Geoffrey's mail.

The words, *Tolway Perry, Solicitors*, were printed on the back of the envelope, which was addressed to *Geoffrey R Greenwood* at *34 Beverley Terrace*. I opened it, intrigued to discover why such an eminent concern was according my Geoffrey the status of a real person. The letter read:

Dear Mr Greenwood

Your tenancy of Flat 34, Beverley Terrace.

We write on the instructions of our client, South East Properties plc, from whom you hire the above flat under a shorthold tenancy agreement.

Clause 24 of the agreement purports to grant you, the tenant, a two-year option to buy a 99-year lease of the flat from our client on certain terms. As you are well aware, it was never intended or agreed that you should be granted such an option. The clause was included in error, is of no force or effect, and is therefore being disregarded by our client.

For the sake of good order, we have prepared an addendum to the agreement deleting Clause 24. This document is enclosed in duplicate, and you are requested to sign and date both copies where indicated and to return them to us in the enclosed self-addressed envelope. We shall then let you have your copy back signed by our client.

As the enclosure indicates, it is only the purported option that is affected. The addendum has no effect on your tenancy as such.

Yours faithfully,

Tolway Perry

I hadn't given the contents of the tenancy agreement more than a glance when I signed it – why look for points on behalf of a tenant who didn't exist? – but now I got out the copy which I kept at the flat and read it through carefully. Yes, Clause 24 did, surprisingly, give the tenant a two-year option to buy the flat, and it was clearly out of context.

I read the letter again, then the addendum Tolway Perry wanted Geoffrey to sign. On the surface it all seemed reasonable and innocent: there'd been a mistake and South East Properties were merely trying to set the record straight. But were Tolway Perry right on the law? Did the mistake invalidate the option? I wasn't so sure.

And why should a high-powered corporate law firm like Tolway Perry have been engaged to deal with so minor a matter as an amendment to a residential tenancy? The letting agents could have handled it competently enough.

I re-read the option clause. It was as much part of the agreement as all the other clauses in the document, including those which obliged the tenant to do certain things and not to do others. And there'd been no negotiations at all about the terms of the tenancy. Tolway Perry were wrong on the law, and they probably knew it.

Then I remembered reading somewhere about a project to create a gigantic 'mini-city' between Kemp Town and Rottingdean. The developer was an international syndicate and the cost would be hundreds of millions. This seemed vastly bigger than the shops-and-offices project Eleanor had talked about. When I got to the office, I rang her.

'Eleanor Downing,' said her voice.

'Eleanor. Geoffrey Greenwood. Remember me?'

'Geoffrey? Of course I do. You took one of those flats.'

'Yes, I did.'

'Do you like it?'

'Yes, it's fine thanks. Look, Eleanor, I'd like to talk to you about some-thing, but preferably not on the phone, and perhaps not in your office.'

'Sounds mysterious. But OK. When and where?'

'In the next couple of days, if that suits you. I'll come up to London. Perhaps we could have a drink or coffee somewhere.'

'Is this business or social, Geoffrey?' I couldn't make out which she'd have preferred.

'Well, it's business, but I *would* like to meet you in person.' That was true; I was curious to see if she'd live up to Mr Clarke's description of her.

As if reading my mind, she said, 'To see what I look like?' I heard that charming chuckle again. 'OK, but you'll be disappointed.'

'I doubt that.'

'I could do tomorrow, after work. Say five thirty.'

We arranged to meet in the lounge of the George Hotel in Victoria, near her office.

An hour or so later, I found myself, yet again – as I'd been doing almost daily for months – standing at my office window and staring at the mangled, half-submerged remains of the old West Pier through the one meagre slice of sea view on offer from the firm's fourth-floor suite in central Brighton. What drew me to the sight of this derelict piece of wreckage had nothing to do with its actual appearance – about which I was ambivalent anyway, since in all its ugliness it possessed a Dali-esque sort of artistic appeal – but the fact that it had become a stark symbolic reminder of the awful disintegration of my precious marriage and family life.

There were blinds on the window but I chose to leave them open, because the view kept me in touch with my thoughts and feelings, just as my visits to the flat let me escape them. That was something I needed, to avoid running too far away and losing the will to stay in control.

3

I'd started seeing Lucy in the eleventh month (by my reckoning) of the 'Great Sulk', or 'GS', as I'd come to think of it.

Marion had always had a sombre side to her nature. It was part of what made her the sensitive, intelligent person she was, and her moodiness somehow went with her kind of beauty – she had dark-brown, brooding eyes and deep black hair, and carried her slender body in a gracious, reaching-up-tall way. But she could be warm and loving – as she used to be with me, most of the time, and always was with Emma and Paulie, the little ones we both cherished. Marion had great depth, and a sensual magnetism that was almost mysterious, as if she had to be made love to in order to be understood. But I had made love to her innumerable times and something of the mystery had always remained. Yet I'd always adored her unreservedly, accepting the enigma about her, and so far not even the Great Sulk had changed that.

The GS was nothing like her earlier mood swings. I'd always suspected that those earlier interludes had had something to do with her father's suicide. She'd told me not long after we met about her father having gassed himself in his car when she was thirteen, and what a terrible shock it had been for her – as well as her mother – especially since it had been so unexpected; he hadn't been noticeably depressed or suffered any sort of misfortune, and there'd been no suicide note or other kind of message from him. And I in turn had told her about my father having been knocked down and killed by a car in Johannesburg when I was nine – the event that had brought me to England, my mother having decided to return to her birthplace with me within months of being widowed. Somehow, Marion and I had avoided discussing these childhood tragedies of ours again except on the rare occasion when the odd passing allusion to one or the other was relevant to some other topic, as if we'd tacitly agreed that the hurt of them should be kept to ourselves and not be allowed to pervade our shared life.

The GS differed from its predecessors in two major respects. One was that it just went on and on, and the other, that it was directed at me, and me alone. When others were present, especially the kids, Marion would behave as if nothing were wrong. But as soon as we were alone together, she'd start sulking and ignoring me except when something needed to be discussed – like things affecting the children, the household, money, or social commitments. We had become strangers living in the same house. She'd avoid me whenever she could, going out somewhere or shutting herself in the 'snug', the small guest bedroom she'd moved into. And worst of all, she just wouldn't talk about the GS or what was behind it. After innumerable futile attempts to get her to do so, I eventually gave up trying. What else could I do, when all I'd get from her was a frown accompanied by a look which said, 'Why do you ask? You know very well what's wrong, and if you don't you ought to. Don't expect me to tell you.' But I did not know. I supposed it could have related to all the petty bickering that had gone before, but I couldn't pinpoint any one argument or topic that could have set it off. In fact, I couldn't even remember what most of the bickering had been about.

I hadn't taken the GS especially seriously, imagining that it was nothing more than an extended version of the kind of mood-swing I was accustomed to, until the day she gave me notice that she was moving out of the bedroom into the snug – 'for a while, just to get the space to think about things.'

'What sort of things, Marion?'

'I'd rather not say, yet.'

'Is this a separation or something? If so, you owe it to me to say so.'

'No, it's not. I'm not leaving you, Charles. Just sorting things out.'

I had no doubt she'd declared some kind of war on me, and I was angry at being made the object of her unexplained antipathy, but decided there was too much at stake for an emotive response from me and that I should let her have the 'space' she wanted. And that was how I began sitting out the Great Sulk and then found myself continuing to do so, week after week and then month after month.

Needless to say, the GS came with a built-in denial of sexual privileges. Sitting out the GS was one thing, but doing so without sex was quite another. Which was why I eventually got involved with Lucy. Or so I told myself. She and Marion were not especially close, but they seemed to like each other and to get on remarkably well – remarkably because they had so little in common. Not only were they physical opposites – Lucy was a shortish, plump but pretty blonde, whose feminine charms were growing increasingly appealing to me in my state of involuntary celibacy, especially once I'd started getting signs that the attraction was mutual – but they were simply different kinds of women in almost every way. Marion had a master's degree in economics, Lucy a handful of O Levels. Marion loved reading – she devoured books of all kinds; I never saw Lucy read anything other than a magazine or a menu. Marion had a dignity that Lucy lacked; Lucy had a lightheartedness that Marion lacked. Marion never lied, about anything; Lucy lied easily and sometimes outrageously.

If I was going to have an extramarital affair, it would have had to be with someone like Lucy. What I'd needed was sex – not the kind that could be bought or the sort of casual one-night stand that was available in abundance from inebriated or thrill-seeking young amateurs, but a liaison with someone who, like myself, was in a relationship that wasn't working physically and needed an outlet for an imprisoned libido, with no strings attached. Lucy Cole had fitted the bill, exactly – at least to begin with.

4

The trip up to London to meet Eleanor wouldn't be wasted whatever happened; there were a couple of things I needed to do there anyway that I'd been putting off.

I made a point of getting to the George Hotel early, because I thought I'd have a better chance of identifying her when she arrived than she'd have of distinguishing me from all the other dark-suited men who were likely to be around at that time of day, especially since she'd told me what she'd be wearing. In the event, I knew who she was as soon as she entered the room. Clarke had been wrong: she wasn't just lovely; she was stunning.

She wore a smart navy-blue trouser-suit with a white silk scarf, and her short dark-brown hair contrasted with alert pale-blue eyes that quickly noticed my raised hand. Smiling radiantly, she came over to me.

'Geoffrey?' Not waiting for an answer, she sat down. I guessed she'd be in her late twenties.

'Eleanor? I'm overwhelmed.'

'So am I, Geoffrey.' Was she genuinely returning the compliment or just being polite?

We ordered – a Scotch for me and coffee for her – and chatted for a while. I asked her about her job and she told me she'd only been in the letting business for about a year; that her real field was in the art world, more specifically in galleries, but there'd been a slump and the London gallery where she'd last worked had closed, so she'd joined her present company, where she'd been put through a lightning training course before becoming a letting manager. She also mentioned that she was a divorcee and lived alone.

'What about you?' she asked me.

'Am I married, do you mean?'

She blushed slightly. 'Well, not that particularly. But are you?' She looked straight at me and her eyes were magnificent.

Was Geoffrey married, I wondered? I decided not. 'No. I'm not.' Although intrigued by her interest in me, I thought it was time to get to the point.

'Eleanor, I need some information about Beverley Terrace, but I don't want you to tell me anything that would compromise you.'

'I'd never do that. Fire away.'

'Has anything new happened with Beverley Terrace since we spoke?'

'Like what?'

'Well, like a sale perhaps – to an international syndicate?'

'Why do you want to know?' Before I could answer, her mouth and eyes opened wide and she exclaimed, 'Hey, you're the tenant with the option!'

'If you mean an option to buy my flat, yes, there is one in my tenancy agreement.'

'Wow!'

'Why the "wow"?'

'Well, this is just what I've picked up in the office. I know very little about the deal itself.'

'What deal?'

'Have you heard about this project to build a new mini-city beyond the marina?'

So, my hunch was right, was it? 'I've read about it,' I replied. 'That's why I'm here.'

'Well, it's a huge thing – much, much bigger than the development I told you about.'

'And Beverley Terrace is to be part of it?'

'The vital part. Fifty per cent of the land they want belongs to SEP – that's South East Properties, your landlord – and Beverley Terrace is bang in the middle of it.'

'So, SEP are selling to the syndicate?'

She smiled. 'The deal's just about done, Geoffrey. The price is enormous, but SEP have got a problem. The buyers have another site on standby in case this deal goes wrong and they've given SEP a deadline to conclude with them or else they go for the other property. And there's been a last-minute hitch.'

I thought I knew what it might be, but said, 'And what's that?'

'Your option, sir. You can't redevelop a property that can be burdened with a ninety-nine-year lease – over even one small flat – and if the buyers find out about your option they won't stick around while the vendors sort you out. They'll just back off and go for the other deal.'

'Am I the only tenant with an option?'

'You certainly are.'

'Do you know how that happened?'

'You were given the wrong form of tenancy agreement to sign. It seems the solicitors who drafted the standard agreement for the short lets made a booboo. They worked from a precedent – a lease they'd drawn up for some commercial property – and failed to delete an option clause and one or two other things that didn't belong.'

I nodded sagely, keeping my silence in case I gave myself away as a lawyer. She went on, 'I'm told they're in the clear. They discovered the error after the document was printed and immediately contacted the owners. That apparently lets them off the hook.' I was inclined to think it did. 'Anyhow,' she said, 'all existing copies of the defective document were supposed to be shredded, but one or two somehow got mixed in with the batch of reprinted copies – which is how you got one of them.'

'I see.'

'So now SEP have been holding back all the tenancy agreements, pretending they've been mislaid, while they deal with the tenant who's got this option. Haven't you heard from anybody about this yet?'

'Heard what?'

'Well, I've been told that SEP's solicitors have consulted two QCs about the matter.'

Mentally, I echoed her earlier 'Wow!' Aloud, I said, 'Yes, I have had a letter from a firm of solicitors.' How safe was it to let her know more? After all, there was really no reason for her to keep this conversation confidential from her employers. I looked at my watch. 'Oh, hell, I've got another appointment. Eleanor, please excuse me. I must rush off. You've been very helpful.'

She gave me a knowing grin. 'Geoffrey, you don't have to make excuses for not wanting to answer my questions.'

I grinned back, feeling foolish. 'Well, yes, you're right. I apologize. But if you don't mind, Eleanor, I do have a reason for not saying too much at this stage.'

She gave me another winning smile. 'Is there anything else you want to know from me?'

'No, not at this stage. Once again, you've been very helpful, Eleanor.'

'So is that it then?'

'Is that what?'

'I thought,' she hesitated – was she blushing again? – 'well, I sort of thought it would be nice if we could get to know each other better. *I* don't have another appointment.' She was very direct, the lovely Eleanor.

'Do you mean that?' It was a highly tempting invitation, but unfortunately not one I could possibly accept. My life was complicated enough as it was, and even if it weren't, how could I possibly get involved with someone who thought I was Geoffrey Greenwood?

'Yes, I do,' she said. 'Does that bother you?'

'No. On the contrary. I'm highly flattered, and I'd love to get to know you better – much better in fact – but I should have told you, when you asked me if I was married, that I *am* in a relationship.'

'Oh, that's great – I mean great that you have someone.'

'Thank you, Eleanor. You're really lovely, and I'm truly grateful for your help.' I reached for her hand and held it for a moment; it felt warm and welcoming. 'But I'd better leave now – or else I'll never be able to.'

We exchanged looks and smiles again, then I forced my eyes away from hers. 'I'll just get the bill.'

'You go. I'd like another coffee before I leave.'

'I'll pay at the desk.' I stood up.

'Don't you want to leave me a contact number, Geoffrey? In case I hear anything more about Beverley Terrace?'

'Yes, please. I'll give you my mobile number.' I did so. There was no risk in that; I never answered a telephone with my name, or identified myself on an answering message.

'By the way,' she said, 'you sound less South African in person than you do on the phone.'

I realized that I'd lapsed into my normal accent. Did it really matter? 'Is that so? It's probably because I've been over here for a while on this visit.'

I looked back at her after paying. She smiled and lifted a hand in farewell and I grinned and waved back. It would have been fun, I thought, if the lovely Eleanor could have become part of my secret life as Geoffrey Greenwood, but that was out of the question. Wasn't it?

5

My thoughts on the way back to Brighton swung between pleasant reflections about Eleanor and mixed ones about the option.

She was not only exceptionally attractive, but plainly intelligent – and not averse to making the kind of forward moves that would normally come from the man's side of a new acquaintance. Yet the way she did so wasn't brash or unfeminine, simply direct, and quite disarming. This wasn't meant to have been a personal meeting – though I had to admit I'd been a little ambiguous about that – but she'd somehow turned it into one, and I was trying to understand why. Sex was certainly part of it – the airwaves between us had hummed with it – but she didn't seem like the type who set out to seduce men. In fact, she'd made it clear – especially with her questions – that her interest in me went further than that. She'd said she was divorced, and there was, I felt, a hint of hurt in her, of loneliness, of a need, perhaps, for a worthy lover. If it wasn't something like that, then Eleanor Downing did not make sense. The fact was that she'd made a huge impression on me, resistance to which would require a strong effort of will on my part.

As for the option, Tolway Perry's letter was a shameful misrepresentation of the law and deserved to be challenged. Had I rented the flat in my own name, I'd not have hesitated to take on both them and their clients, SEP. If they'd been honest and open about their problem, I'd have felt inclined to co-operate with them because I'd never asked for or expected an option to buy the flat, but I felt that their duplicity had ruled out the need for fair play on my part. They'd chosen to bluff their way to their objective, without realizing they were writing to a lawyer who was equipped to call their bluff, rather than the layman who they believed would fall for it.

Unfortunately, I was in no position to call their bluff, because I'd pretended to be someone other than myself and valid agreements were possible only between real people using their true identities. Which meant that the tenancy agreement was probably null and void, and so was the option. But what, I wondered, would happen if I wrote back as Geoffrey's solicitor, disputing the legal position and saying my client was standing on his rights? Given the situation they were in, they'd *have* to negotiate with me and pay my client out for agreeing to cancel his option.

Of course, if all that did happen and the truth came out afterwards, I'd be in deep trouble: I could be prosecuted for deception and struck off as a solicitor – and I'd have to give the money back. It was unthinkable.

So what next? Geoffrey had received a letter that called for a response. If there was none, they'd surely try and make personal contact with him; so the letter had to be answered, and the only way to answer it was to do what it asked: put Geoffrey's signature on the addendum and send it back.

Despite having made that decision, I continued to brood over the matter. I hated giving in so feebly. There could be a tidy sum in the exercise – though I'd have problems with it. I couldn't bank it in my own account, nor could I open a bank account for the imaginary Geoffrey. And there'd be a tax problem with the gain. But as a first step I could have the money paid into the client account I'd already opened for Geoffrey with the firm; then I'd have time to consider the next move. I was confident I'd find a way of getting the money into my own hands eventually, possibly over an extended period and in a form which would allow me to pay tax on it openly.

Realistically, I asked myself, what were the chances of my being found out if I went ahead? My client need not put in an appearance personally – he lived abroad – and the process could always be aborted if anything went wrong along the way. And once agreement had been reached, there'd be no reason for anybody to want to reopen the matter.

There was also a need for consistency in the way I conducted Geoffrey's affairs. Had there actually been a Geoffrey Greenwood and had I been his solicitor, I'd not have hesitated to advise him to contest the issue. So shouldn't I simply act as if he were real? Or was that just a way of rationalizing the course of action my instincts were urging me to take?

After a sleepless night I drove to the flat in the early morning. The sky was almost cloudless as the sun rose and it looked like being a beautiful day. I made myself breakfast and sat on the balcony eating it. The solution, I decided, was to test the water and see what happened.

By the end of the day the following letter bearing my reference and signature was on its way to Tolway Perry:

Dear Sirs

Re: South East Properties plc and Mr G. R. Greenwood

Our client, Mr G. R. Greenwood, has consulted us about your letter to him.

The matter is receiving our careful consideration and we shall address you further in due course.

Yours faithfully
Brook, Amery and Phillips

6

I got a call two days later. 'Mr Hamilton's on the line for you, from Tolway Perry,' said the receptionist.

I felt my pulse rate surge. Game on. 'Put him through.'

'Mr Brook,' said a well-spoken voice on the telephone, 'James Hamilton, Tolway Perry. I'm due to be in your part of the world tomorrow. Could we meet?'

'Tomorrow's not a good day for me, Mr Hamilton. What's it about?'

'Oh, just this client of yours, Greenwood. Thought it'd be convenient to try and resolve the matter if possible, and I don't often get down to Brighton these days, unhappily.'

'I wouldn't mind coming up to London one day. I am there often – and I'm not really ready to talk about the matter yet.'

Hamilton's agitation was almost visible. 'No,' he said. 'I think you'll realize when we meet that this thing can, and should, be taken further at this stage.'

'I'm always willing to listen, but I've got no mandate, you know, and tomorrow *is* difficult. What time did you have in mind?'

'You tell me. I can arrange my day around it.'

We settled on eleven, and I told him I could only spare him an hour. They really were keen, weren't they? And I was right in it now.

When I got home that evening, Katka, our Slovakian au pair, was giving the children their supper in the kitchen. She looked on with amusement as the two little ones jumped up and down around me, excitedly competing for my attention with unintelligible accounts of their day. Emma was five and Paul – or Paulie as we all called him – three. Emma had yet to adjust to the unpleasant reality of her brother's presence in her life. When he'd been an infant, there'd been some ambiguity in her feelings towards him – he was cute and lovable, but he shared her parents with her, and as hard as she tried to fight that, she'd learned to endure it. Now that he could run and talk and play with things, he was no longer cute in any way, but an out-and-out menace. Nothing of hers – dolls, tricycle, toys, storybooks, whatever – was safe with him around, despite her efforts, and ours, to hide things from him and keep him at bay. 'Daddy, Paul is ruining my life,' she told me one day; she never used the more endearing 'Paulie'.

It was as well she didn't know about some of the things her brother got up to, such as the infamous Easter egg incident. I'd bought them both large chocolate eggs at Easter, one with 'Emma' written on it in white icing, the other 'Paul'. Marion handed these out on Easter Sunday morning. When I went into Paulie's bedroom shortly afterwards, he was sitting on the floor, his face full of chocolate stains, tucking into what was left of his egg – it still included most of the part with his name on it. Half an hour later, I came back and he was still at it, though this time there was noticeably more of the egg left than before. Then I saw the word 'Emma' on its side and admonished him sternly: 'Paulie, you're eating Emma's Easter egg!'

'No, I'm not. It's mine.'

'No, it's not yours. It says "Emma".'

'It does not. It says "Mine".'

What could I do but laugh inwardly, deprive him of the rest of the egg, and rush off to buy his sister another one?

But it wasn't all one-way traffic. Emma gave as much as she got, using to full effect the advantages of the older child to tease and torment him. They bickered a lot, but seldom came to blows and, by and large, they actually got on quite well together – when they got lost in whatever they were doing. All in all, I guessed they were much like all young siblings, although everything about them was unique and special to me. They were a large part of why I went on enduring the GS and waiting for it to pass.

I'd been told Paulie was just like me. I'd have described him as a blue-eyed charming devil. Did that describe me too, I wondered? He certainly had my eyes, and remembering some of the things I'd got up to as a boy – not to mention the dangerous game I was now playing with SEC and Tolway Perry – I supposed 'devil', or perhaps more aptly 'daredevil', was an epithet that did fit me. But was I charming? Marion had thought so – once – and Lucy had actually told me so. Paulie certainly appealed to everyone who knew him – except his sister, of course.

As for Emma, she was a replica of her mother – dark-haired, dark-eyed – but quite unlike her in temperament. She laughed a lot and always had a ready smile and hug for me.

I worried a lot that the GS was having an effect on them, and I put that to Marion once. She disagreed. 'We're loving parents, Charles, both of us. What happens between us takes nothing away from them.'

'But we're hardly ever with them together. And that makes a difference. A big one.'

'We're with them together enough. And anyway, I can't do more, so what's the point? Don't try and use the kids to get to me, Charles.'

'I'm not,' I said angrily. 'That's a nasty thing to say.'

'Maybe. Well, if it is, I'm sorry. But I'm not discussing this any further.'

And she didn't. Nor did I bring the subject up again. I just went on doing all I could to make it seem to Emma and Paulie that all was well between their parents.

'Where's Marion?' I asked Katka, when the hubbub had died down.

'Inside, but she not feel well.'

I found Marion in the living-room, her head in a book. She barely looked up at me. 'Katka says you don't feel well,' I said.

'I think I've caught a cold and I don't want to pass it on to the children. Will you put them to bed, please? Katka must go off now.'

Was her tone a little softer tonight? Perhaps I could try and talk seriously to her a little later. I felt I needed to. There'd been no change in the situation for something like fifteen months now and our marriage was dying on its feet. Marion didn't seem to care whether it died or not; whatever was behind the GS was more important to her. I did care, so it was up to me to make one more determined effort to break the deadlock.

'Sure,' I replied.

'Good. Your supper's in the oven.'

By the time the children were asleep and I'd eaten, Marion had already disappeared into the snug. Tentatively, I tapped on the door and said through it, 'Marion, the kids are asleep. Is there anything else you'd like me to do?'

I'd expected her to answer through the door, not open it, but she did. Putting her head around it, she glared at me, her eyes ablaze. 'I told you I wanted to be left alone,' she snapped, spitting the words out at me. 'Why the hell don't you just leave me in peace?' She closed the door again and I heard her lock it from the inside.

I stood there, stunned, then began seething. I didn't have to put up with this kind of humiliation any longer. She'd become impossible to live with. The sooner I divorced her the better. But I quickly pulled myself up. Was I really ready to end my precious marriage? It would be so final, and so awful for the kids.

I ran myself a hot bath. As I lay soaking in it, I tried to reconcile this Marion with the person she'd been before the GS and threw my mind back to all the good times we'd had. Like the things we did together in those early days after we'd met at college. I recalled her rich laughter and the delicate tenderness of her lovemaking. Then later, the way she shared the burden of my mother's illness with me, and consoled me when the end came. Afterwards, there'd been those years together in the London flat, so fulfilling for me, with Blackfords, the City law firm, but so miserable for Marion. 'Teddy,' – her pet name for me, which she never used any more now – 'I hate London. It's overwhelming,' she'd complain. So eventually she got her way and we moved to Brighton and Hove, where she'd been born and grown up, and where her mother still lived. And for me it was bye-bye Blackfords and the junior partnership, and hullo old Herbert Wharton and his one-man solicitor's practice in the Lanes. But it had been worth all the change and sacrifice because it worked for her. She got, and kept, a good job, and we bought a flat, and Herbert Wharton retired and the practice grew, and then we got married and had Emma and Paulie, and bought the big house in Hove in which we now lived.

But a year or so later the bickering had started, then the GS, and things had been going downhill ever since.

Getting out of the bath, I asked myself where to now? It was clear I couldn't change the situation. One day she'd say something to me, I was sure, and it wouldn't be conciliatory. I should resign myself to the inevitable. But I still wanted to hang in there, just in case there was a chance of the old Marion, my Marion, coming back to me. Meanwhile, I had a second life to live now – Geoffrey's – and I could go on as I was. Why not?

Then, standing there wet and naked, towel in hand, I thought again of Eleanor.

7

James Hamilton arrived promptly, but I deliberately kept him waiting for ten minutes before emerging to escort him into the small conference room. I offered no apology for the delay.

He was looking uncomfortable and annoyed. I gestured to him to sit down and offered him coffee, which he declined. He seemed a little stuffy and stereotyped, but I knew better than to underestimate a legal colleague.

'You're short of time today, Charles,' he said, having proposed we use first names, 'so let's get down to business. This is all without prejudice, of course?'

'Of course, assuming you're here to negotiate.'

'Er, yes, you could say that,' replied Hamilton, obviously disarmed by having to make this admission before establishing a position. 'Now, it would be unfair of me not to put you fully into the picture.'

'Definitely, and not merely unfair.'

'Quite so. My clients are close to concluding an advantageous sale of their property and the transaction would be facilitated if they were able to divest the property of as many encumbrances as possible. Your client's option to buy his flat, albeit lacking validity, is one such encumbrance.'

What a pompous way of stating a fraction of the truth, I thought. Aloud, I said, 'With respect, James, I have advised my client that I don't share your view about the option being invalid. Right now I'm preparing a brief to counsel on opinion.'

'Have you read the case law yourself yet, Charles?' Bluff number two: the case law did not support Hamilton.

'In fact, yes, I have, though not as thoroughly, I'm sure, as my counsel will – or, for that matter, as your counsel undoubtedly has already done.'

'What makes you think we've taken this to counsel?'

'Haven't you, James?'

Hamilton looked down at his lap. 'Counsel has expressed the view – orally – that the matter is arguable.'

'Almost anything is arguable, as you know – but be candid now, James:

which argument does he favour?'

Hamilton sighed. 'Yours, I'm bound to say.' I could almost see him thinking this seaside lawyer was no dummy.

'So, James, can we drop the legal debate?'

'At this stage, yes. I'm really here to talk about money.'

'I'm listening.'

'That flat's worth well over a hundred thousand – which is what your client would have to pay for it if he exercised the option. There'd be no resale profit in it for him.'

'That's not the point, is it?'

'Not entirely, no. What I take you to mean, Charles, is that he'd be entitled – assuming the validity of his option – to say, "I have a right which you want me to give up, for your reasons, not mine, so you may buy my right for what it's worth".'

'Exactly. Well, what do your clients think it's worth, James?'

Without hesitating, Hamilton replied, 'A hundred thousand pounds.'

Now it was I who sighed. 'You came all the way here to offer that? I don't believe it.'

'Why not? It's very generous, in the circumstances.'

Here we go, I thought. 'What circumstances, James? You've just admitted your clients must get rid of that option or else they'll lose a massive deal, and you're offering my client a hundred thousand pounds?'

'I never said anything about a massive deal, nor did I say your client's supposed option was the critical factor. I said it was one of—'

'James, I'm not relying on what you've told me this morning. I have other sources of information.'

Hamilton frowned. 'Other sources? What sources?'

'Without wishing to sound rude, that's my business. But you can't expect to keep things quiet around a big deal like yours. Tell me, James, who's running the matter in your office?'

'I am. Why?'

'Why? Because I find it hard to accept that the lawyer in charge of this enormous deal would leave his office for a day – or the best part of one – just to dispose of a minor side-issue when the deal is in crisis.'

'It's not in . . .' Hamilton started to say. Then he lowered his eyes again and spoke more softly, 'As I said a few minutes ago, I came here to talk about money.' He looked up. 'Two hundred?'

Just like that? How much higher would he go? But how far did I want to take this? I must be careful, not for fear the negotiations would collapse –

that was unlikely – but to be sure there'd be no comebacks once a deal was done. I wasn't selling an option as much as exploiting a situation, and to do so to excess could leave a sour enough aftertaste for someone to want to know more about this shrewd lawyer and his extortionate client. It was time to make a pretence of being fair.

'James,' I said, 'I'm not enjoying this auction, or your apparent discomfort. I do want the best for my client, but not by taking undue advantage. At this stage, why don't we both take instructions from our clients and then lay our cards on the table?'

Hamilton seemed relieved, though still on his guard. 'Yes, that sounds sensible.'

'Then this is what I suggest. I'll go back to my office and call my client from there. You stay here and do the same. When you've talked to your people, write a figure down on a slip of paper. I'll do the same, and we can exchange slips when we resume and see where we stand. What do you think?'

Hamilton hesitated before answering. 'That's fine with me.'

'Good. I'll leave you now. Please feel free to use this telephone here if you wish.'

'Thanks, but I have my mobile.'

'Right. When you're ready, just use this phone and dial my secretary on two-two-one. Her name's Cindy.'

Back in my office I considered the state of the negotiations. Two things were clear: one, both parties wanted the matter resolved that day – it didn't suit me to drag this out any more than it did Hamilton and his clients – and two, Hamilton's last offer would be raised, even perhaps up to half a million. But that would be too high, given the risk of the after-taste factor. What would be the right mark? Three-fifty, I decided. What figure would Hamilton write down? Not less than two-fifty, surely – more probably three hundred. I tore a slip off a notepad on the desk and wrote '£400,000' on it, then leaned back and waited. A few minutes later Cindy told me Hamilton was ready if I was.

Back in the conference room, we exchanged pieces of paper. '£300,000,' said Hamilton's. Neither of us could suppress a knowing smile.

'Split the difference?' asked Hamilton. I nodded and we shook hands across the table. It had been as easy as that.

'I'm instructed to get this in writing today,' said Hamilton.

I'd been expecting – and hoping – he'd say something like that. 'I don't think I can reach my client again before tonight,' I replied.

Hamilton frowned briefly. 'Look here, Charles, I have the authority to conclude this settlement and I'm prepared to sign for my client right now. If you're willing to do the same, we can get our clients' formal confirmations later.'

'I'm happy with that.' The proposal suited me perfectly.

While we waited on the typing, I asked Hamilton how long he thought it would be before Greenwood would have to vacate his flat. 'Nothing will be happening on the site until next year,' he replied. That was good to know; not only had I come into a nice sum, but I'd have more time to enjoy the flat.

The settlement note signed, Hamilton departed hastily and in excellent spirits. I returned to my office and, like a tennis player who has just won a crucial point, put my left leg forward and punched the air with my fist.

The ringing of the direct phone on my desk aborted my celebrations. It was Lucy.

'Charles,' she said. 'Malcolm has accused me of having an affair.'

Oh, hell, I thought. 'Well, haven't you?' I hadn't meant to sound callous.

'Yes, of course I have. But with you.'

'Well, who does he think it was with?'

'That Greenwood chap.'

8

I was struck dumb.

'Are you there, Charles?' asked Lucy.

'How on earth did he come up with that?'

'He rang me at work this morning and demanded I meet him at home at once. When I got there, he was wild. He asked me straight out if I was having an affair and when I denied it he called me a liar. Then he mentioned Greenwood's name and I was stunned.'

'What did you say?'

'I told him he was talking rubbish – about me having an affair, that is. But he shoved a private investigator's report under my nose and told me to read it. He'd had me followed.' (Why hadn't I considered the possibility?) 'They saw me park my car in the bay reserved for flat thirty-four. And they claim they saw Greenwood go up to the same flat. How can that be?'

'They must have mistaken me for him.'

Lucy seemed to consider this. 'Yes, I suppose they must have. Charles, what am I to do?'

What was *I* to do, I wondered? This ridiculous development, just when I'd done the deal with Hamilton, was alarming. With the imaginary Greenwood caught up in Lucy's marital affairs, how long would it be before it came out there was no such person, and where would that leave me? In a huge pile of crap, that's where. SEP and Tolway Perry would show me no mercy. I was thinking fast. It would be far better for me if Malcolm knew that Lucy had been seeing me. Given the state of my marriage, how much would it matter if Marion knew too? She'd be upset that it was Lucy, but she could hardly complain about my infidelity. It might even be the thing that would kick-start our marriage back to life, seeing nothing else was doing so. And if it brought about the end, then so be it.

'Lucy, you'd better tell him it was me. I can't let Geoffrey get involved in this.'

'No, Charles, it would be fatal if I did that. He told me he'd employed the investigator because he'd suspected that I was seeing you. He'd watched us together and picked up the vibes between us, and he's jealous as hell of you. If I admit it was you, my marriage is over. I don't want to admit anything right now. What I need is an excuse for having gone to the flat.'

'And parking your car in a reserved bay? Besides, you can bet they waited till you came out.'

'Yes, the report said so. Oh, hell, Charles, my whole life's at stake here and I don't know what to say or do.' This was the woman who, only a month or so earlier, had been ready to leave her husband.

'Lucy,' I said, 'it's hard for me to advise you, because I don't know Malcolm well enough. What I do know is it won't do anyone any good if Greenwood is implicated.'

'He is already.'

'That's not so. It's me you've been seeing. Besides, if confronted, Greenwood would deny it all – convincingly. And since you can't explain away the investigators' report, Malcolm will soon find out the truth.'

'Maybe not. He still loves me, I think, and if I go on denying everything, he may give me the benefit of the doubt.' The line went silent, then she said, 'That's all I can do – keep denying the whole thing and brazen it out.'

'Do you really believe that can work?'

'Yes, if I can convince him the report's a lie. There was no mention of any pictures – of the two of us together, I mean – and private investigators do have a bad reputation, don't they?'

'Some of them.'

'Well, anyway, I'm going to brazen it out.'

'Will you let me know what happens?' I needed to stay in touch with developments so as not to be taken by surprise when Malcolm came looking for Geoffrey Greenwood. Her decision to 'brazen it out' was risky – for both of us – but there was nothing I could do about it. I could hardly go to Malcolm behind her back and confess of my own accord; I had to respect her right to do what she thought best in relation to her own marriage.

'Yes, of course,' she replied.

My mobile rang not long after Lucy's call. It was Eleanor.

'How nice to hear your voice again, Eleanor,' I said.

'Yours too, Geoffrey.'

'To what do I owe this pleasure?'

'Could I see you again?' She added quickly, 'It's about Beverley Terrace.'

The last bit sounded like an excuse, but I was happy to play along. I'd been hoping to hear from her. Things had changed since we'd last met and there was no reason not to meet her again – as Geoffrey. There'd be no problem about that in vast, anonymous London. I couldn't think of telling her who I really was, and needn't at this stage. If anything developed between us, I could reconsider the position later. And I could stop the whole thing in its tracks whenever I wanted to.

'I'd be delighted to see you again,' I said. 'What about having lunch with me in London?'

'That would be lovely. When and where?'

I suggested an Italian restaurant in Kensington and we arranged to meet there on the following Tuesday. I said I'd make a booking.

Meanwhile, I put Geoffrey's signature on the settlement with SEP, and the following day, Friday, saw the conclusion of all the formalities, including the transfer of £350,000 into the firm's client account. It was time to tell my partners what I'd done for the client Greenwood, and finding them together in Jonathan Amery's office, I did so.

'Well done, Charles,' said Jonathan. 'I'd love to have been a fly on the wall when you humiliated that tight-arsed City shyster.'

Jonathan was vociferously biased against the big-law-firm fraternity of London. At forty, he was the oldest of the three of us, which, along with his appearance – he was thin, with greying hair, slightly taller than me, and wore heavy dark-rimmed glasses – gave some people the impression that he was really the senior partner, despite his name featuring after mine. In fact, we were all equal partners. At least that was the case as far as profits and status were concerned, but equality didn't extend to our contributions to the practice; I brought in more business and earned more fees for the firm than both of them put together, and they didn't seem to mind that at all.

Their rationale, I knew, was that it was bound to be so because I was the commercial lawyer, with a background and connections in the corporate world, whereas they were left to graft away at other, less lucrative and more tedious things, like conveyancing, litigation, and seeing to the firm's administration. The fact that all of that hardly justified an egalitarian approach to rewards was conveniently overlooked. The truth of it all was that it was I who led the firm and drove the practice, and I knew full well it was my own fault that I'd made a bad deal into the bargain. It was something I'd been meaning to change for a long time.

'What are you going to charge this Greenwood chap?' Jonathan asked.

'I thought ten thousand.' It was a large fee, but given all the circumstances – the need to keep up the appearance of being at arm's length with the client, the amount of the settlement, my own share of the fee, and the fact that I might have to keep the money in the client account for some while yet – I thought it would be wise to err on the side of generosity to the firm. But having set the ball rolling, I had, it now seemed, opened myself up to my partners' greed.

'Ten thousand?' Jonathan looked at Barry Phillips. 'What do you think, Barry?'

'Well,' replied Barry, the youngest of the partners, 'there ought to be a substantial add-on for a resounding success like this.'

'That's how I came to my figure,' I said. 'There was hardly any work as such.'

'Nobody at Tolway Perry would hesitate to take ten per cent of the proceeds under similar circumstances,' Jonathan volunteered.

'I don't know about that. But I suppose fifteen thousand could work – that's close to five per cent.' I was buying peace of mind, albeit resentfully.

'Sounds better,' said Jonathan, 'but it's your call, Charles. By the way, when do we get to meet Greenwood? Keeping the best clients to yourself as usual?'

As a generalization, this remark was both unfounded and unfair, but it was certainly true in Geoffrey's case. 'No, not at all. He's been to these offices' – an untruth which it would be difficult to disprove – 'and anyhow, he lives in South Africa and when he's here he travels about a lot.' Then, as a calculated afterthought I added, 'In fact, he's got a couple of things coming up which are very much in your domain, Jonathan, so I expect you'll be meeting him soon enough.'

'What does he want us to do with the money in the client account?' asked Barry, the partner responsible for clients' balances. 'Are you intending to pay it to him right away?'

It was funny, I thought, how cliquish Jonathan and Barry had become, especially seeing I'd known them both longer than they'd known each other. I had very little social contact with either of them and hardly knew Barry outside the practice. He was affable enough, but somehow serious and a trifle bookish. His appearance was nondescript – he was of medium height and build and had a forgettable face – and he seemed to have no special interests, though he did live with someone: a similarly unexceptional young woman called Betty whom he sometimes brought along to office occasions.

'No,' I told him; 'he'll let us have his instructions, but I expect he'll want us to hang on to it for a while. Free of interest – there's some exchange control angle to foreign currency received by South African residents.' No sooner had I said that than I knew I'd made a mistake.

Jonathan frowned. 'I hope we're not getting implicated in anything dodgy. What about all that reporting stuff in the Proceeds of Crime Act?'

'There's nothing illegal about this money, Jonathan. It's come to us from a major British law firm via a UK bank, and we know all about why it's been paid.'

'Yes, but I'm talking about this South African currency business.'

'It's just an administrative thing, nothing more.'

Barry chimed in, 'Are you quite sure, Charles? I mean, what do we really know about this chap?'

'Everything we need to, Barry. We've verified his ID and that's all we're obliged to do.'

'Well,' said Jonathan, 'I only meant we have to be vigilant.'

'That goes without saying,' I retorted, not attempting to hid my irritation.

The discussion left me feeling uneasy. It had unearthed yet another potential source of difficulty around the Greenwood pretence. Now that Geoffrey's affairs were no longer seen within the firm to be the relatively petty business of a minor client, Jonathan and Barry would undoubtedly become more inquisitive about them, and the new legal rules about solicitors' duties to report suspected irregularities regarding money in client accounts didn't help. Shouldn't I try and do something about Geoffrey's missing identity documents in case Barry started sniffing around? Perhaps, but what? Forge a passport for him? Hell, no. There was a better solution – a split with my partners – and not only for this reason. I must give the matter some serious thought, and meanwhile keep Geoffrey's file out of the way – at home, or better still, at the flat.

9

The next day, I played golf for the first time in ages. Saturday was usually my day with the children, but this Saturday Marion's mother, who lived not far from us, in Hangleton, was taking Emma and Paulie shopping for clothes. I had no idea what Marion was doing; she and I might as well have been inhabiting different continents now. Except for dining together at home occasionally – usually in silence – we had lost virtually all contact. But I'd noticed how she'd sometimes look out for me, as if seeking reassurance that I was still around.

So I went to the club, joined a fourball, and was soon wrapped up in the game. My partner was Henry Harper, a pleasant fellow, also in his thirties, who, despite being slight of build and no more than about five feet six tall, was an accomplished golfer who carried me for the first nine holes and then inspired me to play exceptionally well off my twenty handicap over the second nine. During the round, Henry, a computer programmer, told me about a new anti-virus device called 'Jab' which he and a colleague had developed. After starting to go into some of the technical details, he suddenly laughed and said, 'Have I lost you, Charles?'

'I'm afraid you have but the concept sounds interesting.'

'Charles,' said Henry on the next fairway, 'can I come and see you professionally? My colleague and I have got a serious problem with Jab and you may be able to help us.'

'Of course, Henry. Call my secretary and she'll set it up.' I wrote the number down on the back of his scorecard.

It was quite late when I got to my car and switched on my mobile. The monitor told me I'd missed three calls from the same number, which I didn't recognize. The phone rang in my hand. It was Lucy. 'Charles, I've been trying to reach you for hours. I'm in a phone booth in Hove.'

'I've been on the golf course. What is it, Lucy?'

'I've confessed.'

'What do you mean?'

'I've admitted I had an affair – with Greenwood.'

'What? Why did you do that?'

'Malcolm was giving me a terrible gruelling and eventually I just gave in. There were things I couldn't explain away, like what I was doing at Beverley Terrace. Brazening it out didn't work.'

'So what exactly *did* you tell him?'

'That I met Greenwood through my job. That I'd done some work for him. That I found him physically attractive, that we had sex twice in his flat, and that I broke it off after that. I said I was deeply sorry, that I still loved Malcolm, that it had never happened before and never would again. And so on.'

'And how did he take it?'

'Badly, very badly. But I think he'll get over it. I'm not sure of anything, but my marriage has definitely got a better chance now than if he'd found out it was you. He may well accept it was a blip with Greenwood. He's gone away for a few days to "think things over".'

'Do you think he'll try and contact Greenwood?'

'No, Charles, he won't. I'm positive about that. It just wouldn't be Malcolm.'

'Maybe I should warn Geoffrey.'

'No, Charles. Please don't do that. If you did, he'd want to clear himself. It suits me better this way.' But not me, I reflected. I hoped Lucy wasn't wrong about Malcolm not wanting to follow up with Geoffrey. 'Promise me you won't tell Greenwood anything without first speaking to me,' Lucy urged me.

'OK, if that's what you want, but if—'

'Sorry, Charles, I have to ring off. Someone keeps tapping on the booth – they want to use this phone. I'll keep you informed. Bye.'

10

In the flat on Sunday evening, I opened my laptop. It was time Geoffrey Greenwood had a proper background. When he'd been a name on a tenancy agreement, it had made sense to keep his details vague and flexible, but now that it was vital to sustain the impression that he was real, inconsistencies and uncertainties had to be avoided. The sooner I made up a suitable biography for him, the more plausibly and effectively I'd be able to run his life and financial affairs.

As I had to be sure his life story differed sufficiently from my own – particularly because of our common links with South Africa and the necessary similarity in our ages – I started by typing a brief résumé of my own personal history. Under the initials CJB I typed my date of birth followed by 'Johannesburg', then 'Father: JCB, SA citizen, b. Jo'burg, accountant. Mother: EB (b. Wilson in Leeds), Brit. & SA citizen. Both deceased, father in car crash when CJB 9, mother of cancer 12 yrs later. No sibs. After father's death, moved back to England with mother. Schools: King Edward prep, Jo'burg, then Ainsley Grammar, north London. Won bursary to St Paul's, then BA Hons, Cantab, then LLB. Met MF. Blackfords, City of Lon. Moved Brighton & H., joined HW who later retd, firm now B, A & P. Married MF (the date appeared). 2 children, E & P, now 5 & 3. Anglican by birth. Hobbies: golf, bridge, reading. Sport at school & college: rugby, cricket, swimming.'

That was about it for myself. Now for Geoffrey. This must be more detailed, otherwise names, dates and places could be forgotten. I opened a second document and typed the heading 'GRG (Geoffrey Robert Greenwood)' on it. Now, date of birth. I inserted the date I'd put into the Beverley Terrace application. Next, 'Birthplace' – much trickier because of complications around official records, nationality, and taxation. Also, I'd given Eleanor the impression Geoffrey was an Englishman living in South Africa. But still he needn't, and indeed shouldn't, have been born in England, because the register wouldn't reflect his birth. And the same would apply to South Africa. The right choice would be an English-speaking country in southern Africa with less efficiently kept public records. A few years earlier, I'd needed a birth certificate from Harare in connection with a deceased estate and had great difficulty getting it; my correspondent there had reported that the system was flawed. I typed 'Harare, Zimbabwe'.

Religion? 'R Cath', I decided. Family? Geoffrey must definitely not have any living close relatives. I typed, 'Both parents dec'd. No sibs'. Did it matter how his parents had died? Not at this stage, I decided. Their names, likewise. Where lived and when? Given 'his' accent, he'd have to have grown up in England. So, 'Family moved to the UK when GRG 6 yrs old. Went to school in London.' Which schools? Did it matter? Not really – too much to remember. '3 A levels, then trained as stockbroker and commodities trader. Moved to SA at age 23.' Current business? Here vagueness for the sake of flexibility seemed advisable. 'Import-export agent, for own account.'

Marriage and divorce? Yes, both. Geoffrey had to be single now but ought to have had at least one important past relationship. Why not a childless marriage followed by a divorce? I typed as much. Leisure interests and activities? 'Tennis and squash. Jazz enthusiast. Follows English football (Arsenal).'

I did a spell-check, read through what I'd typed, deleted my own biography, and saved Geoffrey's on a CD.

11

On the Tuesday, I took the train up to Victoria and a cab to the restaurant. I was five minutes late and Eleanor was waiting for me at the bar, looking radiant in a light-grey suit and a pink silk blouse. I noticed one or two men eyeing her. It was safe being Geoffrey in London – the likelihood of my being greeted by name there was remote – but I did have to be careful about details, like having enough cash on me to avoid having to use my credit card in her presence.

I'd booked the table in Geoffrey's name and we were shown to it as 'Signor Greenwood' and '*signorina*'. I'd noted previously how the staff of better Italian restaurants always made the tactful choice of '*signorina*' in preference to '*signora*' when addressing ladies of unknown status.

When I'd ordered the wine, she said, 'I hear SEP settled with you. I don't want to know the details, but are you satisfied?'

'Yes, I am. My solicitor did a good job for me. And once again, many thanks to you too, Eleanor. You helped a lot.' I grinned at her and said, 'That's why I'm buying this lunch.'

She smiled back at me. 'And why I'm accepting it. Thank *you*.' After a short silence, she put on a serious look and said, 'I wanted to see you, Geoffrey, because I found out quite a lot about the schedule for Beverley Terrace. You should have masses of time. . . .' She looked across the table at me, paying careful attention to her words, stopped talking, and burst out laughing. 'You're not really taken in by any of this, are you?' she asked.

I laughed too. 'No. Not really. I'm overjoyed that you wanted to see me, Eleanor. I was going to contact you myself.' Staring into her eyes as I spoke, I decided I'd never met a more attractive, charming, sexually appealing woman. How easy she'd be to fall in love with!

'What about your other relationship?' she asked.

'Oh, that. It's over and done with.'

During lunch – and afterwards, when we took a taxi to Hyde Park and sat on a bench talking – we traded biographies, or rather, she told me the truth about herself and I told her some of what I'd made up about Geoffrey. It was an unfair exchange, but I could hardly have trusted her with my dangerous secret. She said she'd been born and brought up in a village near Cambridge and had a degree in fine art, not from Cambridge. She'd married in her early twenties but been divorced within eighteen months. Her mother had died a few years ago, but her father, a retired senior police officer to whom she was very close, still lived in the house in which she'd grown up. She had an older brother living in Australia. Without the backing of her father – a strong man of considerable will – she'd have lacked the courage to break with the man she'd married. After the divorce, she'd reverted to her maiden name, Downing. She'd had one or two meaningless relationships since but was now quite unattached – this last piece of infor-mation imparted with a glowing smile.

For my part – or rather, Geoffrey's – I stuck to the bare essentials and sidestepped her questions, finally escaping them by inviting her to the cinema. She'd taken the afternoon off and we went to see a movie at Marble Arch, then had a drink at a nearby pub, where we held hands. Afterwards, we shared a taxi which dropped her off at her flat and took me on to Victoria station.

I wasn't surprised that she hadn't invited me in – this was our first date after all – but she let me kiss her goodbye in the taxi, softly on the lips, and whispered, 'Please call me soon.' I promised I would.

As I was leaving the house the next morning, I got a call from the office to say that my first appointment for the day had been cancelled, so I went into the conservatory – a large, bright, colourful room full of potted plants nurtured by Marion, a keen and quite accomplished gardener – and settled myself in a chair. I needed to do some serious thinking about what I was going to do with Geoffrey's money.

The longer it stayed where it was, the more difficult and inquisitive my partners were bound to get. Had it been a much smaller sum to cover the firm's disbursements for Geoffrey – like ten or twenty thousand – there'd have been no problem; holding money in trust for clients to cover payments made on their behalf was part of the normal business of solicitors. And now that Geoffrey had his own funds, I could discontinue the clumsy arrangement by which I'd been using postal orders, ostensibly emanating from Geoffrey, to reimburse the firm for its outlays of rent and other expenses in connection with the flat. The size of the amount was what mattered, and the sooner I could move the bulk of it elsewhere, the better. The question was, where?

I'd been considering various possibilities and had so far dismissed them all. The kind of strategy I'd used to cover up his lack of identity within the firm wouldn't work anywhere else, and it was far too dangerous to think of putting the money into my own name yet. I could draw up, and sign as Geoffrey, a deed making the money over to myself as his trustee, but such an arrangement would have tax and banking complications. And as for trying to set up some sort of trust with one of my offshore connections, the amount was too small to warrant the cost, even if I could get around the problem of convincing the prospective trustees that my client was a real person.

So, what was I to do with the money? I had no idea; I'd just have to keep on thinking about it.

12

When Henry Harper arrived to keep his appointment, he was accompanied by a small, thin young woman with mousy hair whom he introduced as his co-director, Brenda Barber.

'Not easy to get to see a lawyer these days,' Henry quipped as he sat down. 'Passport, utility bill – next thing you guys will be wanting blood samples.'

'Well, this ID business isn't really new, but many solicitors weren't too bothered about it until the money-laundering laws were tightened up recently. It's a pain, I agree, not only for the clients, but for us too. But you're in now, Henry, so what can I do for you?'

'Well, it's about the third shareholder in our company – an impossible fellow by the name of George Gragorin—'

'Sorry to butt in, Henry,' said Brenda, removing her jacket, hanging it over the back of her chair, and donning a pair of heavy-rimmed spectacles, as if these were essential preliminaries to her participation, 'I'm not sure how much Henry has told you about Jab, but maybe we should explain what it does.'

'Please do.'

'Well, it's a revolutionary anti-virus device. It uses neural networking to predict new patterns of viral activity on a PC. With Jab, you don't need virus definition updates. With traditional anti-virus software, programmers can never react fast enough to new viruses. Jab uses its own learning intelligence to monitor in-out interfaces and detect any malicious activity on a computer before it can take effect.'

'You're way over my head with the technical stuff, Brenda, but I think I get the general idea. You're saying Jab's a jump ahead of present anti-virus technology.'

'Yes, in a sense. More accurately, ours is a different technology. And it's cheap to manufacture.'

Henry took over. 'Jab was our brainchild, Charles – Brenda's and mine. We stumbled across the idea when we were working together for a software company, so we quit our jobs and set up our own project. We formed a company, put all our own savings into it, and got bank facilities, but we ran out of money just when we were making a breakthrough. Then our accountant found Gragorin, who seemed to be rolling in cash. He offered to lend the company the money we needed if he got one third of the shares for nothing. It was an offer we couldn't refuse. That was about a year ago. Now we're due to fly to the States in three weeks to make a presentation to Hall Computers and run tests with them. They're one of the world's biggest computer manufacturers and they're very interested in Jab. If they like it, they'll offer it to the market with every PC they sell.'

'So what's Gragorin's problem?'

'He's a peculiar fellow – obnoxious and irrational, in fact a bit crazy, we think. The company owes him about three hundred thousand pounds of capital and interest, and he wants it all back now, plus another two hundred grand for his shares. Says he's going to put the company under if we don't agree.'

'I don't understand. What's bothering him? You seem so close to cracking the jackpot.'

'We suspect,' said Brenda, 'he's in trouble with some gambling syndicate in London. He's a heavy gambler and he's frantic for the money.'

'Is the full three hundred thousand due and payable?'

'Yes. And we can't repay any of it right now.'

'You could oppose proceedings, you know, and stall him for a while.'

'We realize that, Charles. The trouble is, Hall will drop Jab like a hot cake if they find out there's a dispute between the shareholders, let alone litigation. Big corporations like that won't touch technology where there's any sort of controversy around it. And our bank will call in our overdraft the moment they learn Hall have backed off.'

'Can't you find a buyer for his shares?'

'Not soon enough. There are a couple of venture capitalists who've shown interest, but they want time to look into it – more time than we have.'

I suppressed a thought that had started germinating in my mind. This was no place for Geoffrey's money, and anyway he didn't have £500,000. As if reading my mind, Henry said, 'Charles, you don't perhaps know someone – a client maybe – who'd like to replace Gragorin?'

'I'm afraid not. At least, I can't think of anyone.'

'That's not why we're here, Charles,' said Brenda. 'We came for your advice. Can you think of any way we can deal with this impossible madman before he blows the whole thing up?'

'Any chance of bringing the Hall demonstration forward?'

'None at all.'

I stared across the room in thought, then said, 'Look; this isn't really a legal problem. All I can suggest is trying a new approach with Mr Gragorin. Do you think it would help if I met with him and tried to talk some sense into him? Or maybe his solicitor could be persuaded to make him see reason.'

'He hasn't seen one yet – at least, that's our impression.'

'Well, he'll have to, if he's serious about proceedings. But, on second thoughts, it may be better to see him alone at this stage. You never know the kind of lawyer he'll get. The wrong kind may see this as a pot of gold. Of course, I can't stop him from bringing a lawyer to the meeting if he wants to – in fact, I ought to encourage him to do so.' I paused. 'Where do you stand with him at this moment? Is he expecting to hear from you?'

'Yes. We told him we had an appointment with a solicitor today about a prospective buyer for his shares – a bit of a naughty lie, but it was all we could come up with. He'll be on the phone by tonight at the latest.'

'OK. What do you think about me writing to him, saying you've come to see me about – what's the company's name?'

'Jab Enterprises Limited.'

'Right, Jab Enterprises Limited, and that I'd like to invite him to my office for a meeting. I won't say exactly why, only that I believe it would be in his interests to attend. Which is true. I'll suggest he rings to make an appointment, but I'll mention I'm fully aware of the urgency. How do you think he'll react?'

'Hard to predict, but he may bite, given our white lie.'

'Well, I certainly can't mislead him about having a buyer once he gets here.'

'Of course not. But what will *you* tell him?'

'I'll play it by ear. I can't promise anything, but this kind of approach sometimes works – I mean bringing a lawyer into the picture. It sort of changes the dynamics. And we don't need to get a final result; all we want is to keep him at bay till after the presentation, don't we?'

'Will you want us at this meeting or not?' Brenda asked.

'Yes, please, both of you. Now, I'm going to need some more information before I write that letter.' I picked up my pen.

After the conference with Henry and Brenda, I drove out to Beverley Terrace. Clarke was at his desk in the lobby. 'A Dr Cole was here to see you, Mr Greenwood. He left this phone number.'

Who on earth was Dr Cole? Oh, hell! Malcolm. Lucy had been wrong; Malcolm *was* following up with Geoffrey. But what exactly was he after? He wasn't the type to resort to physical violence with his wife's supposed lover. Nor did he have any legal rights: the courts didn't award damages to wronged husbands any more. He probably wanted to find out whether Geoffrey confirmed Lucy's story, and if not, who else could have been using the flat. Was this the time to put him right? I could easily ring Malcolm – as if spontaneously, of course – and tell him the truth. That would get him off Geoffrey's trail, but unless Lucy was wrong about this too, it would also end all hope there was for her marriage. And I couldn't do that to her. For the present, all I could do was keep on ducking Malcolm. It might be an idea to stay away from the flat for a while after this visit.

'I'm going abroad,' I told Clarke. 'Just came to pick up a few things. I've no idea who this fellow Cole is and I don't want to ring him. If he comes round again, Mr Clarke, please tell him I've gone overseas and you don't know when I'll be back – which will be true; I don't know myself.'

I rang Eleanor from the flat and accepted an enticing invitation to have supper with her at her place on the following Monday evening.

13

Eleanor came to the door in a short beige skirt, white high-heeled shoes, an off-white, semi-transparent blouse, and, very obviously, no bra. The lightly tanned skin on her superbly shaped legs and bare arms was smooth and unblemished, as was also the paler, visible soft cleft in her bosom. Everything about her was sensually compelling.

I gave her the wine and flowers I'd brought and she kissed me softly, letting her lips linger a little. She offered me a drink and, when I said Scotch, invited me to pour my own and a dry sherry for her. Then she sat down on the sofa and beckoned to me to join her there.

'Geoffrey,' she said, fixing me with her irresistible eyes, 'I can't tell you how happy I've been since we met. How about you?'

'What do you think?' I answered with a broad grin.

'I hope you have. Because I'm crazy about you and I'd hate it to be one-sided.'

'It isn't.' I took her hand and she moved mine onto her bare thigh.

'I asked you here because I wanted to be kissed and loved by you – later, after supper. But now. . . .' Deliberately, she put her drink down on the coffee table and, reaching up, placed her hand behind my neck, drew my mouth to hers, and let me pull her body into mine. Next thing we were feverishly kissing and grasping as much of each other as possible and stripping off clothing – our own and each other's – until she lay on the floor beneath me. Afterwards we just stayed there, on the carpet, exchanging soft kisses and caresses, and saying nothing, until she bit my ear tenderly and said into it, 'It's suppertime, lover.'

We made love again at around eleven, in her bed; then I left to take the last train back to Brighton, as Geoffrey Greenwood the lover, soon to return and make love again to the lovely Eleanor.

14

I couldn't stop yawning at the partners' monthly lunch meeting. 'Been staying up late?' Jonathan asked me.

The truthful answer was yes and no. Yes, I'd been having very little sleep. And no, I hadn't been up; I'd been in bed, with Eleanor, for much of the last two nights, and in railway carriages between Brighton and London for most of the rest of them. The car would have been much easier, but I didn't dare use my own vehicle – like my credit card, it identified me as myself. The situation was tricky, but I was determined the deceit would be short-lived. This wasn't just another chapter in the alleviation of my sexual frustrations, and Eleanor wasn't just another Lucy. We'd been doing more than just making physical love; we'd been talking a lot and laughing and listening to music and drinking wine, and becoming friends as well as lovers. Eleanor, like Marion, was an intelligent woman of the world with whom I could share things, and I was convinced I was falling seriously in love with her.

'Geoffrey,' she'd said last night, lying next to me, 'this is becoming important to me, you know. I feel very close to you, as if we'd been together for years.'

'Yes, my love. So do I.'

'I hope so. Because I don't want to be hurt. And I'm scared I will be, what with you living in South Africa and just visiting here, and me knowing so little about you and your life there.' She paused, as if hesitant about going on, then said, 'You know, my marriage and divorce left me badly shaken. It was over nearly five years ago, but it's still with me – which is why I haven't got involved with anyone since. Well, not until now.'

'What kind of man was your ex-husband?'

'The less said about him the better. He was just a bastard, that's all. But he got his comeuppance. My father saw to that.' I waited for more, but she fell silent.

'Well, about South Africa,' I said, then hesitated.

'Yes?' She looked at me expectantly.

'I'll have something to tell you quite soon.'

'Really? Are you moving to England then?'

'I'm sorry, Eleanor love, I can't say more just yet, except that I hope you'll like my news when you hear it.'

'OK, then, I'll try and be patient.' She smiled and said, teasingly, 'So I'm not just a sex object to you then?'

'Oh,' I laughed, 'you certainly are. The best ever.' I kissed her lips softly. 'But I love you too – very, very much.' Was I going too far too fast?

'Do you mean that?'

'Yes, I do. Every word of it.'

I'd been on the point of taking her into my confidence, but had held back. I desperately wanted her to know the truth about me and no longer feared that my secret wouldn't be safe with her, but I had to be absolutely certain I was ready to leave Marion and face the consequences of doing so. If I wasn't, I must break with Eleanor, very soon, without her ever having to know the truth.

Before I left, she'd suggested that we spend the weekend together in Brighton, but I'd forestalled her by offering to take her away instead – to a little place I knew in the Cotswolds – and she'd agreed.

I answered Jonathan's question: 'I suppose you could say that. I've had a spell of insomnia. Got a lot on my mind.' Jonathan and Barry exchanged glances. The state of my marriage was an open secret in the office. 'Is there anything else to discuss?' I asked them. 'I've got a two-fifteen appointment.'

Barry cleared his throat. 'There is just one more thing, Charles.'

'What's that?'

'I don't imagine you've seen this yet.' Barry passed me the latest issue of the Law Society's *Gazette*, flagged and open at an article headed 'Trust Funds and Money Laundering'. I skimmed through the text. A solicitor in Birmingham had been removed from the register for allowing his client account to be used for money-laundering. A disciplinary hearing found that, although he didn't know what his clients were up to, he ought to have suspected something was wrong and reported it. The article contained a stern warning to the profession to be constantly vigilant so that client accounts were not abused.

I looked up. 'Well?'

'Well,' replied Jonathan, 'it's this Greenwood chap's money we're concerned about. You said something about South African currency controls.'

I tried to keep calm. 'Yes, but the money wasn't obtained illegally. You know how it got there.'

'As we see it, Charles,' said Barry, 'that may not be good enough. If

Greenwood's not supposed to keep that money out of South Africa, or if he has to make some sort of return to the authorities there but is evading them, that falls squarely into the scope of this article.'

I'd have loved to say something like, 'You idiots. This money's got nothing to do with the South African authorities. It's mine. Greenwood doesn't exist.' But it also occurred to me that if it had been my own money and I were evading UK tax by keeping it in a false name, they'd certainly be right to object to it being with the firm. What I did say was, 'I'm pretty sure Greenwood's not evading South African controls or whatever, but I'll speak to him and ask him to satisfy us about that or take his money away.'

'Thank you, Charles,' they both said, Barry adding, 'How soon can you do that?'

'I think he's in South Africa right now. It might not be prudent to raise it with him till he gets back.'

'When do you expect that to be?' Barry persisted.

'Within a fortnight or so, I think – based on what he was saying when I last saw him.'

'OK,' said Jonathan. 'Then we'll leave it to you to sort it out.'

After they'd left the room I sat and simmered for a while. This was the last straw. As soon as my personal life was sorted out, I'd be moving out of this partnership. Meanwhile, I had two weeks to find another home for the money.

My mind went straight to Jab and the Gragorin problem. Gragorin had taken the bait; he'd called in response to the letter and made an appointment, mentioning he'd be coming alone, he didn't need a lawyer to hold his hand. He wanted £500,000 altogether, which was much more than I had in the Greenwood account. On the other hand, he seemed desperate for money, so maybe some sort of compromise would be possible; after all, his shares would be valueless if nothing came of the Hall Computers deal, and they'd cost him nothing anyway. Perhaps he'd be open to taking the £300,000 he was owed now and parting with his shares on the basis that he'd get the £200,000 he wanted for them only if the Hall deal materialized. That would be eminently affordable to me-alias-Geoffrey. Of course, investing in Jab would be extremely risky, but all I'd be risking was money I'd come into by an amazing stroke of luck and was having problems keeping. And if Hall did buy Jab, I'd have a much larger amount and could then think more seriously about an offshore trust as a home for the proceeds.

I'd see how the meeting with Gragorin went.

15

The weekend in the Cotswolds had to be postponed. Eleanor rang me on my mobile to tell me her father was being admitted to a London hospital on Saturday morning for some tests and she wanted to accompany him and stay around. I phoned Marion and told her my plans for the weekend had changed and we dined at home together on the Friday evening, when she seemed to come out of her shell somewhat and was surprisingly amicable. Then, she surprised me even more by saying, 'Charles, shouldn't we talk?'

'Now?'

'No. I don't mean now, or even this weekend. I mean next week if possible. We're drifting along and going nowhere. And that's bad for everyone, especially the children.'

At last, I thought. 'I know. You're right. When do you suggest?'

'Can you come home early one day, say Monday or Tuesday?'

'Tuesday will be better.' The meeting with Gragorin was scheduled for Monday afternoon. 'I can be home by four.'

'That'll be fine.'

I found the sudden change in her disconcerting, if not a bit scary.

George Gragorin was indeed a disagreeable man, in both character and appearance. His most notable features were a totally bald head, a bloated, blotchy, pockmarked face, a stocky body, and a belligerent bearing. He looked to be in his fifties, spoke gruffly – in a foreign accent which I couldn't identify, mentally classifying it as possibly Balkan or Baltic – and smoked one cigarette after another, blandly ignoring both the notice on the conference table saying, 'Thank you for not smoking' and my barely polite request that he comply with it. I decided not to press the smoking issue for fear of evoking a reaction that might mar the progress of the meeting. Gragorin's hands, I noticed, were not only nicotine-stained but decidedly dirty, a fact which did not deter the fellow from biting his finger-nails with an intensity that suggested they were not part of his anatomy but some vital source of nutrition. His whole demeanour was aggressive and uncontrolled, and it was altogether unpleasant being in his presence.

After an hour of unproductive discussion, Gragorin's contribution to which had been almost entirely obstructive and irrational, I said, 'I think I may have a solution to all this. Mr Gragorin, would you mind if I stepped outside with Henry and Brenda for a minute?'

Gragorin sniffed and nodded, and I ushered Henry and Brenda out of the room.

Over the weekend I had more or less decided that, if Gragorin would agree to take the £300,000 unconditionally now and the other £200,000 if and when a deal was done with Hall, I'd buy him out with Geoffrey's money. In the corridor, out of Gragorin's hearing, I told Henry and Brenda, 'I've got a client in South Africa called Geoffrey Greenwood who's wealthy and likes new challenges. He's been on the look-out for what he calls a 'dynamic opportunity'. I've told him about Jab and he's very interested.' They were locked into what I was saying. I continued, 'He's got technical people out there who'd like to see a full description of the Jab device and some basic financial information. They'll sign a secrecy agreement.'

'All that stuff's available. It's exactly what we prepared for Hall. We can get it to you within half an hour.'

'If you do that, I can fax him this afternoon. If he's happy, he'll move immediately, but he won't risk more than three hundred thousand up front.' I told them the terms which I wanted to offer Gragorin.

'I'm pretty sure he'll go for that,' said Henry. 'What do you think, Brenda?' She nodded.

'How soon can your client get here?' asked Henry.

'He won't come over at all. If he likes the deal, he'll leave it to me to tie up the legal angles and put everything to bed. I've got his power of attorney' – I realized I'd better draw one up quickly and put Geoffrey's signature on it – 'and he's got money here.'

'That all sounds great. But what do we tell Gragorin now?'

'The truth – except about the terms, which come later. It should keep him quiet until we hear from Geoffrey.'

Gragorin remained seemingly determined to be as difficult as he could. He wanted to know all about the man who might be buying his shares, but I told him I could say nothing more for the present except that if there was to be a deal it would be done quickly.

'He must buy at his risk,' said Gragorin. 'I give no warranties, nothing.'

'That won't be a problem, Mr Gragorin,' I replied. 'He'll be looking to Henry and Brenda for warranties.' Henry nodded.

16

Marion was waiting for me in the conservatory.

'Charles,' she began, 'I've started seeing someone.'

'Seeing someone?'

'No, not in that sense. I've started having sessions with a therapist, a woman who's helping me deal with our difficulties.'

What a welcome development, I thought. 'That's very good,' I said enthusiastically.

'I'm still angry and upset, about a number of things, but I'm confused, because something else keeps getting in the way. I'm talking about my father's suicide.'

'Yes, I'm sure that still troubles you. That kind of tragedy never goes away.'

'No, it doesn't, but that's not what I mean. I thought I'd come to terms with it years and years ago, but now − just when we've been having these troubles − I've started brooding over it again, in a different kind of way. It's like I'm fixated on it. I don't know why. I can't get it out of my mind, and I don't want it there. It sort-of stops me from thinking clearly about anything else, especially the things I need to be thinking about − I mean you and me, and the kids and whether we can sort everything out and whether I even want to. I just keep seeing my father on that last night before he went out and did it. Merle − that's her name − says I've got 'unfinished business' over my father's death which I have to deal with. I've no idea what she means, but she says we'll get round to it. You know, my mum and I both saw a therapist after it happened, but I only had a few sessions with him. Mum went on seeing him for at least a year.'

'What else does Merle say?'

'That something's probably triggered it off and I must work with her on finding out what that is. The only thing I've noticed − and it probably means nothing − is that I sometimes feel strange when I see you playing with the kids, as if there's a kind of ominous sign hanging over the scene. It's almost like I'm watching a horror movie − you know, the kind of scene that's accompanied by eerie, off-key childlike music sung in a high-pitched female voice − and next thing I see my father's face and I know he's going off to kill himself.'

'How strange – and awful.'

'Yes, it is. But Merle thinks – and so do I now – that you and I should come to an understanding while I try and sort this thing out with her.'

'What do you suggest?' I asked her, gently.

'I don't want us to break up – not yet anyway. Oh, you can stay away, as much as you wish, lead your own life as they say, be free. I won't interfere.' She'd never said anything like this before. 'We don't have much of a marriage any more, but I don't want a. . . .' – she was searching for a word – 'a fracture just now, and I don't think anything definite should happen one way or another until I can focus properly.'

'That's fine with me.' What she was proposing was fair and practical.

'I hope you do understand,' she said. 'I'm suggesting we, say, call a truce – not that we're at war or anything, but something like a truce. An under-standing that we just let things stay as they are for the present.'

Should I tell her about Eleanor? Yes, I decided, I should. After all, she was being open with me. 'No. I don't want to force the issue,' I replied, 'but there's something you need to know. I've started another relationship.'

She pretended not to react, but there was a noticeable change in her expression. 'I'm not surprised, Charles, but that doesn't change what I'm saying. We're having this conversation because we have to reach some sort of understanding, even if it's only an understanding not to change anything – and when I say 'anything' I include your relationship.' She almost spat the last word out. 'What I want is that we both know where we stand – I certainly do now – and leave it at that until we're ready for the . . . fracture.'

'Or reconciliation?'

'I don't think so. Other relationships don't usually help there, do they?'

'I still love you, Marion, more than anyone.' Now why did I say that? I hadn't intended to.

'Yes, I believe you. I'd say the same if you didn't have someone else. Anyhow, let's just wait and see, shall we?'

Then, after a short silence, I asked her, 'Are our financial arrangements still working for you?'

'Oh, they're fine – while we're living in the same house, that is.'

'Good. But please let me know if you there's anything you do want.'

'Yes, I will. Thank you, Charles.'

Afterwards, I regretted having mentioned another relationship. It had been an unnecessary disclosure and one that had certainly cooled the air. But she'd been right that we needed an understanding, and I felt better now that we had one.

Alone in the master bedroom, I switched on my mobile. There were two messages, one from Eleanor for Geoffrey, the other from Lucy for me. Both had left mobile numbers. I tried Eleanor's first.

'Geoff darling,' she said, 'I've got two pieces of good news. First, my dad's fine.'

'I'm really glad to hear that.'

'Yes. I'm so relieved. The other is, I've got a job interview tomorrow – for the position of manager of a new elite gallery in Chelsea. It's absolutely right for me, Geoff. It's what I know and love best. And the money's good too.'

'That's terrific. What are your chances?'

'Pretty good, I think. The agency say they're impressed with my CV. If I get the job, I'd like to move. My flat's not ideal.'

A thought struck me. Travelling up to London all the time was a hassle, and sooner or later Marion and I would be separating and I'd no longer be living under the same roof as Emma and Paulie, though I was determined to keep them fully in my life and to see and be with them as often as their interests would allow. I wanted to be with Eleanor, and here was the opportunity. There'd still be a healthy balance in Geoffrey's account with the firm one way or another, so I said, 'What about our sharing a flat?'

'What a wonderful idea, Geoff darling. I'd love that.'

'Yes, so would I. I'll have to move out of Beverley Terrace sooner or later, and I can't think of a better place to stay when I come to the UK than with you.'

'Geoff, how much time *will* you be spending in the UK?'

'A lot more than I have been now that I've got you in my life. What time's your appointment?'

'Ten o'clock. I won't know the answer tomorrow, of course, but come to my place tomorrow night and I'll tell you all about it – and stay over. You won't need pyjamas.'

'You've just twisted my arm, Eleanor darling.'

Then I called the number Lucy had left. She answered. 'Where are you?' I asked her.

'At a friend's – a girlfriend. I'm glad you got me here. I was about to switch this phone off and go home. Charles, Malcolm won't stop going on about Geoffrey Greenwood. I thought you should know. Perhaps you *should* warn Greenwood after all.'

'He's already—' I stopped myself; Geoffrey would hardly have told me about a message he'd received to phone a Dr Cole.

'Already what?'

'Gone back to South Africa.'

'Well, I'm sure Malcolm won't try and contact him there, but he probably will when he gets back.'

'What does he want of him?'

'All he'll tell me is that he wants to talk to him, but I think he's after Greenwood's version of the facts. He's got his doubts about my story.'

'Where's he staying?'

'He's back home, but it's all very strained. It's a mess, you know.'

'I imagine it is. And I'm truly sorry for you.'

'Thank you for saying that. I miss you, Charles. Don't you miss me, even a bit?'

'Of course I do.' I made no attempt to hide my irritation. Lucy was out of line.

'It would be nice to be with you again – just once.'

'Lucy, that would be stupid, especially now.'

'I know. Just testing. By the way, how's Marion? I haven't seen her for a while.'

'Fine. She's just fine.'

'Must be nice to have a good marriage still,' she said cattily. 'Or *is* it a good marriage, Charles?'

'Bye, Lucy.'

'Sorry, Charles. I shouldn't have said that. It's just that you always seemed to get so little out of your marriage. I can't understand why you want to cling to it. Or is there someone else who's taken my place now?'

'Lucy, you're out of order.'

'Oh, well. Sorry again then. *You're* never out of order then, are you?'

'This conversation's going nowhere.'

'That's clear. Very well, Charles. Should I still keep you in the picture? About my problem, I mean.'

'Yes, please do.'

17

Doing the deal with Gragorin turned out to be easier than I'd imagined. The man was so hungry for money that it didn't take long before he'd accepted my terms. His initial reaction to the proposal was one of feigned incomprehension, which was followed – after I'd made it clear that my client wouldn't buy on any other basis – by an animated show of petulance and then rapid capitulation. He couldn't wait to sign the relatively simple agreement I then drew up, brushing aside my suggestion that he show it to a lawyer before committing himself to it. I signed for Geoffrey under my purported power of attorney, which I showed him but he ignored, and by the end of the day he'd left with the firm's cheque for £300,000 in his hand, having signed over to Geoffrey his shares in and claims against the company and resigned as a director.

Jonathan had signed the cheque with me. He and Barry were visibly relieved to see the bulk of Geoffrey's money leave the firm and quite amenable to the balance remaining in the client account, the more so since it would be reduced even further by another charge for fees.

Henry and Brenda were delighted with the outcome and gave me an exaggeratedly pompous welcome to the board of directors in Gragorin's place – an appointment which, I'd informed them, Greenwood had asked me to accept in view of his own distance from the company's affairs.

I spent the whole night with Eleanor. She told me the interview couldn't have gone better and that she was optimistic about getting the job.

'That's great,' I said. 'And how's your father getting on now?'

'He's still complaining about the same aches and pains. They assured him there's nothing seriously wrong with his health – he's got a bit of arthritis, that's all. One of the doctors told him he's just suffering from retirement syndrome.'

'What's that?'

'It's not a medical condition, just a name for a form of stress that affects people who retire and feel they've become useless. In my dad's case, it's particularly bad because he held such a high position – he was second in command of the whole Cambridgeshire Constabulary, you know, and he's a control freak. He's very clever and he's always had authority, and he

54

loves taking charge of things and manipulating people. He says he's just an old man now, living alone, which isn't true because he still behaves the same way and still has friends – mainly ex-colleagues.'

'How do you get on with him?'

'Oh, I love him dearly, and he loves me – sometimes too much, I think. I've always been the apple of his eye, and he's always been my big daddy, my protector. But I try and keep him out of my life as much as I can, because he likes to run it for me. He sort of just takes charge and I somehow find myself going along with him and his ideas, because he's so self-assured and dominant – and usually very logical and convincing. It's only afterwards that I realize I haven't done my own thing, but his.'

'Does he know about us?' What I certainly did not need in my life right now was an interfering policeman.

'No. I haven't said a word to him about us, or you. And I don't intend to until I feel I must. As it is, he's always going on about my lack of judgement when it comes to men, and how naive I was to be taken in by Tom – my ex-husband – and how I'd still have been in that relationship if it weren't for him. I'd hate to think what he'd say if I told him I'd fallen in love with someone I'd just met who lived overseas. He'd want to know all about you, and about your intentions. No, Geoff, I'll introduce you to him when the time's right and I've managed to prepare the ground for both of you. Meanwhile, you'll remain my secret love.'

'That's OK with me,' I said. 'He sounds interesting and I'd like to meet him, but from what you've just said, I'd rather he didn't know about me yet.'

In fact, her approach suited me perfectly, because by the time her father did get to hear about me, I'd no longer be Geoffrey Greenwood to her and there'd be no need for him to be told I ever was.

As far as she herself was concerned, I was convinced now that my marriage was over and that I should tell her everything. It was simply a matter of timing and preparation – the occasion had to be right and I had to be fully rehearsed, not only about what to say and how best to put it, but also with the answers she'd want from me once she'd heard it. It wasn't going to be easy, but I was banking on her feelings for me prevailing and making it possible for her to accept me as myself instead of the person she thought I was.

I still loved Marion – I always would – and was pleased she might be coming to terms with her problem, but even if she *was* emerging from the Great Sulk, it had happened too late. I now shared with Eleanor the complete relationship – love, sex, and companionship – as I'd once done with Marion but no longer did. The only thing it lacked was that Eleanor wasn't the mother of my children. But I was determined to minimize the damage to Emma and Paulie of my now inevitable fracture with their mother and to see that I remained their father despite it, in every sense and way. And I was confident that both Marion and Eleanor would be willing to help me bring that about.

The next afternoon there was a message from Eleanor on my mobile to say she'd got the job and given in her notice at Lawtons, and that she was taking some holiday leave owed to her so that she could look at flats. She asked me to call her back. When I did, I congratulated her and she said, 'Can you come up for the weekend and help me, Geoff?'

'I can get there on Saturday night, which will leave us all of Sunday.' She was happy with that. I couldn't mention – yet – that I had two small children with whom I spent a large part of every Saturday.

It was time to find out whether Malcolm had put in a second appearance at Beverley Terrace, so I rang Clarke and told him I was calling from abroad. 'No more visitors, Mr Greenwood, but a few letters have arrived for you.'

'Mister Clarke, please put them in a large envelope and post it first-class to my solicitor, Mr Charles Brook.' I gave him the address. 'You've still got a cash float there for me. And if you wouldn't mind, could you continue doing the same for me on a weekly basis until I get back to Brighton?'

Clarke's envelope was on my desk the next afternoon. Only one of the letters in it was of any interest. It was from Malcolm and read:

Dear Mr Greenwood,

We have not met, but that is not for want of trying. You are a difficult man to get to, so I must write to you. My wife Lucille (Lucy) has told me she had an affair with you and I have evidence to bear out that she visited your flat a couple of times. I need to know if you admit to having had a relationship with her. I have reason to believe that she may have met someone else in your flat. My marriage and family life are at stake. If you are a man of honour you will contact me, one way or the other. If you don't I will keep on trying to see you. You are the only person who can help me sort all this out.

Yours sincerely
Malcolm Cole

The letter was handwritten on notepaper bearing Malcolm's home address and telephone number. A thought struck me: I could write back to him as Geoffrey. But what could I say? That I hadn't had an affair with his wife? If so, I'd be telling him what he suspected: that someone else had been using my flat – exactly what Lucy didn't want him to hear. And what would he do next? Try and get me, as Geoffrey, to tell him who'd been using his flat, and probably also confront Lucy about me again.

No, writing to him would only stir up things more. There was nothing I could do but make sure I kept dodging him and hope he'd eventually give up the chase, though I somehow doubted he would – unless, of course, he and Lucy became reconciled. Failing that, the situation continued to be a dangerous one.

18

Henry's call from New York came about two weeks later.

In the meantime, Eleanor had found a flat in St John's Wood which we'd viewed together on the Sunday and both liked a lot. It was a bright, newly decorated two-bedroomed apartment situated a block away from the High Street, very near Regent's Park. Afterwards, we discussed how we'd arrange everything and I knew I ought to be making my disclosure now – how could I possibly contemplate living with her as Geoffrey Greenwood? On the other hand, how could I just become someone else while we were busy setting up home together? There we were, talking about furniture and financial arrangements, and there she was, happy and excited about it all, and there I was, waiting for the chance to make the astonishing revelation that I wasn't the nice single fellow from South Africa she'd fallen in love with and was about to start living with, but a married solicitor with two young children who'd been lying to her and cheating on his wife. This was probably the worst possible time for me to be breaking the news to her. Better to do so once we were installed in the flat.

We agreed we'd each pay half the rent and other outgoings, but that she should apply for the tenancy – my suggestion, which I justified to her on the basis that my being a non-resident could diminish our chances of getting the flat as against competing resident applicants. I insisted on paying for the furniture and other things we'd need, pointing out that she'd be bringing in all her stuff from her present flat. 'Oh, Geoff,' she laughed, 'that's all old trash. It's got no value.' Reluctantly, however, she gave in, but only on the clear understanding that whatever was bought with my money must belong to me.

She was overjoyed to learn a few days later that she'd got the tenancy. I transferred into her bank account an amount sufficient to cover my share of the first six months' rent and an additional £15,000 of Geoffrey's money for purchases. She asked me if I wanted to help her choose any of the furniture or other things and seemed pleased when I said I didn't, and she enthusiastically offered to take charge of all the moving and other arrangements, asking me to do no more than show up on the day.

As it turned out, I wasn't even able to do that, because I was on my way to America.

It was a very excited Henry who called me from New York on one of my rare evenings at home.

'Charles,' he shouted across the Atlantic, 'they're crazy about Jab. They want it so badly they won't let us come home till we've done a deal with them. How quickly can you and Greenwood get here?'

'Please slow down, Henry, and tell me exactly what's happened.'

'Here's Brenda. Speak to her.'

'Charles,' came Brenda's voice. 'It's unbelievable. The presentation went like a bomb and they're already talking about money.'

I felt a surge of excitement. 'What sort of deal. . . ?'

'They want to buy us out, Charles – partly for cash and partly for their own stock. Henry and I must remain full-time, but over here. The business must move here.'

'And the price?'

'They're talking about four thousand dollars a share – that's for all nine thousand shares in Jab Enterprises – which means they're valuing the company at thirty-six million dollars!'

That made Geoffrey's shares worth $12 million. Incredible! 'That's probably just their starting figure,' I heard myself saying. 'Hold them off. I'll be there as soon as I can get on a plane.'

'What about Greenwood? They want all the shareholders here.'

'I'll call him right away.' There'd be time to let everyone know Geoffrey wouldn't be coming. And Hall Computers would surely not let an opportunity like this go by just because they'd have to deal with Geoffrey's lawyer acting under his power of attorney rather than the man himself.

Henry came back on the line. 'Charles, Brenda and I want you to know how much we appreciate what you've done for us. Everything's turned the corner for us since you came onto the scene.'

'Slowly, Henry. We're not there yet, you know.'

'We are, you know,' replied Henry.

I was on a flight the next day, having seen to various preliminaries, which included an apologetic phone call to a disappointed Eleanor about an urgent business deal in New York – she reassured me she could handle everything in my absence and wished me luck – and a brief explanation to Marion about a business trip for a client, as well as a rather longer one to Emma and Paulie about having to go somewhere in an aeroplane for my work but not being away too long. Marion, too, wished me luck and I told her I'd keep in touch. I'd also arranged for Merriwether and Clayton, a New York law firm specializing in IT mergers and acquisitions, to have a team standing by.

Rooms had been booked for Geoffrey and me at a Manhattan hotel. When checking in, I told the receptionist Mr Greenwood had been delayed and would be arriving the next day. There was a message for me to call Henry on a particular number as soon as I arrived.

'Are you guys there?' Henry asked.

'Well, I am. Greenwood's been delayed.'

'Oh, hell. Hall are insisting on meeting all three shareholders personally.'

'As far as I know he's coming, but not today. Meanwhile, I've got his full authority to negotiate – as well as his power of attorney – and I can reach him by phone.'

'Charles, you have to see he comes. Anyway, Brenda and I are at Hall's offices on West Fifty-Seventh Street. Can you grab a cab and come over right away?'

'Yes, as soon as I've showered and changed.' Henry gave me the address and told me to ask for Conrad Reiman when I arrived.

There were seven people sitting around a conference table when I was shown in – Henry, Brenda, three other men and two other women. The men rose as I entered, and one of them, a balding giant, greeted me. 'Mr Brook, Charles Brook? I'm Conrad Reiman, vice-president in charge of acquisitions, Hall Computers.' He introduced each of the other four to me. They were all Hall executives.

I sat down, declining an offer of coffee, and Reiman said, 'Charles, if I may call you so,' – I nodded – 'we're disappointed Mr Greenwood's not here. We're told he has one third of the company's stock, which we can't think of buying in his absence.'

'He's been delayed, unavoidably, but I'm expecting him here tomorrow.' I was still working out the excuse I'd be giving for Geoffrey not showing up at all; it would have to be illness or an accident of some kind, but the details had to be convincing.

'Well, I hope he does,' said Reiman, 'or else we may just have to post-pone everything until he finds the time to get involved.' Henry and Brenda were looking alarmed.

Reiman asked one of the women present, an in-house lawyer, to outline his company's proposal. Reading from notes, she said they'd pay $36 million for Jab Enterprises, $24 million in cash and $12 million in quoted stock of Hall Computers at current market value. Henry, Brenda, and other key personnel would be expected to sign employment contracts. Stockholders' loans would be repaid, which meant I'd get back the £300,000 I'd already paid Gragorin in addition to Geoffrey's one-third share of the price, out of which I'd have to pay Gragorin the other £200,000. Hall's external attorneys were drawing up the full, formal offer.

'Conrad,' I said, 'it all sounds fine. The only problem my clients have is with the price. I'm not saying it isn't acceptable, but they've got no idea of the market value of something like Jab.'

Reiman hesitated before replying. 'As a lawyer, Charles, you know better than I that the market value of anything is what a willing buyer will pay for it and a willing seller will accept. Technology like Jab is no different from anything else. We're willing buyers here and the price we're offering is what we think Jab is worth to us. This city's full of financial consultants who think they know all about deals around technology. You can go and talk to any one or more of them but it won't help you much – unless, of course, they put you on to another buyer, and if that happens we back off. We're not about to enter into an auction for Jab.'

He paused, nodded at one of his colleagues, who nodded back, then continued: 'We want to do this deal and the sooner the better, but just as we don't want to overpay, so it doesn't suit us to be buying cheap, because unhappy sellers can become bothersome afterwards, even when everything's signed and sealed. Besides, it's not going to do us much good if Henry and Brenda, who'll be running Jab for us, start thinking they got a raw deal. Our offer will be open for seven days, during which time your clients are free to get all the advice they want – financial, technical, legal, you name it. There'll be only two conditions: one, you don't negotiate with any other buyers behind our back, and two, you guys stick around so that this thing stays on track' – he looked at me – 'and that includes Greenwood.'

The meeting was adjourned, and Henry, Brenda and I were given a room with a telephone and secretarial assistance, which we used to set up appointments for the next day with Merriwether and Clayton and an investment bank recommended by that firm. Henry and Brenda told me they were both anxious to accept the offer and tie the deal up; they'd never expected to see this kind of money and didn't want to run the slightest risk by delaying their acceptance.

'Geoffrey's as keen as you people are,' I replied, 'but he never believes in grabbing the first offer too quickly, and besides, Reiman's committed now for the next seven days, so we've got nothing to lose by making a few enquiries.'

'At this moment,' said Henry, 'I'm more worried about what will happen if Greenwood doesn't show up.'

'I expect him to get here, Henry, but rest assured that nothing will derail this deal now.'

Even as I said these words, I wasn't as sure about that as I had been before meeting Reiman. He was a shrewd, experienced operator, quite capable, if his suspicions were aroused, of seeing right through me to the invisible Geoffrey Greenwood.

19

Marion made her dramatic breakthrough in therapy shortly after my arrival in New York.

As I was to learn from her later, it happened towards the end of a particularly taxing session during which she'd been feeling increasingly anxious without knowing why. Then the therapist, Merle, had suddenly averted her eyes and taken a deep breath.

'Marion,' she said, 'exactly where were you when your father kissed you goodnight?'

'In my bed. Why?' Marion felt a sharp pang of foreboding.

'You say your father was crying?'

'Yes.'

'And you held his face in your hands and comforted him?'

'Yes.'

'And where was he?'

An avalanche of emotions came tumbling down on her. And then, with sickening horror, she remembered.

'Where was he, Marion?' Merle repeated.

She could barely let herself answer the question. 'On top of me,' she whispered. And then she shouted, shaking all over in her rage, 'He was in the bed, on top of me, the fucking bastard!'

20

It was just after midnight in London when I rang Eleanor from New York. She'd made me promise to call her from there, no matter how late it was in London. I asked her what she was doing and she said she was tucked up in bed, thinking of me, and had been hoping I'd phone. I told her I'd had a good flight and a busy afternoon, and might be tied up for a couple of weeks.

'I miss you, Geoffrey darling, terribly.'

'So do I, my love. I miss you too. Tell me about the flat.'

She did – about the stuff she'd been buying and the moving arrangements, and how exciting it all was. Then we exchanged more endearments and she asked me for the name and number of my hotel. I was prepared for the question, and though I was anxious to avoid compounding the lies I'd already told her, I had no alternative. So I said I was moving hotels in the morning but wasn't sure of the details yet, all the arrangements having been made by my American hosts. I promised to call her again in a few days. 'But if you want to reach me in the meantime, sweetheart, by all means ring me on my mobile. The number's the same. I'm using the international roaming facility.'

It was, I reflected after the call, tricky enough trying to conclude a multi-million-dollar deal for an absent, non-existent client without also having to manage a complex communication problem with someone from whom I was concealing my identity. At all costs, I had to continue evading requests by Eleanor for particulars of where I was staying – imagine her trying to reach me at my hotel as Geoffrey Greenwood! My intended disclosure to her, which had been forestalled by my unexpected departure, must now await my return to London, and meanwhile the pretence had to be sustained. What I'd have to do if necessary was tell her that I was very busy on this trip and couldn't have too many personal calls. When I did eventually make the disclosure, I'd have to do some serious apologizing and be very convincing about the reasons for having delayed my revelations.

As for the deal, I was about to become a multi-millionaire, but as Geoffrey Greenwood – a complication the only possible solution to which was an offshore trust. I'd considered the idea once before when looking for a home for the money in the firm's client account and rejected it, but now the amount involved was large enough to warrant the cost factor. The trouble was that I would have to find some way of establishing Geoffrey's identity and credibility – and do so without delay, because everything had to be ready before the deal was completed.

Fighting off the sleep I so badly needed, I stayed up for hours, thinking. At five in the morning I consulted my diary and rang a number on the island of Guernsey.

'Citadel Trustees. Good morning,' said a pleasant female voice.

'Is Jeremy Lefarge available?'

'Yes, sir; he is. Who may I say is calling?'

'Charles Brook, solicitor.'

The familiar voice of Jeremy Lefarge came on the line. After the initial greetings, I said, 'Jeremy, I'm in New York, tying up a big deal for a South African client. His name's Geoffrey Greenwood.'

'Sounds like a nice lucrative job for a hungry lawyer,' said Jeremy with an audible grin, 'especially if you're busy with it at this hour. It must still be dead of night over there.'

'Just after five in the morning. This thing's on the point of being tied up and my client would like the proceeds to go into trust. Can you help?'

'That's this company's business, if I'm not mistaken, and I'm still its chief executive in Guernsey. So how much do you want to tell me now, Charles?'

'Quite a lot, if you have the time.'

'Fire away.'

'My client needs a trust in which to hold between twelve and fifteen million dollars in cash and quoted stock, and I've recommended you guys to him as trustees.'

'Thank you for that, Charles. That's big money. Discretionary trust, I presume?'

'Yes.'

'And the beneficiaries?'

'The client himself, for one.'

'And who else. Children? Grandchildren? Wife? Mistress?'

I'd anticipated the question and decided on Eleanor. Greenwood was supposed to be childless and single, so the person nearest to him would be the woman with whom he'd soon be living. As a beneficiary under a discretionary trust she would not have any rights, but merely be *eligible* to benefit – though I'd be happy for her to participate if she and I formed a lasting relationship. If we didn't I'd have lost nothing by having her name appear in the trust deed.

'At this stage,' I told Jeremy, 'there'd be two named beneficiaries – Mr Greenwood and his partner, a woman called Eleanor Downing. But don't bother with those details now, Jeremy. I'll be faxing or emailing all that to you. Right now, I just want us to establish the fundamentals. My client is selling his interest in a UK company to an American corporation and wants the proceeds to bypass him and go straight into the trust. What would you need to set it up and be ready to receive the money and the stock?'

'Well, as I'm sure you know, we'd have some preliminary requirements. The size of the trust fund – and your introduction, of course – make it very attractive to us, but we must know about the source of the funds and exactly who we are dealing with – I mean this Greenwood fellow. I think we'd have to meet him personally.'

'That might be difficult for a while. It's unlikely he could get over to you for a few months.'

'Hmm. I've got a problem with that.'

'There must be a way around it surely, Jeremy? This thing can't wait.'

After a short silence, Jeremy said, as if thinking aloud, 'Charles, you're on our panel of referring professionals and you're vouching for him, I presume. So I suppose a personal meeting with him could be delayed for a few months, but we'd need identification and references before we could accept any cash or other assets.'

'I could let you have a certified copy of his passport as well as a formal introductory letter from my firm.'

'Yes, that would do. But we'd also have to have something independent about the source of the money.'

'How about a letter from the company making the payment? Confidentially, it's Hall Computers.'

'That'll be fine.'

'Good. My client's here in New York with me, so I'll get the details to you in writing in the next couple of days.'

Here I was, telling Jeremy that Geoffrey was in New York while simultaneously pretending to everyone involved in the deal that he wasn't. But I had no choice.

'Great. Meanwhile I'll prepare a draft declaration of trust and email it to you there. Can you give me an address?' I gave him the hotel's email and said, 'Thanks, Jeremy. It's always a pleasure doing business with you.'

'Thank *you*, Charles. This one sounds very nice.'

Next, I rang Cindy in Brighton and asked her to make a search in the firm's archives for a file I'd closed off a year or two earlier – that of the estate of the late Paul Morrison, a citizen of Zimbabwe who'd died of a heart attack at the age of forty while living in the UK – and to courier to me in New York the copy of the deceased's passport which should still be in the file. I also told her to see that any post for Mr Greenwood which had been redirected from the client's flat should be included in the parcel.

Then I lay down on the bed and thought about my night's work. Assuming I could create Geoffrey's 'passport' as I hoped to, there should be no further obstacles to the setting up of the trust. With the aid of my laptop and the amenities of the hotel's business centre, I could prepare all the paperwork Jeremy would be expecting to receive from me, sign it all – as Geoffrey where necessary and as myself where appropriate –and leave it to Jeremy to establish the trust by means of a declaration by the trustees.

From my point of view, the document that would really matter was Geoffrey's letter of wishes to the trustees, because that was the means through which I'd be able to take control of the trust. In this kind of situation trustees didn't really want to make the key decisions; they preferred to leave them to their client, the founder; though legal control had to be with the trustees. So the usual procedure was for the founder to write the trustees a letter expressing the founder's wishes as to how the trustees should run the trust. The letter of wishes wouldn't bind the trustees legally, but in practice they would willingly comply with it, unless they had good reason not to, such as illegality. Geoffrey's wishes would be designed to suit my objectives.

As for the problem of Jeremy receiving a personal visit from Geoffrey in the next few months, I'd have to see to it that Geoffrey couldn't make that visit, or any later one.

21

The next week was a busy one. After two days of meetings with advisers, Henry, Brenda and I were persuaded that Hall Computers' offer was not at all unfair. We were told that Jab had an uncertain lifespan, because anti-virus technology was in a constant state of research and development. Hall were keen to get it because it could conveniently be sold with their computers, but it was too susceptible to competition to become the corner-stone of a gigantic new business. The advice we got was to ask for another $10 million and then take whatever came our way.

By now Geoffrey's arrival was three days overdue.

'I'm afraid Geoffrey Greenwood can't get here,' I told Henry and Brenda.

They both looked crestfallen. 'Why?' asked Henry.

'He was in a motor accident the day he was booked to fly here from Johannesburg. At first his injuries didn't seem too severe, but then there were complications and he had to have surgery, and now he's all plastered up and unable to travel.'

'That's awful for him,' said Brenda, 'and pretty bad for us. Did you know about the accident?'

'Yes, but he'd asked me not to say anything because he didn't want to rock the boat unnecessarily.'

'How do you think Hall are going to react?' asked Henry.

'I can't see Reiman dumping the deal, especially now it's clear Geoffrey can't help himself. Anyhow, we must let them know. Let's mention it to the Merriwether team and they can pass it on to Hall's attorneys.'

The news about Geoffrey was not well received by Reiman. He rang me as soon as he'd heard it. 'It's too bad about Mr Greenwood and I wish him well, sincerely, but we remain very unhappy about doing this thing without him.'

'Well, he genuinely can't fly and it's going to be some time before he can.'

'Where is he exactly?'

'At home in Johannesburg, I believe.'

'Could I speak with him on the telephone?'

Oh, hell. This guy's just not giving in, I thought. I chose my next words carefully. 'If you think you should, I'm sure you can.'

'I certainly do think I should. Is there any reason why I shouldn't?'

'Well, Conrad, if I were advising you, I'd say it's about the worst thing you could do. You tell me you don't want any comebacks from this man, but how's it going to seem to him when you, vice-president of Hall Computers, call him across a distance of ten thousand miles because he can't get here? I know the man, and he's bound to be unsettled by your call, no matter what you tell him. I'm here in New York – his lawyer, with his power of attorney – and he and I are in daily contact, so why should you need to call him personally? To put him under some kind of pressure – that's what I think he'll think – and the first thing he'll do is phone me and ask me what's going on. Then one of two things will happen. Either he'll be scared off, which I doubt, but he might be – remember, this deal's not as crucial to him as it is to Henry and Brenda – or he'll want to go ahead but be uneasy. Which is exactly what I think you want to avoid. You don't want any comebacks, Conrad, and you won't get any from Geoffrey Greenwood – as things stand now – but make him suspicious and who knows?'

There was silence at Reiman's end of the line, then he said, 'You're making sense, Charles. I'd like to consult my colleagues about this.'

'What about the deal?'

'Oh, that must go ahead, full steam ahead. We'll think of something regarding Greenwood.'

The conversation left me wondering about the level to which I'd managed to raise my capacity for deception. I'd enjoyed being inventive when taking on Tolway Perry and SEP, but maintaining the illusion of a real Geoffrey Greenwood had become a considerable strain. It had reached the stage now where I was just telling one lie after another. Sooner or later I was bound to slip up. And as for the moral aspect of it, I was beginning to dislike myself; I'd been cheating and lying ever since I'd conceived Geoffrey and it felt as if I was on a treadmill: the more I lied the more I had to.

The money was good, though.

22

The negotiations were due to resume on the Monday. Meanwhile, there was welcome respite over the weekend. I spent Saturday afternoon browsing around Manhattan and doing some shopping, picking up gifts for the children, Eleanor and Marion, and very nearly making the mistake of signing the card to accompany Eleanor's 'Charles' instead of 'Geoff'. Or would it have been a mistake? Not if she got the card after I'd made my revelation.

That evening I went with Henry and Brenda to Greenwich Village, where we had supper and saw a show. I wondered about Henry and Brenda; they weren't just partners but good friends; the question was how good? I knew they occupied separate rooms at the hotel, but in the short time I'd known them I'd never heard a word about any other relationships and they seemed to be together most of the time. Anyway, it wasn't any of my business; they were entitled to their secrets as much as I was to mine, though the truth about mine would have shocked the lights out of them both.

On Sunday we all attended a barbecue lunch at the home of Nathan Mann, the partner in Merriwether and Clayton who was leading the legal team. The occasion was spoilt by some inclement weather but was otherwise quite enjoyable.

'This always happens,' Nathan Mann told me, 'whenever we entertain clients. The office joke is that it wouldn't if we changed the firm's name to "Gloomy Weather and Clayton".' I smiled. Nathan was turning out to be a likeable person as well as a competent lawyer.

I'd called Eleanor at the flat that morning – she'd moved in the previous day – and after she'd told me about some of the attendant hassles and how she hoped to have the place in a fit state to impress me when I got back, we'd had a lovers' conversation so intimate that I was able, at the end of it, to convince a purring Eleanor that it would be difficult for me to speak to her again until the next weekend – assuming I didn't get home before then. She hadn't asked me again for the name or phone number of the hotel, and it occurred to me that the omission might actually have been deliberate. Perhaps she'd decided that pressing me for information I didn't care to volunteer, especially at such a great distance, might do more harm than good to the harmony of our still-blossoming relationship.

Then, before leaving for the barbecue, I'd composed and typed two documents on my laptop. One was a letter from me to Jeremy Lefarge which read:

Dear Jeremy

Here are the promised details of the proposed new trust for my client, Mr Greenwood:

It is to be called THE GREENWOOD TRUST and the first beneficiaries are to be GEOFFREY ROBERT GREENWOOD of Flat 6, Washington House, 10 Lilac Avenue, London NW8, and ELEANOR MARY DOWNING of the same address, but the Trustees should have the power to appoint additional beneficiaries and to exclude beneficiaries. If so directed by GEOFFREY ROBERT GREENWOOD, the Trustees should treat as a beneficiary any company designated by him.

Mr Greenwood is here now and I shall let you have the following within the next couple of days:

1. a certified copy of his passport

2. a letter of reference concerning him

3. a letter from Hall Computers Incorporated confirming that subject to contract Mr Greenwood will become entitled to certain stock and monies as the proceeds of the sale by him of his shares in a UK company called Jab Enterprises Limited.

An advance copy of the letter of wishes signed by Mr Greenwood accompanies this fax.

Kind regards

Charles Brook

The second document was a letter of wishes in which Geoffrey Greenwood requested the trustees to carry out their powers in accordance with his wishes as conveyed to them from time to time, either by himself or by 'my legal adviser, Mr Charles Joseph Brook, who you may always assume will be acting on my full authority'. The letter went on to say that in the event of Geoffrey's death or if anything else happened to him which suggested he had ceased to be capable of communicating with the trustees, they should act on 'the wishes of the said Charles Joseph Brook in all respects as if they were mine.'

I saved both documents on a floppy disk, then went down to the hotel's business centre – having previously checked that it would be open on Sunday – where I printed them out in duplicate. I signed the fax as myself and put Geoffrey's signature on the letter of wishes, which I inserted in an envelope addressed to Jeremy. Then I handed the envelope in for posting and the fax for transmission.

23

Conrad Reiman and his people reacted to the suggestion that the price should be increased with all the expected protestations and posturing, but didn't take too long to concede another $9 million – which everyone knew they needn't have done but had decided to do because their first offer had not been their last and, as Reiman had said, keeping vendors happy was important to Hall. This brought the price of Geoffrey's shares up to $15 million.

Meanwhile, there'd been a few other developments unconnected with the deal. First, the couriered parcel had arrived from Brighton with two unexpected items, both of them letters in sealed envelopes. One was from Marion to me, the other from Lucy to Geoffrey at Beverley Terrace. From Cindy's covering note I learned that Marion had particularly wanted her letter sent on to me in New York. Lucy's letter had been in Geoffrey's mail redirected from the flat. Despite my curiosity about Lucy's letter to Geoffrey, I read Marion's first.

To my surprise it began *Dear Teddy*, the pet name she hadn't called me by for at least a year; then it went on:

> *I'm writing to you on the advice of Merle Watson, my therapist. She says I owe it to you, myself and the children to tell you something I've been repressing for twenty years. It's quite horrible. So here goes.*
>
> *My father took his own life when I was 13 because he had just raped me. He did it very gently but he did hurt me and make me feel dirty and guilty. I got into the bath afterwards and cleaned myself up, but I forgot about that, too. He cried afterwards and then went off in his car to gas himself. I had repressed the sex part entirely until now, but Merle has helped me open my mind to it – I want to tell you in person exactly how, when you're back here. It might have happened more than once, though I can only remember the one time. Merle thinks there may have been more, because he was always kissing and cuddling me. My mother knew nothing*

about it, though I think she must have suspected at the end. Anyhow, she's never given me any hint of that, and I don't want to tell her now because it will only hurt her, like it has hurt me all these years. Please never let her know any of this.

I'm sorry, Teddy, very sorry, that you, too, have had to be a victim of my father's disgusting lust. According to Merle, most of my anger towards you had nothing to do with you, it was about my father. She also believes that what set off my fixation on my father's suicide after all those years was seeing you in the role of a father to our kids, especially Emma. Whenever I saw you playing with them, my mind would start connecting what I was watching with what had happened to me and bringing the whole awful thing back into my consciousness. That's what she says and it seems about right to me.

Merle, you, and I are now the only people who know about this awful business and I know I needn't say this but it must never go any further than the three of us. Merle is surprised that I managed to have a normal physical relationship with you afterwards. She says girls who've had similar experiences are often turned off sex for life. Besides you (and my father, curse him) I have never had sex with anyone, man or woman.

Teddy, I know this has been what has dragged me down, because even with the horror of knowing, I feel much better now, better in fact than I've ever felt as an adult. I've written to you about this because it's easier than telling it, and after we've talked about it on your return I never want to speak of it again.

About you and me, I don't know if we still have a marriage, or if we ever really did have one, because I feel as if I have to learn anew about love between a man and a woman. I do believe I have loved you and I think I still do, even though it's complicated now because I drove you away and you've found another life for yourself. But I must also tell you that I don't take all the blame for what's happened between us: there were other things that upset me which I still want to discuss with you. The important thing is that I now know I want to stay in this marriage and make the effort, with you, of trying to redeem it, for our own sakes and those of our dear little ones, and nothing will please me more than to hear that you feel the same way.

I don't want to say any more for now, nor do I expect a reply from you while you are still away. What I'd like is for us to discuss everything when you are back.

All my love

Marion

The letter left me feeling stunned, shaken, and deeply sorry for her, but for myself, somewhat to my own surprise, happy and uplifted. She still loved me and wanted to rebuild our marriage – all that I'd longed for until

I'd met Eleanor. Could Eleanor really ever mean as much to me as Marion? Wouldn't it be wonderful if Marion could indeed become herself again and we could work out whatever difficulties we still had? As for her shocking experience, incestuous rape was reputedly common, but here it was, in the life of my own Marion. What a sick, heartless monster this so-called father of hers must have been! Taking his own life had been almost as selfish and cruel as the act – or acts – that had led him to it. And what an ordeal she must have suffered, and for so long too! She'd been brave to write to me like this. And she said she thought she still loved me. I must phone her at once, not to discuss anything in detail but just to let her know my reactions to the bad and the good news in her letter. No, it was too late in England; I'd call her tomorrow.

But what about Eleanor? What a mess! Then, thinking about her, I was confused. Did Marion really mean more to me than she did? My love for Marion was somehow in the past and would need to be revived, and there was no guarantee it would be. My love for Eleanor was fresh and new, and untarnished. But then, of course, there were the children, and regardless of what I arranged about them, the dynamics of my relationship with them would change if Marion and I split up. I needed to suspend my emotions until I got home and spoke to Marion face to face, and only then could I really start thinking clearly about it all.

I turned my attention to Lucy's letter to Geoffrey.

Dear Mr Greenwood

You don't know me but my husband believes that I have had an affair with you. We both know it's nonsense but I have admitted it. I can't explain why in a letter. It's very complicated.

I believe he has been trying to contact you. I don't know what he's after from you. You can, of course, ignore all this if you like but I'd be pleased if we could just have a short conversation.

It is quite safe for you to ring me on my mobile telephone (number above) any time of day or night. Please do so.

Yours sincerely
Lucy Cole

What was Lucy up to? If she had a good reason for wanting to talk to Geoffrey, why hadn't she asked me to pave the way? She had my mobile number and could have reached me wherever she thought I was. She obviously didn't want me to know. Her availability to take a call day and night suggested she and Malcolm weren't together any more. What, if anything, should I do? As myself, clearly nothing, because I ought not to have seen the letter. As Geoffrey, perhaps write back to her in Geoffrey's handwriting, but say what? And she'd specifically requested a phone call, not a letter.

I crumpled the letter up and threw it in the bin.

24

The copy of the late Paul Morrison's Zimbabwean passport was the next item in the parcel to receive my attention. It wasn't a bad copy – all the vital personal information was more or less legible – and the photograph, although a bit blurred, as I'd expected, was that of a man in his thirties, the passport having been issued some years before Morrison's death. All in all, the document was ideal for my purpose, so I put it in my briefcase to take with me to a store on Forty-Fifth Street called Fototrix which I'd come across the day before.

There'd been a sign in the window saying the establishment specialized in digital reproductions and reconstructions of pictures and documents 'for strictly legal purposes'. I'd gone inside and spun the sales clerk a story about a stag party for a friend who was getting married and how we, his pals, wanted to send him on his way with a 'passport to matrimony'. I asked the clerk whether, if I brought in a copy of the groom's passport, Fototrix would be able to reproduce it in the desired form. The clerk replied they certainly would, though the final product would look like a photocopy, not an actual passport. That would be fine, I said.

The clerk remembered me when I returned with the copy of the Morrison passport.

'I wasn't able to get a copy of the bridegroom's own passport,' I told him, 'but his cousin, who looks a lot like him, gave me a copy of an expired passport of his own to use.' I showed him the document. 'It's from Zimbabwe in southern Africa. He and the groom were both born there.'

The clerk examined the copy. 'Yeah. We can work with this. What exactly do you want?'

'Well, I'd like another copy of the passport with some changes.' I explained that the cover page should say 'Matrimony' instead of 'Zimbabwe', the bridegroom's name, Geoffrey Robert Greenwood, should replace the name of his cousin, Paul Morrison, and three dates should be changed – those of issue and expiry, so that it would be currently valid, and the holder's date of birth.

The clerk asked, 'Would you like any of the inside pages changed to say Matrimony – which he pronounced matri-*mo*-ney – 'instead of Zim-what-ever?'

I pretended to consider this suggestion. 'No. I don't think we need go that far. The matrimony message will be clear enough from the cover.'

The clerk wrote out an order, noting all the required changes, worked out a price for the job, took payment in advance, and told me my 'goods' would be ready for collection in forty-eight hours.

I'd ordered a wake-up call for 5.30 a.m. and rang Marion when I got it.

'I received your letter,' I said. 'I'm so sorry, Marion darling.' I hadn't called her 'darling' in a long time. 'What a monstrous ordeal you've been through, and for so long! I'm very angry for you – and for us, as you say.'

'Thanks, Teddy. I'd prefer to wait till you get back before we discuss anything.'

'Yes, of course. But I want you to know I love you.'

'Thank you, Teddy. I love you too. But there's a lot of ground for us to cover. When will you be back?'

'Difficult to say. It's all going well, but I'd guess another week to ten days.'

Then she told me the latest about the kids and we chatted for about ten minutes, more warmly than in years, but with an element of reserve in each of us – in her, I sensed, because she was unsure of herself and afraid of moving anything forward yet, and in me because of Eleanor. And probably in her too.

The 'passport to matrimony' was perfect. After collecting it, I took it back to my hotel room, removed the inside pages from the cover, detached the page with the photograph and the holder's particulars from the rest of the document, wrote on it, 'Certified a true copy of an extract from the original passport of Geoffrey Robert Greenwood,' and put my signature and the date underneath those words, followed by 'Solicitor and Commissioner for Oaths'. Strictly speaking, I wasn't competent to certify documents outside the UK, but that technicality wouldn't bother Jeremy Lefarge.

Using the firm's letterhead saved on my laptop and, again, the facilities of the hotel's business centre, I typed, printed out, and signed a letter to Citadel Trustees Limited in St Peter Port, Guernsey, for Jeremy's attention.

Dear Sirs

We are very pleased to be able to introduce to you our valued client Mr Geoffrey Robert Greenwood and to assure you that he is a person of means, standing and the utmost integrity. We have a considerable acquaintance with his financial interests and affairs and do not hesitate to recommend him to you as a client.

Yours faithfully
Brook, Amery and Phillips

Despite Conrad Reiman's reservations about the absence of Mr Greenwood, he'd been perfectly willing, when approached by me the day before, to let me have the following letter:

To whom it may concern

This confirms that Hall Computers Inc is in negotiation with the shareholders of a certain UK company for the acquisition of their interests and that if agreement is reached between the parties Mr Geoffrey R Greenwood will become entitled to receive a consideration of some US$15 million for his interest in the company in cash and Hall Computers stock. This will be available to Mr Greenwood's order subject to the terms of the relevant agreement.

Yours faithfully
Conrad G Reiman
Vice-President Acquisitions
Hall Computers Inc.

I'd been entirely satisfied with the declaration of trust which Jeremy had emailed me, so I printed it out, wrote, 'Approved by me', and the date in Geoffrey's handwriting on the front page, and put Geoffrey's signature underneath those words. Then I wrote Jeremy a short covering letter enclosing the declaration of trust, the certified copy of the extract from 'Geoffrey's' passport, and the letters from my firm and Conrad Reiman. Finally, I put everything in a large envelope addressed to Jeremy and handed it to the concierge to be couriered urgently to Guernsey.

*

My little excursion into passport forgery had also served the additional purpose of providing me with the identity document that should have been kept in Geoffrey's original file. Before putting the certified page of the passport in the envelope to Jeremy, I'd made a photocopy of it to take back to the UK and put it into the file, which I could then safely return from the flat to the office, where it would be open to the eyes of my partners and anyone else who might care to pry into it.

Eleanor called me on my mobile. 'Geoff, I know you're madly busy there, but I have to ask you something.'

'Fire away.'

'I'd like an answering machine at the flat, with a personal message on it. BT's answering service is too anonymous. Are you OK with that?'

Was I? Nobody would be phoning Geoffrey – other than Malcolm or Lucy perhaps, but not at the flat surely – so did it matter? The real question for me was whether I was going to continue being Geoffrey to Eleanor after I got back. Marion's letter may have changed everything – or it may not.

'With *your* outgoing message, or mine?' I asked her.

'Well, mine – I mean in my voice – but the message would be ours. How about something like this: "You've reached the London home of Geoffrey and Eleanor. Please leave your message after the tone".'

'Sounds fine to me.'

'Good. I thought I'd ask because I don't know how you monitor your calls.'

'I won't be giving the number of the flat to my business contacts. I use my mobile. So, as I say, it's fine. Eleanor love, I'm sorry. I do have to go into another meeting.'

'Just one more thing, Geoff. I've put two entries in the phone directory, one under 'Greenwood, GR' and the other 'Downing, EM'. I meant to clear it with you before, but I sort of just went ahead, thinking you wouldn't mind.'

I did mind. Building up Geoffrey's identity as a real person was one thing: publicizing the fact that he had a home in London and its whereabouts was another. But there was no point in objecting now.

'I don't mind at all, so don't worry,' I said. 'Bye, my love.'

' 'Bye, Geoff. And take care.'

25

My partner Jonathan phoned me early one morning at the hotel. 'How's it going there in the Big Apple, Charles?'

'Very well.'

'We're under a lot of pressure here, you know. Could use you. When do you think you'll be back?'

'Another week, more or less.' I was annoyed. 'Hell, Jonathan, what do you think I'm doing here? Going to Broadway shows? The fees from this thing are going to be huge.'

'I realize that, Charles, and it's great, but we're running the whole show here, you know.'

This was the last straw. 'Fine. If you guys think I'm not pulling my weight, why don't we just call it a day? I have had it, Jonathan. We can discuss the terms of the dissolution as soon as I get back.'

'Hey, hey, Charlie, what's all this about? Who said anything about a dissolution?'

'I did, and I meant it – as soon as I get back,' with which I put the phone down and smiled to myself. I'd enjoyed that. And how nice it was to be breaking away from those two pieces of baggage! The phone rang again.

'Charles,' said Jonathan. 'Please don't take it that way. You're overre-acting.'

'No, I'm not. This isn't something new. It's been on my mind for a while. But we can talk it through there when I'm back.'

After a short silence, Jonathan said, 'If you're serious about this, then I suppose we've got to talk about it. But you're right: let's wait till you're back.'

The conversation ended on a cool note, but I'd got the message across, and happily, it seemed as if my partners might not make it too difficult for me to split with them. On reflection, though, perhaps I should slow things down a little, take one thing at a time: the deal, Eleanor, Marion, Geoffrey, my partners. I had a lot on my plate.

Although Reiman appeared to have put his concerns about Geoffrey's absence to one side for the present, it would be foolish, I thought, to assume that Hall and their attorneys would be content to conclude a deal of this magnitude with a vendor whom they'd never met or spoken to and whose lawyer would be signing the sale agreement under a general authority. Something must be done to make it look as if Geoffrey was actively involved, even if only at a distance.

So, using my laptop and the internet connection in my hotel room, I quickly set up an email address for Geoffrey with 'hotmail.com', then rang Nathan Mann. 'Nathan, can you please have the final draft of the sale agreement emailed urgently to my client in South Africa? Just the agreement itself and the warranty schedule – the other stuff doesn't really affect him. I want to go through the agreement with him on the phone.'

'Sure. What's his email address?'

'It's geoffgwood@hotmail.com.' I spelt it out for him.

'Hotmail? Does he have the storage capacity?'

'More than enough, I'm sure.' I already had an electronic copy of the same documents and knew they were within Hotmail's free limit.

'Any particular message to go with it?'

'Oh, just that it's at my request and I'm expecting him to call me as arranged.'

'Take it as done, Charles.'

About an hour later, I signed in to hotmail.com as Geoffrey. The message from Merriwether and Clayton was there, with the attachments. I typed the following document:

To whom it may concern:
I, Geoffrey Robert Greenwood, record that I have received from Merriwether and Clayton the attached email message and the accompanying draft sale agreement and warranty schedule and fully understand the contents of those documents, and authorize my solicitor Charles Joseph Brook to bind me to the agreement set out in those documents, with or without modification, under the general power of attorney already given by me to him.

The next morning, I printed the document out in the hotel's business centre, went back to my room, wrote 'Johannesburg' and the date in Geoffrey's handwriting at the bottom of it, and then signed it as Geoffrey. In the afternoon, I took it with me to a meeting and gave it to Nathan Mann. 'I got this by express courier an hour or so ago,' I told him.

Nathan read it. 'Very good. I'll send Thorstens a copy and table it at the signing.' Thorstens were Hall's attorneys.

Another problem overcome.

The signing meeting was scheduled for the Wednesday afternoon. That morning, Conrad Reiman phoned me and invited me to lunch with him in his office.

He greeted me warmly when I arrived and we had a cold lunch with white wine in a small dining room adjoining his office. No one else was there. We chatted pleasantly about this and that – New York compared with London, the financial markets, holidays in Europe – while I waited for him to get to the point. Eventually, over coffee, he excused himself and returned with a sealed envelope which he gave me. On it was printed, 'Mr Geoffrey R Greenwood'.

'Charles, could you see that Mr Greenwood gets that?'

'Yes, of course.'

'It's an invitation from Hall Computers. We'd like him and his wife or partner to be our guests here in New York as soon as he's well enough to travel.'

'That's very kind. Is there any special reason why?'

'There certainly is. I want to meet him personally and talk the deal over with him face to face.'

I went cold inside. 'Are you saying you're not going to do the deal until you've discussed it with him in person?'

'No.' Reiman shook his head. 'Not at all. The deal will be signed this afternoon as arranged. We want Jab and we're not about to let it get away just because your client hasn't come to the party. But as I've told you, Charles, we must have personal contact with every individual with a substantial stake in a deal like this, so there can be no comebacks later when they find out how well we've done out of what they've sold us.' He paused. 'Charles, you've played your part as Greenwood's representative admirably, but you're not your client' – he should only know, I thought – 'and I still need to meet him face to face.'

'Conrad, forgive me, but I don't understand. The deal will be history by the time you meet him.'

'Charles my friend, you're talking as a lawyer, I'm talking business. People are afraid of giant corporations – they don't trust us – so at Hall we have a code of conduct that makes us do fair deals. Meeting people like Greenwood personally when we do this kind of deal is part of that code, and seeing I couldn't meet him before doing the deal, I have to meet him afterwards because we can't afford exceptions to the code.'

'But what would you do if he were to tell you afterwards that he didn't like the deal?'

'Good question, Charles, but one I'm throwing right back at you. Have you any reason to think he'll do that?'

'No, of course not. He's not that kind of person.' Actually, I reflected, he's not any kind of person, and he's not going to show up in New York, ever.

'Yes, I'm sure that's so,' said Reiman, 'so shall we leave it at that? I mean, the guy has choices – he's not bound to accept the invitation – but if he doesn't I might worry a little, or perhaps even a lot.'

I was tempted to ask, 'What about?' but didn't. Instead, I said, 'I'm sure he'll be glad to come and be delighted to make your acquaintance.'

Reiman laughed. 'You're much too polite for a good lawyer.'

The agreements were signed that afternoon in Thorstens' main board-room, after which there were congratulations all round and champagne. Henry and Brenda made no attempt to conceal their elation, to the point in her case of an embarrassing display of near-hysteria brought on by the mistaken impression that everyone else was drinking as much champagne as she was. She was obviously as unaccustomed to alcohol as she was to sudden wealth. Henry, while not celebrating to similar excess, was nonetheless sufficiently overcome by the occasion to go around the room unabashedly heaping his praise and gratitude upon almost everyone who had played any part in the deal, including me. Then, as if that were not enough, he went on to say, for all to hear, 'What a pity Greenwood's not here today. He's the only one missing, and I'd really like to have met him before we sold the company,' and then, turning round to face some of the others, 'Do you know, Brenda and I have never even met the fellow?'

'That's because he only bought his shares very recently,' I announced, realizing as I did so that Reiman must now be wondering why this Greenwood guy had not only sold, but also acquired, his shares in absentia. And what further questions would go through his mind, I asked myself, when it transpired that Mr Greenwood would not be coming to New York at all?

I deliberately avoided looking in his direction.

26

I flew back to Heathrow the next afternoon, travelling alone since Henry and Brenda had to stay over for another couple of days. Eleanor had been delighted when I'd called to say I was coming home, and was expecting me to take a taxi straight from the airport to St John's Wood – especially seeing that the flat there was now supposed to be my UK home.

I'd have preferred to be able to go home to Marion and the kids first, because my conversation with Marion could affect both relationships. But was that really so, I wondered? The truth was that I wasn't coping with my ambivalence. I had this peculiar sense of actually being two people, one of whom, Geoffrey, had missed Eleanor a lot and was keen to be with her again, and the other, Charles, was eagerly looking forward to a reunion with the new 'old Marion' and excited about the prospect of a reconciliation with her. In the event, I'd had no choice but to call Marion and tell her I'd see her over the weekend as I had to attend to something in London on the way home.

On the flight, I sat back and allowed myself, for the first time really, to savour the pleasure of my newly acquired riches. As Geoffrey, I'd come out of the deal with $15 million in cash and stock. I'd still have to pay £200,000 to Gragorin and a meaningful fee to my firm, but that would all be more or less covered by the £300,000 I'd be getting back from Hall for the loan which I'd taken over from Gragorin. I was a very rich man and need never again have any financial worries. There was still, however, a lot to do and think about.

My Greenwood adventure was definitely nearing its end. I could no longer sustain the illusion of a real Geoffrey Greenwood. To do that I'd have had to be an illusionist in the true sense of the word. When my imaginary client failed to show up in either New York or Guernsey and Malcolm Cole found out that his wife's supposed lover didn't exist, I'd be in deep trouble – unless something else happened in the meantime. And I'd known all along what that was going to be.

I switched my mobile on in the taxi and checked for messages. There was one, from Lucy. I called her back.

'He's left me, Charles,' she said, 'for good.'

'I'm truly sorry about that, Lucy.'

'And I'm bloody sorry for myself. He's left the house and he's threatening to fight me for everything, including custody.'

'He hasn't got a hope on that. How old's your daughter again?'

'Sarah? She's four.'

'You haven't anything to worry about as far as she's concerned.'

'Thanks for that, Charles, but I didn't phone you for legal advice. You don't do divorces anyway, do you? Professionally, I mean.'

I didn't react. She was being catty again. The conversation was unpleasant, but I wanted to know if there had been anything further about Geoffrey. As if reading my mind, she said, 'Your Geoffrey Greenwood's a difficult man to get hold of.'

'Oh? He's been with me in New York. I've just got back. In fact, I'm in a taxi from the airport at this moment.'

'Is he with you now?'

'No. He's on his way back to South Africa. Why do you want to know?'

'Well, Malcolm wanted to speak to him – I told you that, didn't I? – but when Greenwood didn't return his calls or answer his letters, he went round to the flat a couple of times but couldn't find him. Then the other day he just said he'd had enough of me and my lover, and couldn't live any longer with a woman who'd betrayed him.'

'That's awful, Lucy.' I paused. 'I suppose he'll give up on Geoffrey now.'

'I doubt it. He's going to stay angry for quite a while. And he seems determined to find out who my lover was. I don't know but maybe he's still thinking about a reconciliation – if it was Greenwood, not you.'

'Well, when he does contact Greenwood, he'll find out someone else was using his flat. I don't think Geoffrey'll mention me, but Malcolm will soon make the connection. After all, I am Geoffrey's solicitor.'

'Maybe.'

'Lucy, now that things have reached this stage, you really should tell Malcolm the truth. It's unfair to Greenwood not to.'

'No, Charles. Sorry and all that, but I haven't given up yet. It's not over till it's over, but it will be if I do as you say. Anyway, I thought I'd just bring you up to date, and that's it.'

It was interesting that she hadn't mentioned her letter to Geoffrey.

Eleanor was wearing a transparent pale yellow nightie and nothing else when she let me in. She put her finger to my lips, took me by the hand, led me straight into the bedroom, pulled off my jacket, pushed me onto the bed, undid my shirt buttons, opened my belt and trouser zipper, pulled out my now bulging penis, lifted the nightie over her head, spread her legs over me, and thrust herself upon me ravenously. Afterwards she lay in my arms and told me how much she'd missed me, and we exchanged kisses and lovers' talk. A while later we made love again, this time more slowly and caressingly, then she left me to sleep off the effects of both the flight and the sex while she busied herself about the flat.

At three in the afternoon she woke me with a soft kiss on the mouth, and I gave her the present I'd got her in New York: a silver watch with a setting of small emeralds. It was the first thing I'd given her and she was thrilled with it. Then we went out and had a salad lunch in the high street, over which I told her that I'd had a highly successful visit to America and was setting up a substantial trust in Guernsey for our joint benefit. I didn't know why I was divulging this to her; I'd brought the subject up only because I'd imagined she'd expect to hear something about my trip, but then got carried away, even mentioning the $15 million. It was just that when I was with Eleanor I felt very close to her, and if it hadn't been for the latest turn of events with Marion, I'd have been talking to Eleanor now about all sorts of things to do with our future plans.

She smiled at me across the table. 'How generous of you, Geoffrey darling, but I don't want that sort of thing from you – your love is all I need. Anyway, I don't even know what a trust is, and I don't really care to.'

Now I managed to change the subject. 'Eleanor darling, I have to go down to Brighton in the morning for an urgent business meeting, but I'll be back in London on Monday afternoon – that is, until I leave for South Africa again on Friday.'

'South Africa? For how long, Geoff?'

'I'm not sure. Could be as little as a week, but perhaps two or three.' She looked disappointed, but then brightened a little. 'I'd love to come to South Africa with you, and one day I will, but there's my job – I couldn't leave it for so long yet – but I could come to Brighton with you tomorrow.' She gave me a little girl's smile. 'Couldn't I?'

'We wouldn't be back till Monday afternoon.'

'Oh. I have to be at the gallery first thing Monday, but I could get a train back on Sunday.'

'That wouldn't be much use. My meeting is scheduled to run well into tomorrow night and then continue on Sunday.'

'Such long business meetings over a weekend?'

'I'm afraid so. It's because this thing has had to be fitted in between the

American trip and my work in London next week. I'm due for meetings here from Monday afternoon, and I fly to South Africa on Friday. There's no other time.'

'Well then, we'd better make the most of what's left of today, hadn't we?'

So we went into the West End and saw a live musical, then had a late dinner in a smart restaurant, and returned to the flat to make love once more.

I took an early train from Victoria in the morning, having bade her an affectionate farewell as she lay curled up drowsily in the bed. 'Expect me here at around seven on Monday evening.' I blew her a kiss from the door and she blew one back.

27

When I arrived home I got another warm reception, though of quite a different kind. The children were thrilled to see me and Marion let me kiss her cheek and hug her. I handed out the gifts I'd bought in New York and the two little ones rushed to open theirs and become engrossed in them.

Marion made us all brunch and suggested we go out for the day, as a family. It was amazing how much she'd changed since I'd last seen her; she was almost her old self again. While I ate, Emma cuddled up on my lap, her newly dressed Barbie in her hand, and Paulie plied me with a three-year-old's questions about the aeroplane I'd flown in.

Saturday with Marion and the kids turned out to be as enjoyable as Friday had been with Eleanor, though very different, of course. Today I was the family man; yesterday I'd been the lover. The children were delighted to be with both their parents together. We all went to a playground on the beachfront, then played games on the beach, and – when the weather turned – drove to an indoor play area in Hove, where conversation was impossible above the shrieks and screams of scores of wildly active kids. After we got home Emma and Paulie were allowed to stay up late, then I told them a long bedtime story which I made up as I went along, with bits of help and encouragement from them. Marion stood by the open door for a minute or two, watching us and smiling.

Then she and I had evening drinks and a late supper, over which we chatted about all sorts of things we hadn't discussed for ages and I told her about my trip and that it had been very successful – for the client, whose name I didn't mention. It was only afterwards, in the living-room, that we got around to serious conversation.

'Teddy,' she said, 'I'm sorry for the way I behaved towards you—'

'There's no need—' I interrupted, but she held up her hand.

'I was wrong to take it out on you, though not altogether – but I'll get back to that. I just want you to know there was a door in my mind which was shut tight all those years. Merle, my therapist, opened it with one question, when she felt I was ready for it.'

And she told me about the question and the shock it brought her – and the anger. How, through the anguish that followed the revelation, she began to understand herself; how she'd shut out her father's evilness and her own shame – and then to emerge from it all, with mixed feelings of pain and the lifting of a burden long carried. How she was working now, with Merle, to put it all behind her and to try and repair the damage it had caused, especially to our marriage, and to me.

'But, Charles – I mean Teddy, or do I? – I can't accept all the blame for that. We had a togetherness before the kids came along, but especially after Paul was born, you got more and more wrapped up in your practice and less and less involved in our marriage, and I think that's what led to all that quarrelling between us. Remember?'

I nodded, but wondered as I did whether I really agreed with what she was saying. There may have been something to it – I wasn't sure. She went on, 'Oh, you were always very good with the kids and very involved with them, but I felt I wasn't part of your life any more – it was all about your career and your clients and your kids. Anyway, I don't think we should go into all that now. What I'd like to talk about is where we go from here. But maybe you've moved too far out of the marriage. Have you?' She looked at me expectantly.

I took my time. The truthful answer was that I had no idea; I was utterly confused, because I was two people. 'I was moving out of it, I suppose, till I got your letter. But now – after a day like today and being here with you – I don't feel that way any more. I know I still love you and I do think we should make a special effort – and not only for the little ones, as you say.' Yet again, as with Eleanor the day before, I found myself going further than I'd intended.

'What about your other relationship?'

'What?'

'You told me you were in another relationship.'

'Oh, that. It's just physical. You and I haven't had sex in a long time, remember.' Why the lie? Why not simply tell her the truth about Eleanor?

But what was the truth? And how could I tell it without mentioning Geoffrey? I was sure she'd have disapproved of the whole Greenwood thing. And why should she know about any of it if I was going to leave her for Eleanor?

'I can understand that. Is it with Lucy Cole?'

How had she guessed? The same way, I supposed, that Malcolm had – from the signs. Lucy would never have told her anything, surely. 'No, it's not with her.'

'Well, I'm glad about that. I'm fond of her, you know, but I always thought she fancied you – and she was having an affair, with some chap from overseas. She doesn't like to talk about it. Did you know she and Malcolm have separated?'

'Yes, I'd heard.'

'Well?' said Marion.

'Well what?'

'Are you going to tell me any more about your relationship?'

'Well, I don't think it would be fair to tell you her name, but it's not anyone you know.'

'Is she married?'

'No.'

'Charles, if we are to make a go of things, you must know other relationships are out.' 'Teddy' had lost out, I noticed. 'Maybe I'm taking this too fast,' she said. 'We haven't lived as a married couple for a long time. Perhaps we need a kind of trial period.'

'What have you got in mind?'

She looked thoughtful. 'I can't share my bed with you yet – here at home, I mean – not until you're ready to give her up, whoever she is. But Merle's suggested something. She thinks we should go away together, for a weekend say, and see how it works out.'

I considered the idea, unsure how I felt about it, but realizing there was no way I could turn her down. 'OK. When?'

'You're the busy one. How about next weekend?'

'Yes. That'll be fine.' By then the deal would have been completed and the money and stock would be in the trust. And I'd already told Eleanor I'd be away.

'Good. I'm sure Mum will stay with the kids, and Katka will be around too.'

We discussed where to go and settled on Cornwall, leaving on Friday and returning on Sunday. Marion said she'd ask Merle for the details of a place she'd been enthusing about – a small inn-type hotel near Penzance where she and her husband had stayed recently.

Lying in bed afterwards, I realized I was feeling guilty towards Eleanor. How ironic! As my wife, Marion was supposed to be the woman to whom I owed fidelity. But then, she wasn't Geoffrey's wife, and as Geoffrey I had no business going away with anyone other than Eleanor – let alone somebody else's wife. Abruptly, I pulled myself up. What nonsense was I thinking now?

When I came downstairs in the morning, Emma and Paulie were having breakfast with Katka. Marion was still upstairs.

'You're not supposed to be working today, are you?' I asked Katka.

'No,' she replied cheerfully, 'but I like to do kids getting up and breakfast. It's fun.'

'Katka, can you stay with them till Marion comes down?'

'Of course. I will love it.'

'Thanks. And please tell her I've gone to the office but I'll be back for lunch. She can reach me on my mobile.'

I drove to Beverley Terrace. There was nobody at the porter's desk and no sign of any mail for me. I assumed what had arrived since the last batch had all been redirected to the office as I'd requested. I should cancel the instruction to Clarke, I thought. Despite what Lucy had said, Malcolm's determination to confront Geoffrey must surely have abated now that he and Lucy had split up, and even if that wasn't so, I couldn't go on avoiding the flat indefinitely for fear of encountering him.

The flat was much as I'd last seen it. I'd left the cleaning lady's money with Clarke and by all appearances she'd been doing her job. It was a bright morning and sunlight stretched across the living-dining area. I sat down at the desk to think and make notes.

From the beginning, I'd intended to see that something happened to Geoffrey one day that would give me direct access to his money, and I had set up the trust with that intention in mind. That day was now approaching, given the expectations of Conrad Reiman and Jeremy Lefarge and the persistence of Malcolm Cole. The sooner I brought the day forward the better. When it came, everyone must believe either that

Geoffrey had died or that he'd disappeared and was probably dead. One of my reasons for putting Geoffrey's fortune into a trust had been that there'd be no need to prove Geoffrey's death; I'd simply get effective control of the trust fund in terms of the letter of wishes. Had the money and the Hall shares belonged to Geoffrey personally, I could have done nothing with them until his death could be presumed, and that could have taken years.

I'd been considering two possible ways of disposing of Geoffrey. One was to simulate an accident or other tragedy. The other was simply to tell everyone – Reiman, Lefarge, Lucy, and my partners – that he'd died, of a heart attack, say, in South Africa. But if I chose the latter course, there'd be nothing at all to corroborate my story and the whole Greenwood fiction could be exposed if anyone was moved to look into it. Jeremy Lefarge would certainly not be able to act on my say-so alone where the trust was concerned. No; I'd have to stage something and create some convincing circumstantial evidence to bear it out. And it couldn't be Geoffrey's death as a certainty, because that would require a dead body. It would have to be his disappearance and presumed death. A disappearance in water while swimming or boating off the Cornish coast might well be the ideal scenario for something like that, and I could examine the prospects during my weekend there with Marion.

When I got home, the weather allowed us to have a family barbecue in the garden and I saw to the fire and the cooking, then spent most of the afternoon with the kids while Marion went to a book club meeting. After supper, she and I watched television together for a couple of hours, and when she'd gone to bed I stayed downstairs for a while, sitting in the dark and doing more thinking and planning.

28

By the time I got to the office on Monday morning, I'd decided that, unless Jonathan raised the subject with me, I'd say nothing further about a dissolution for the present. Sorting out my personal life and getting rid of Geoffrey were more pressing priorities. I was, however, determined to pursue the matter as soon as I was ready.

Not unexpectedly, Jonathan didn't even allude to our last conversation and I found both him and Barry effusively friendly and welcoming. It didn't take Barry long, however, to raise the matter of the fee for the Hall deal.

'There's still some work to be done,' I told them, 'on the completion, in London. I'm going up there at midday and staying for possibly the rest of the week. But I would like to settle the fee now, because it's to be paid by Hall Computers and we can bill them on completion. I was thinking of a hundred thousand dollars.'

'What the hell, Charles!' exclaimed Barry. 'Look at the size of the deal and how much time you spent on it. We're entitled to at least twice that.'

I had to rein my reaction in. 'Hall may be a big cow, but it's not going to let itself be milked like that.' I'd lose Conrad Reiman's trust by blatantly overcharging his company. 'Don't forget,' I added, 'I didn't do any of the documentation. All of that was done by two American law firms.'

We eventually agreed on a $150,000, but the discussion fortified my resolve to leave the practice. I resented being accountable like this. It was bad enough that these two miserable hangers-on were getting more than their fair shares of the fees being earned from other clients, but there was absolutely no reason why they should continue to benefit financially from my own personal affairs.

I bought a *Financial Times* at the station. The Jab-Hall deal was reported and briefly commented on alongside a photograph of a smiling Conrad Reiman shaking hands with Henry and Brenda, both beaming. There was no mention of Geoffrey Greenwood.

In the afternoon I worked at the City offices of Hall's accountants. At around 4.30 I got a call from Cindy, who sounded shaken and upset. 'Mr Gragorin's rung for you three times. He's insisting you call him back and he won't wait. He's been very rude and he said something about getting Greenwood. Can I give you the number? I don't want to have to speak to him again. He frightens me.'

I asked for a room where I could make a private call and rang the number. Gragorin answered and directed an avalanche of words at me. 'Nobody steals from Gragorin. Your Mr Greenwood, he's a thief. Henry and Brenda too. Maybe you too. They wait to get me out cheap, then they sell – for millions. That Greenwood, he's not getting my money—'

'I don't understand, Mr Gragorin,' I interrupted. 'All you're entitled to is another two hundred thousand pounds, which you'll be getting next week.'

'That's just crap, lawyer. You make me sign, but nobody tell me about a deal for forty-five million dollars. I come to your office by myself without a lawyer and you make me sign contract. Nobody say nothing about this deal, then you all go off and Greenwood he gets my money.'

'You knew all about the negotiations with Hall.' I was getting annoyed. 'And I invited you to bring your lawyer and told you to take legal advice, more than once. No one made you sign anything. You wanted to sell. All you were interested in was getting paid out. You can't come along now—'

'Don't you tell me I can't. I can. I already speak to my lawyers about this, now, and they say I have very good case. I want my money from Greenwood or else I sue him. He must give me my fifteen million dollars and I give him back his dirty three hundred grand.'

His demands were outrageous and I doubted he'd consulted any lawyers. 'George,' I said, hoping the informality would help, 'you're wrong and out of order. As I've already said, you'll be getting a cheque for two hundred thousand pounds next week. But that's all you're getting. Now I'm very busy and I'm going to put the phone down.'

'Put down if you like. Just first give me Greenwood's number. I speak to him. If he refuse to pay, I sue him.'

'I won't give you any information at all, Gragorin. You're entitled to nothing and you know it.'

'If you won't give his number, then tell him to ring me. Same number you use now. By tomorrow. Or I sue. Goodbye, Mr Chips.' With which he ended the call.

I was mildly amused by the 'Goodbye, Mr Chips'– he pronounced 'Chips' as 'Cheeps' – which must have had some peculiar connotation in his own mind. Anyway, the whole thing was a try-on; he had absolutely no leg to stand on and no self-respecting solicitor would pursue the matter for him. On the other hand, it could get tricky if he continued making a nuisance of himself and wanting contact with Geoffrey.

While doubting that he would, I realized I now had yet another reason for expediting Geoffrey's demise.

By early Tuesday afternoon, all the formalities to complete the Hall-Jab deal had been carried out other than some automatic processes and I was able to ring Jeremy Lefarge in Guernsey to confirm that he could expect to receive the money and stock due to the trust within days. I told him Greenwood wanted most of the cash placed on a two-month deposit with a first-class bank and the rest on call. We discussed interest rates and Jeremy asked for faxed confirmation of the instruction, which I immediately sent him – signed by me on behalf of Geoffrey, as authorized under the letter of wishes.

My work done, I phoned Eleanor at the gallery and she said she could get off early and meet me at the flat at around 4.30. Meanwhile, I went out and did some shopping – for Geoffrey – in Regent Street managing to pick up a suit, a jacket, and a pair of trousers, all made in South Africa.

I got back to the flat before her. The answering machine showed there'd been two messages. I played them back. The first was for Eleanor from her father, and the second for Geoffrey from Gragorin.

'Mister Greenwood,' it went, 'this is Gragorin. I'm not sure your lawyer give you my message. But you don't ring me, so I give you my number again' – he did so – 'and you phone me quick or I sue. Goodbye Mr Chips.'

How, I wondered, had he got the number of the flat? The new BT directory had surely not come out yet? Or maybe it had. But even if it hadn't, there were so many other sources from which the number would be available once Eleanor had applied for the phone and directory entry, including the directory centres that could be reached by telephone or on the internet. Nowadays, information like the particulars she'd have supplied was widely and rapidly disseminated for marketing purposes, and there was a healthy trade in lists of names and addresses of house-holders in Britain – in spite of the Data Protection Act, which somehow operated so perversely that no one's personal information was confidential except when one wanted to access it oneself.

No matter. I wasn't going to ring Gragorin back, either as Geoffrey or as myself.

Then Eleanor came home and made love to me.

29

When I awoke the next morning, Wednesday, with Eleanor asleep next to me, I wondered why on earth I'd agreed to go away with Marion this weekend. Living with Eleanor in the flat these last couple of days had been little short of paradise. Here I was, lying beside an extraordinarily attractive, intelligent woman who made love delightfully and adored and respected me and wanted to spend the rest of her life with me, and what was I doing? Trying to repair my shattered marriage. Shouldn't I just phone Marion and call the weekend off? And then follow that up by calling the marriage off and telling Eleanor who I really was and that I wanted to marry her? Before going to America, I'd already accepted the inevitability of the fracture that Marion had spoken about and concluded that everyone would be better off that way, including the kids. The only thing that had changed since then was that Marion had uncovered her repressed memories, but that didn't mean she would come to terms with them or that we could actually rebuild – or, perhaps more correctly, build for the first time – the kind of loving relationship that was needed to keep us both happy and create a sufficiently stable environment for our children to grow up in. Considering all that had gone before – as well as the fact that I was in love with Eleanor now – that outcome was highly improbable.

Well then, why wasn't I doing that – breaking with Marion right now, I mean – instead of just thinking about it? Because – I answered myself – of my bloody duality again. I was Geoffrey right now, and Geoffrey loved Eleanor. Charles loved Marion, and when I was being Charles I desperately wanted to save my marriage, whatever the difficulties. And besides, I couldn't take it for granted that Eleanor would react positively to the news of my real identity. Would she love me as Charles? Could she?

Over breakfast she and I arranged to meet for lunch in Chelsea, after which she was to show me the gallery. I decided to spend the morning in the flat. When she'd left for work, I rang Cindy at the office, who told me there'd been a message from Jeremy Lefarge to say that the Greenwood money had been received along with confirmation that the Hall Computer stock was now held for The Greenwood Trust. She also said that several clients had been calling for appointments – people who particularly wanted to see me personally, some of them having been waiting for me for weeks – and I instructed her to start making appointments from the following Tuesday. Then I lay down on the sofa, stared up at the ceiling, and forced myself to think rationally and constructively about how and with whom I should spend the remainder of my life.

Half an hour later I'd decided not to cancel the arrangements for the weekend, for two very good reasons. One, I'd make the weekend in Cornwall the decisive factor in my choice between Marion and Eleanor – just as Marion was doing, on Merle's advice, in relation to our marriage – and two, there was its other, crucial purpose as an opportunity for reconnaissance in terms of my plans for Geoffrey.

At lunch, I told Eleanor I had to leave for South Africa a day earlier than I'd planned. She was visibly disappointed but didn't ask me any questions. Instead, she proudly showed me around 'her' gallery and afterwards, in the flat that evening, treated me to a grand farewell candle-lit dinner followed by another night of erotic bliss.

30

The next morning, Thursday, I decided the weather was conducive to some badly neglected outdoor exercise and went for a brisk walk in Regent's Park after Eleanor had gone off to work. When I got back, Andrew, the porter on duty, told me I'd had two visitors during my absence – a gentleman who fitted Gragorin's description and spoke with a foreign accent, and a taller, well-dressed fellow who'd been with him and hadn't spoken at all.

'The foreign gentleman asked me when you'd be back, Mr Greenwood. I told him I had no idea. They waited about twenty minutes – on the pavement – then the foreign gentleman came into the lobby again and said they were leaving but would call again and I should give you a message if you returned before they did.' Andrew consulted a note. 'I am to inform you, sir, that George came see you, with a friend, and that they'd be back. You'd know what it was about.'

It didn't surprise me at all that Gragorin had found out the address of the flat as well as the phone number, but whatever the source of his information, it was clear he wasn't suing Geoffrey, at least not yet. Had his threat of litigation been at all serious, there'd have been a letter from his solicitor, not a visit from the man himself. No, like Malcolm, he wanted to confront Geoffrey, but, unlike Malcolm, Gragorin was unstable and irrational, and hence capable of anything. The fact that he'd been accompanied might imply a threat of violence, or it might not. Whatever it was that he had in mind, Gragorin had now become rather more than just a nuisance. If he got the slightest sniff that there might not be such a person as Geoffrey Greenwood, he'd have no need for litigation. Blackmail would become the means to his end, and it might not even stop at $15 million.

Just as I'd needed to evade Malcolm Cole, so I must now avoid Gragorin – only Gragorin was a far more dangerous proposition. It was a good thing I was going back to Brighton that very day, and highly desirable that I leave the St John's Wood flat at once and stay away until the coast was clear – meaning until I'd disposed of Geoffrey. Which made Geoffrey's disappearance a matter of great urgency.

On the train to Brighton, I wondered how Marion must be feeling about the weekend.

As she would tell me later, she'd been anxious about it. The revelation about her father had been therapeutic, but it had also forced her to wrestle with all sorts of feelings she'd suppressed, like the humiliation and the shame, and the persisting, irrational sense of her own guilt: she'd been thirteen when it happened, not a small child. And she'd by no means come to terms with all that yet. She had been considering postponing the weekend and wondering about my other relationship, and about where I'd been staying in London, and with whom.

Although Merle had encouraged her to have sex with me during the weekend if I wanted her to, she'd decided she couldn't – and wouldn't. I'd have to extract myself from my other relationship before that could happen. But even without the sex complication, the weekend was a daunting prospect for her. No matter how much we still might feel for each other, we *had* grown apart and the rebuilding process, if there was to be one, would need time.

But in the end, her decision had been to go ahead with the arrangement. The weekend had been Merle's idea and Marion trusted her judgement. It was necessary, Merle had said, because it would tell us both what the chances were. Without it, we'd just blunder on.

The need for Geoffrey to have a complete wardrobe and his own personal effects having now become pressing, I did some more shopping when I got to Brighton. I bought more new clothing from a store in Churchill Square, then went to Oxfam for some second-hand items and to Boots for a razor, toothbrush, and other toiletries. Then I took a taxi out to Beverley Terrace and told the driver to wait while I deposited my purchases in the flat. That done, the taxi dropped me off at the pier and I walked to the office, getting there just before 3.30. I started going through my mail and messages, but soon decided that the task was too formidable to be tackled now and went home.

When I got there, Marion was trying to look cheerful, but she did seem pleased to see me. She asked me what time I thought we should leave in the morning.

'As early as possible. It's going to be a long drive. Six or seven hours – longer maybe, if there's traffic, or if we stop for meals. Can you be packed and ready by eight?'

'I'm almost packed already and the kids will be fine.'

We left at 8.30. The little ones watched us go, standing by the front gate with Katka, squealing excited farewells and blowing kisses at us. Marion remarked as we drove off that they really did seem happy that their mummy and daddy were going on holiday together. 'Small children have got a lot of instinctive insight, you know,' she said.

After an hour or so the sun came out and I switched on the car's air conditioner. 'How about some music?' she said. I nodded and she put on a CD we'd both always liked, and soon we were singing along with some of the tracks and laughing as each one ended. We argued over the words and laughed about that too. We were friends again.

It was a long journey. We stopped three times at Services and shared the driving, talking a lot. We reminisced about various things and swapped anecdotes about the children. I told her about my dissatisfaction with my partners and she was responsive and supportive, just as she'd always been in earlier times. It struck me that I could never have *this* kind of companionship with Eleanor, one that was built on a background of years of shared experiences and augmented by the bond of shared children. Oh, my never-ending ambivalence!

In fine spirits, we reached our destination earlier than I'd expected. We found the hotel with little difficulty, leaving the A30 a few miles beyond Penzance to join a B road bordered for much of the way by high hedgerows, and then following signs along a narrow, twisting strip of tarmac which descended southward towards the ocean. The hotel, which was called The Cuckoo's Nest, nestled on a slope overlooking the sea and a range of cliffs to the left. At the foot of the slope, where the cliffs began, stood a large sandy beach, and spreading away from it along the coastline, a number of smaller beachy coves sheltered below the cliffs.

The Cuckoo's Nest turned out to be full of character and exceptionally clean and well kept, with only about a dozen bedrooms, all with *en suite* bathrooms. We were welcomed by a jovial, ruddy-faced man of middle age, very much a caricature of the typical landlord, who even introduced himself as 'your landlord, Martin Jones.' There was a Mrs Jones too, whose first name, we soon learned, was Trudy and who made her appearance in the dining-room that evening, along with two or three other members of staff, one of whom was especially conspicuous – if not to Marion, then certainly to me and by all indications to most of the other male diners too.

She was a young woman – in her mid-twenties, I guessed – who doubled as waitress and barmaid and whose appearance was quite strikingly voluptuous. She had a mop of lustrous dark red hair piled up on top of her head, shimmering, smiling green eyes, a beautiful oval-shaped face with rosy cheeks and a pouting lower lip, and a shapely figure, and moved about the dining-room with erotic elegance in a uniform consisting of a white frilly blouse above a dark-green miniskirt that showed off an admirable pair of black-stockinged legs. From overheard snatches of her conversation with others, I made out that her name was Jenny and that she had a slight West-country accent but spoke grammatically and articulately, suggesting she must have attended a good school as a child. I was mildly disappointed that we were being served by the other, similarly attired but rather less appealing, barmaid-waitress.

The attractions of Jenny the barmaid were, however, of less interest to me than the layout of The Cuckoo's Nest and some of the establishment's arrangements for its guests. When checking in, we'd been given a set of three keys to share, one of which was for our bedroom, a second for our wardrobe, and the third for the back door of the hotel. Attached to the central keyring was a small metal tag embossed with our room number, sixteen. Martin Jones explained to us that the only access to the building after pub closing time was through the back door, as the front and pub entrances were both locked from then until the morning. We should feel free, he said, to come and go as we pleased, using the back-door key as necessary. It was this facility in particular which most interested me.

The meal was good and so was the wine, and we lingered in the pub afterwards, each uncomfortably aware that our next move would be upstairs to share a bedroom for the first time in ages. Marion had stopped talking and appeared ill at ease. I suspected she was worried that I might be expecting to have sex with her and that she wasn't ready for that. She needn't have been; I wasn't at all in the mood for sex – well, not with Marion, yet. She was looking lovely and I felt a deep bond of love with her, but she'd become a stranger to me physically and the only bond of lust I had now was with Eleanor.

Then Marion leaned towards me, took my hand, and in barely more than a whisper said, 'Teddy, would it matter awfully if we didn't make love tonight? Let's just go upstairs and be together, shall we, at this stage of things? What do you think?'

I gave her an understanding smile and nodded, trying my best not to let her notice how relieved and grateful I was.

31

I got up early the next morning, managed to shower and dress without waking Marion, and went down to breakfast, which was served in a bright, pleasant conservatory. Marion had told me she'd be sleeping late and missing breakfast, and I welcomed the opportunity to do some reconnoitring on my own.

Trudy Jones, Martin's wife, took my order and asked me what we were planning to do. I told her we might go to the beach.

'Excellent idea. It'll be a perfect day for that and you don't need to drive anywhere. Just walk down the hill and take the footpath to the main beach.'

'What about the other, smaller beaches out there?'

'Yes, they're more secluded, if that's what you're looking for, but they're not easy to get to – and there aren't any lifeguards there. At low tide you can get to two or three of those coves from the main beach by simply walking across a sandbank, but once the tide starts coming in, those coves get cut off – on the sea side, that is. You can still get on and off them by the cliff paths behind them.'

'How's the swimming?'

'The water's pretty cold, even on a nice warm day like today, and the depth's erratic. There's a sudden drop quite near the low-tide water-line. On a good day the sea's pretty calm off the main beach, but currents tend to occur off the rocks lining the coves. Are you a good swimmer, Mr Brook?'

'I get by – in a swimming pool.' I chuckled.

'Well, then, my advice'd be to stick to the main beach and swim between the beacons put up by the lifeguards. My husband's a regular in the summer – until the end of this month, September – but he never swims off the coves. You'll be wanting beach towels, I presume?'

'Yes, please.'

'We provide them at no charge. Just ask for a couple at the front desk as you go out.'

After breakfast, I made my way out into the garden behind the hotel. Eleanor wouldn't have left for work yet, so I called the London flat on my mobile.

'Hullo, my darling,' she said. 'Where are you?'

'In Johannesburg.' There was no way she could tell I was still in the UK; I could be using the international roaming service, as I'd done in New York. Nonetheless, I asked, for effect, 'Can you hear me clearly enough?'

'Yes, very. It's as if you were in London.'

'Eleanor, can you take a half-day off next week?'

'I suppose I can, but why?'

'I need to talk to you – about something important. I'm leaving here tonight and flying into Gatwick from Paris on Monday with a business associate, and I won't be back in London till next weekend, but I'd like to see you as soon as possible. Is there any chance you can come to Brighton on Monday or Tuesday afternoon and meet me at the Beverley Terrace flat?'

'Yes, if it's important as you say, I can leave the gallery for the afternoon. Monday'll be good.'

'Great. It's flat thirty-four.'

'I've never been there before, remember?'

'Yes, I know. You should be ashamed, letting me a place you'd never even seen,' I chided.

'I can get a train and taxi, and be there around 2.30. How will that do?'

'Perfectly. You can come straight up. I'll be waiting for you in the flat.'

I was being swiftly decisive now. Geoffrey's time was fast approaching and I had two choices where Eleanor was concerned: either to break up with her before it happened, letting her hear the news of Geoffrey's fate afterwards, or tell her everything. I didn't know yet which of the two it was going to be, but I was determined to have stopped vacillating by Sunday night at the latest. The venue for my discussion with her had to be Brighton because I was avoiding the London flat. (I had decided Beverley Terrace was safe from Gragorin; he'd already established his point of contact, and besides, the telephone at Beverley Terrace wasn't listed, and couldn't be, seeing it was only an extension from the front desk.)

As for Geoffrey's fate, what Trudy Jones had told me had been encouraging. I must inspect those coves. If one of them proved suitable, I'd be ready to finalize my plan of action. I went up to the room and opened the door as quietly as I could. The curtains were still drawn and Marion still in bed. She murmured 'Teddy' drowsily and I said, softly, 'You don't have to get up yet. I'll go for a walk and come back later.' She responded with another, unintelligible murmur and turned over.

Leaving the hotel, I walked down the hill and took the footpath to the main beach. There was an ugly concrete structure near the top of the beach which I examined. It housed some toilets and changing rooms, above which there was a viewing platform for the lifeguards. Some beach chairs and umbrellas were stacked against one of the walls behind a sign reading, 'For hire. Ask lifeguard.' A tanned, well-built young man in a T-shirt and swimming trunks was about to mount the ladder leading up to the platform. I approached him and said, 'Excuse me. You are a lifeguard, aren't you?'

'Yes, part-time. I'm a university student.' He looked up at the sky. 'Lovely day.'

'Yes, it is. My wife and I are thinking of spending the morning here. We're staying up at The Cuckoo's Nest.'

'With the Joneses? I know them well. Very nice people.'

'Tell me, those other beaches – in the adjoining coves – does anybody ever go there?'

'Well, one's a naturist beach – not the very next one, but the one after that. That means it's legal to swim in the nude there. But it's usually deserted.'

'What about the others?'

'The other coves? Well, at low tide people do move between this beach and the adjoining cove, but that's not possible when the tide comes in. Before that happens, though, one of us usually goes round there and warns anybody that the beach is going to be cut off – well, from the seaside anyway.'

'And the ones beyond that?'

'Oh, those. They're pretty deserted most of the time.'

'I'm surprised there's a – what did you call it? – naturist beach along here. Wouldn't a nude swimmer be visible from the cliffside above The Cuckoo's Nest?'

'Not really. There's only one spot up there from which you can see these beaches, but it's overgrown and difficult to get to, and too far away to notice details like that.'

'Well, cheers then.' I strolled down the beach, which was deserted at this early hour except for one scrawny male bather who was emerging from the water. The lifeguard-student's information had been very helpful. It was sounding more and more as if one of the coves beyond the naturist beach could well be the perfect setting for Geoffrey's accident.

I sat down and removed my shoes and socks, then stood up and resumed my walk, carrying them. It was low tide and the beach extended beyond the cliff and rocks to my left – as I faced the sea – making the adjoining cove accessible across the sand. Using that means of approach, I made my way to the front of the cove. It was entirely deserted. Unlike the main beach, it was surrounded on all sides – except where it met the ocean – by hills, cliffs, and rocks. It was also a lot smaller than the main beach. I walked to the water's edge where small waves lapped the shore, and looked at the sea. It appeared calm, but it wasn't hard to see that, given a moderate breeze and a rising tide, the conditions could quickly become rather less benign, especially if the depth of the seabed was as erratic as Trudy Jones had said. There were clusters of large rocks to either side of the cove and several others protruded from the water in various positions. It was pretty obvious too that conditions on the remoter beaches – with regard to both swimming and privacy – would be at least as satisfactory. I looked at my watch. It was time to go back. Marion must be up and about by now.

I found her on the veranda, waiting for me. 'Where've you been?' she asked me. 'I tried your mobile.'

'Just for a walk, down to the beach. My phone didn't ring.' I pulled it out of my pocket and the monitor told me I'd missed two calls. 'Sorry,' I said. 'There's obviously no signal down there' – another favourable development.

'That's OK. I haven't been waiting long. I'd like some tea and toast. The dining-room's closed but Mr Jones says there's a nice little tearoom in the village about a mile away. Do you mind? I know you've had breakfast.'

'Yes, I have, but I'll drive you down there.'

On the way, I told her about the main beach and we agreed to spend the morning there. To save time, I dropped her off in the village and drove back to the hotel to fetch our swimming things and a pair of beach towels, so we could go straight to the beach and use the changing-rooms there.

Jenny's presence in the room caught me unawares. 'Oh, good morning,' I said. 'I've come to get a few things.'

'Good morning, Mr Brook.'

'It's Jenny, isn't it?'

'That's right.' She'd been making the beds and now moved over to the door, which, as if to give herself more room to work in, she pushed with her bottom so that it was barely ajar – leaving us together in virtually a closed room. I unlocked the wardrobe and peered inside, trying to concentrate on locating the two swimsuits but distracted by her proximity.

'How long are you staying with us?' she asked.

'Only till tomorrow.' As I spoke she brushed past me from behind, touching my arm lightly on the way. I found the swimsuits and when I turned around with them in my hand, I had a good view of the greater part of her plump bosom as she bent forward to tuck in the bedclothes.

'Have you got what you came for?' she asked, bending lower and revealing even more of her breasts; then, holding that position, she lifted her head and smiling coquettishly at me said, 'Or is there anything *I* can do for you?'

I was amazed at how blatantly she was coming onto me. She had incredible sex appeal, but this wasn't something I was going to get into.

'Er, not really, thank you,' I replied. 'I just need a couple of things from that drawer next to you.'

'Fine,' she said, still smiling, but making no attempt to get out of my way and forcing me to come around the bed and approach the drawer from behind her. And as I did so, she turned around and there we were, standing face to face, our bodies touching. Fighting the surge of arousal inside me, I summoned up the will to keep dead-still and say to her, as politely yet firmly as I could, 'Can you please excuse me?'

'OK,' she said, moving to one side to let me squeeze by her, our bodies still in full frontal contact, especially at the level of the bulge that had begun to form in my trousers. 'My, my,' she said, with a broad grin, letting her hand stray down to rest on my hip, 'what a big man you are, Mr Brook!'

The natural thing for any warm-blooded heterosexual male to have done at that point was take hold of this irresistible female and make the most of the moment, but, with my heart pumping hotly, I forced myself to reach down and pull her hand away gently, then edge past her towards the drawer, half-fearing as I did so – and half-hoping in the devil-part of me – that she'd move along with me and maintain the contact. But she didn't. And when I allowed myself to look at her again, after retrieving the two pairs of sunglasses, she was still smiling openly at me but no longer on the offensive, having seemingly realized that she'd gone as far as she could for the present.

We stared at each other for a few seconds; then she said, 'You're here with your wife, aren't you?'

'Yes, I am.'

'Any chance you'll be coming again – alone?'

She was astonishingly forward, this Jenny, and a bit like some seductive mythical goddess of love. There was every chance I would be back – soon and without Marion – but I was determined not to allow Jenny to get in the way of the crucial purpose of my next visit to this part of Cornwall. So I should have answered the question in the negative, but instead heard myself say, 'Possibly.'

Still smiling, she said softly, 'Please. You must – for my sake,' and opened the door wide. Admonishing myself for having given her this measure of encouragement, I stepped out of the room, trying not to smile back, and made my way downstairs.

32

When I got back to the village Marion was buying a few things in the high street, including some bottled water, a slab of chocolate, and a tube of sun-tan lotion. We drove to the main beach, left the car in the car-park there, and after changing and hiring two chairs and an umbrella from the lifeguard-student, settled ourselves towards the front of the beach, which was now occupied by about a dozen people and had been somewhat truncated by the incoming tide.

'It was silly of you to bring your things and change here,' observed Marion. 'You could have done that in the room.'

'The room was being cleaned.' She should only know how close I'd come to being undressed by the cleaner. 'I'm going for a swim,' I told her.

'Already? Don't you want to sit and enjoy the sun for a bit?'

'I need to cool off.'

As I walked towards the water's edge I noticed that the sandbank leading to the adjoining cove was now submerged. I let the sea wash over my feet. It felt extremely cold, but I waded in determinedly up to my knees, then crouched down, pushed myself forward, and covered a short distance swimming breaststroke. When I stopped and tried to stand up, I found I was chest-deep in water. The dramatic change in depth was astonishing – Trudy had been right about that. After taking a few strokes back towards the beach, I was once again able to stand up in water that reached

no higher than my knees. I did a few more short swims in different directions and concluded that not only was there a sort of reef running more
or less parallel to the shoreline which accounted for the sudden drop in the
level of the sea-bed, but there were also several other, irregular dips and
rises all over the place which could unexpectedly leave a bather out of his
depth. All to the good, I thought.

I looked back at the beach and noticed a strikingly attractive raven-
haired woman in a bright yellow swimming costume sitting on a beach
chair under an umbrella, then suddenly realized I'd lost my bearings
momentarily and that the object of my attention was Marion. Emerging
from the sea, I made my way back to her, then picked up one of the beach
towels and, bending towards her, kissed her warmly on the cheek. She
responded with a glowing smile.

'How was it?' she asked. She'd been taking in the sun, having applied
lotion to her uncovered skin, and was looking marvellous, her gleaming
black hair cascading over her neck and shoulders and seeming to deepen
the gloss on the exposed parts of her slim, shapely body. I *had* lost my bearings, in another sense: I'd forgotten how beautiful my wife was.

'Cold,' I replied, 'and the water depth's a bit tricky. But very refreshing.
I can recommend it. Take care when you go in.'

'I've decided to opt out. I'm happy as I am.'

'Where's the sun-tan lotion?'

'Would you like me to put some on you?'

'Yes, please.'

Her hands felt soft and smooth as she applied the cool liquid to my back
and the backs of my legs. Then she made me turn and face her, lying on
my back, as she leaned over me and did my chest and upper abdomen,
and the front of my thighs. Then, glancing to her right and left to be sure
nobody was watching, she put her hand over the front of my swimming
trunks and held it there briefly. Giving me a flirtatious look she said, 'I'd
like you to make love to me, please, Teddy – at the hotel, as soon as
possible. How about that?'

I grinned back at her. 'Sounds good.' We stood up, packed up our things,
made our way back to the car without bothering to change out of our
swimwear, did the very short journey to the hotel, and in barely ten minutes
after leaving the beach were naked in each other's arms in the room.

I couldn't remember sex with Marion having been more passionate or
enjoyable – in fact, it wasn't just sex; it was a lovers' reunion, a warm and
tender revival of deep mutual love long withheld and, as soon as it was

over, we both knew it had been a significant event. This wasn't Eleanor or Lucy; it was Marion – the Marion I knew so well, my Marion. But also a new Marion. Had this Marion always been there, there'd have been no Eleanor or Lucy – and no Geoffrey. My ambivalence had now been brushed aside, finally. From this moment on, I was fully committed to my marriage, and on Monday I'd be breaking with Eleanor. And there'd be no need for any disclosures to her.

We lay together side by side silently for quite a while, glancing and grinning at each other every now and then. Later, we ordered gin-and-tonics from room service and drank them, sitting on the bed in towelling gowns provided by the hotel.

Should I tell her anything about Geoffrey now, I asked myself. I couldn't talk to her about Lucy or Eleanor, of course, and as I'd already decided, she wouldn't be impressed with my impersonation of a non-existent character for financial gain, but sooner or later I'd have to explain how I'd come into such a lot of money.

Or would I? I didn't intend transferring any large lump sum or sums from the trust to myself – that would be impossible anyway. My plan at this stage was merely to take control of the trust following Geoffrey's supposed demise and then taking years over getting the benefit of the trust fund for myself and my family. It would all have to be done subtly – first, there'd be a programme of investment, in property perhaps, then later there could be loans, leases, and other arrangements. Over the longer term, assets could be moved into other trusts in which Emma and Paulie, say, could become eligible to participate. Nobody would be in a position to object, other than the trustees, but in time I'd be able to move the trust away from Jeremy Lefarge and Citadel, and into the hands of my own trust company maybe. The point was that there was loads and loads of time for all that, and for letting Marion enjoy the fruits of my Greenwood adventure without her having to know all the details of it.

Had I been leaving Marion for Eleanor, it would have been different, of course, because Eleanor would have had to know everything. As a named trust beneficiary, she'd have been my principal means of access to the trust fund and my guess was that she would have been more comfortable with the truth than Marion, though I couldn't be sure of that. But all that was academic now; I was staying in my marriage.

What I did need to tell Marion about, though, were my plans to come back to Cornwall with Geoffrey.

'Have I ever mentioned a client of mine called Geoffrey Greenwood?'

I asked her.

'No. At least I don't think so. You haven't spoken about any of your clients in a long while.'

'Well, he's probably my best client at the moment – the most lucrative in terms of fees, that is. The firm's made a lot of money out of him this year. He lives in South Africa, but he's here often, on business, and he's coming over again this week to consult with me. He's still recuperating after an accident and needs to rest and relax, so he wants us to meet at a quiet seaside resort, and it's just occurred me that this could be the place.'

'This place? You mean this hotel?'

'I actually meant this part of Cornwall, but why not this hotel too?'

'Seems to me it's a long way from everywhere. Surely Brighton or somewhere around there would do as well?'

'He specifically mentioned a quiet place. Brighton's hardly quiet, and the weather here's a lot better. He's used to sunshine and sandy beaches you can swim off, not pebbles and ice-cold, murky water.'

'Oh, Brighton's not as bad as that, Teddy. And anyway, this beach this morning, it's very nice, but it's nothing like the beaches he must be used to.'

'No, of course not. But this is about as good as it gets in Britain, isn't it?'

'Yes, I suppose it is.' She paused. 'Yes, you're right. You could do worse than bring him here. How long will you be away, do you think?'

'Two or three days – maybe four.' It would depend on the weather, I told myself, but hopefully I'd be lucky on at least one of four days given the time of year.

'Can you be away from the office again?'

'Oh, yes. I'll be charging him by the day – at full rates.'

'When will you do this?'

'Very soon. Maybe from the middle of the week.'

'This coming week?'

'Yes.'

There was a short silence. 'It's a pity, your having to go away again, just now, when things may be sorting themselves out.'

'Yes, I know, but it won't be for long, love. It's the sort of tail-end of what I was doing in New York. After this we'll have a lot more time together, I promise you.'

'We'd better, or I'll break your neck.' We both laughed.

We went down for lunch just after two o'clock. When we were leaving the dining-room, I said, 'I think I'll make a provisional booking now – for Greenwood and myself, I mean.'

'How do you know the dates will suit him?'

'I know he'll be back in England on Monday and that he wants to do this as soon as possible. I'll make it provisionally for Wednesday, Thursday and Friday.'

'That's up to you. I'll see you upstairs.' She gave me a sly grin.

Martin Jones, who was at the desk, was delighted to reserve two rooms *en suite* for me and my friend, whose name I mentioned and Jones wrote down. I told him the booking would be confirmed on Monday and asked whether a deposit was required. 'Not at all, Mr Brook, not from you.'

This, I reflected on my way upstairs, was going to be a different – and much more difficult – experience. I'd become accustomed to impersonating someone called Geoffrey Greenwood, but pretending to be two people, myself and Geoffrey, in the same place at the same time, was going to take some doing. I could easily slip up, and the unexpected could always happen. But how much would it matter? It wasn't as if I was doing away with a real person; I'd just be staging something – a non-event, really. All that was needed was the semblance of reality. It should all be fine, as long as the plan was finalized carefully and carried out as convincingly as was reasonably possible.

We didn't have sex again that afternoon; instead, we just lay in each other's arms and then fell asleep. At four o'clock we got up and had a Cornish cream tea on the veranda, and afterwards – at my suggestion – went for a long walk along the cliff paths behind the cluster of beaches. The path we followed took us up to a point above the fourth cove, where it intersected with another, somewhat overgrown path that descended towards the small beach below. I went a short way down this narrow path alone and observed that, although the tide was out, the sandbank that ran in front of the beaches nearer the main beach didn't extend to this cove.

Marion said she was tired, so we walked back the way we'd come – a much easier trip because it was downhill all the way to the back of the main beach.

In the evening we dined, on Martin Jones's recommendation, in the restaurant of a small hotel in the village of Mousehole near Penzance. The meal, the wine, and the service were excellent. On the way back to The Cuckoo's Nest, Marion said, 'Teddy, what happened today – between us – was wonderful for me.'

'For me too.'

'Yes, and I'd love it to happen again tonight. But after we leave here tomorrow, it can't happen again. I mean I can't do it with you again, if there's still going to be another woman. I think I've made that clear already.'

'Yes, you have, but don't worry about that. I decided today that it's over. I'm going to speak to her on Monday and break it off.'

'Oh, Teddy darling. How wonderful! I love you.'

'I love you too – more than you know.'

Then I started thinking seriously about what I was going to tell Eleanor.

33

The next morning, Sunday, after a pleasantly demanding night with the new lover my wife had become, I had an early breakfast alone again and then took the car up the road towards the clifftop above the hotel. I wanted to find out for myself exactly how difficult it was to reach the point on the cliff-side that overlooked the cluster of beaches, and what could be seen from there.

The road was steep and became narrower as it wound upwards, eventually coming to an abrupt end as it opened out onto a viewing site which overlooked the sea on the side facing away from the beaches. The site was small, but big enough to accommodate two or three cars parked side by side. I left the car there and took a footpath that seemed to lead the way I wanted to go. After a while the path became a track, which then grew increasingly indiscernible. Suddenly, I recognized the clifftops above the coves in the distance and made my way over wild undergrowth until I came to a rocky outcrop from which I could look out across the sea towards the main beach and the range of sheltered beaches that stretched out from it to my right.

From where I stood almost all of the main beach was visible. There were a few people on it, but at this height and distance they appeared tiny. The coves were even further away, and it seemed to me that if anyone standing where I was were to watch someone swimming off even the second cove, the observer wouldn't be able to see any details at all. Powerful binoculars, of course, would make all the difference, but only if they were really powerful, and how likely was it that someone with really powerful binoculars would be watching the coves from this overgrown, almost inaccessible vantage point at precisely the time at which Geoffrey's 'non-event' was occurring?

And so, another excursion having been concluded satisfactorily, I returned to the car – experiencing some difficulty on the way in picking up the path – and drove back to the hotel.

Marion was not only up and dressed but had even beaten the end-of-breakfast deadline and was packing to leave. 'It's been lovely here,' she told me, smiling; 'I mean what we've found here. Think we can take it back home with us?'

'Of course we can,' I replied, taking her in my arms.

Unlike the drive down to Cornwall on Friday, the journey back on Sunday proved long and tedious due to traffic delays, but it was followed by a joyful reunion with the children and then an excellent supper cooked by Marion's mother, who was staying the night.

I remained downstairs for a while after Marion had gone to bed. In the car on the way home she'd announced, joyfully and almost with pride, that she'd be moving herself and her things back into the master bedroom the next day. 'Tonight,' she'd said, 'will be my last night in the snug. It's just as well,' she'd laughed; 'I need the rest.'

I poured myself a Scotch and spent the next hour working on the excuse I was going to make to Eleanor for 'ditching' her – a horrible word, but apt. It would be about my – meaning Geoffrey's – ex-wife in South Africa and unresolved issues. In the end, I wasn't very happy with the results of these deliberations, which meant she wasn't likely to be either, and decided it would be better to start off with a broad idea of what I was going to say and then play it by ear as we talked. Too much advance fine-tuning in this kind of situation could have the wrong effect: over-rehearsed excuses never sounded sincere.

Whenever we'd been apart until now, we'd made love as soon as we were reunited. Ought I to let that happen tomorrow, before I said anything to her? I'd be a bit of a heel doing so, but wouldn't it put us both at our ease and underline my reluctance to be parting from her? After all, I was sincerely reluctant to be doing this, and it wasn't as if I didn't *want* to make love to her. So I decided, very well then, I'd just let what happened happen, and take it from there.

In the morning we all had breakfast together – Marion, her mother, the kids, Katka, and I. We were a real family again. Afterwards, I went off to the office and Marion kissed me goodbye.

I rang Eleanor at work at around noon to confirm I was back from my travels and expecting her at Beverley Terrace in the afternoon.

'Geoff,' she said, 'there's a strange message for you on the answering machine in the flat, from some foreign chap. I picked it up last night after I'd been out shopping. It sounded urgent. The machine's on again now and I haven't erased the message, so why don't you phone in and pick it up? The remote access code is one eight.'

The call had been from Gragorin. 'Mr Greenwood,' said his voice, 'Gragorin. Why you never at home? I come other day to see you, with a friend. You can't dodge me, you know. Me and my friends we watch you now. One day we pick you up. If you got sense, you phone me. I give you number once more.' He did so. 'Goodbye, Mr Chips.'

How Gragorin and his friends could be 'watching' Geoffrey was a mystery. They had no idea what he looked like – nor did anybody else. But they were, probably, keeping any eye on the flat – and on Eleanor. And it wasn't impossible that Gragorin would approach her if his efforts at contact with Geoffrey continued to fail.

On the other hand, it was only a matter of days now before Geoffrey was out of the way. Meanwhile, I was about to break with Eleanor. If Gragorin spoke to her after today, she'd tell him she and Geoffrey were no longer together. But what about 'Geoffrey's' things in the flat – mine actually? Wouldn't she – and Gragorin – be expecting him to come and collect them? I must make a point of telling her I'd be round to the flat to get my clothing and personal things in a week or so – not before – and I should try and persuade her to keep all the furniture and other stuff. She'd probably insist I have it, but I could stall her about that too. Then, once Geoffrey was no longer in the picture, I could try and sort it all out as his solicitor – by correspondence, not personally, of course. But that wasn't urgent. First things first.

34

I arrived at Beverley Terrace just before two o'clock and was greeted in the lobby by a sallow-looking Mr Clarke.

'It's been quite a while, Mr Clarke,' I said. 'How are you?'

'Not at all well, I'm afraid to say, Mr Greenwood, thank you. In fact,

I've been rather ill; been off with a mild stroke. This is my first day back.'

I noticed he spoke with a slight slur and his mouth looked asymmetrical.

'I'm very sorry to hear that. Should you be here at all today? You don't look up to it, you know.'

'I prefer being here, sir. Mrs Clarke frets over me at home. Makes me feel worse, not better. It's more peaceful here. Going upstairs?'

'Yes. I've been away, in America. Have you any mail for me?'

Clarke extracted four envelopes from the pigeon-hole for Flat Thirty-Four and gave them to me.

'Thank you. I'm expecting someone, a visitor. You know her, Eleanor Downing.'

'Ah, the lovely Eleanor. Yes, I do. Haven't seen or heard from her in a long while.'

'Please send her straight up when she comes.'

'Of course, Mr Greenwood.'

I wondered if I should offer Clarke any kind of explanation for Eleanor's visit. He wasn't to know that Eleanor and I had been sharing a flat in London or that there was anything between us, and it would probably be best to try and discourage him from believing there was. He'd soon be hearing of Mr Greenwood's tragic accident and might regard the gentleman's romantic involvement with 'the lovely Eleanor' as a tasty titbit worth mentioning to his peers.

'We're having a business meeting, and I'm expecting others too,' I said. Even the seemingly unworldly Clarke was likely to be sceptical about the commercial nature of a private meeting in a flat with a woman who looked like Eleanor, but letting him think others were coming might give him a different impression, and the fact that nobody else actually arrived wouldn't matter, as Clarke often left the lobby and didn't witness every single arrival there.

Eleanor rang the bell promptly at 2.30. Seeing her again now in the flesh, I knew at once that my ambivalence was far from banished. She smiled at me and said, 'Hullo lover. I've missed you,' and I started wondering all over again why I was giving her up.

'Me too,' I replied, and next thing she was in my arms and we were kissing, then in no time we were both naked on the bed.

I heard the door being opened with a key just as I was poised above her in the missionary position, so I looked up. Lucy was standing by the open door, staring at us across the room.

As I watched, she closed the door, came a couple of steps closer, and said, 'Hullo, Charles, or is it Geoffrey? May I join you?'

Eleanor pushed against my chest and sat up, then reached for her dress and pulled it on. 'Who is this?' she asked me.

Lucy answered. 'I'm Lucy – Lucy Cole – and, as you see, I've got a key to this flat. Who are you, may I ask?'

How on earth had I forgotten to get the key back from her?

'My name's Eleanor – Eleanor Downing. What's all this about?' She looked at me, then at Lucy.

'I'd be delighted to answer that, Ellen darling,' said Lucy – the 'Ellen' was spitefully deliberate – 'as soon as I've finished saying something to our mutual friend here.' She sat down on the end of the bed, prompting Eleanor to stand up and move away. I stayed where I was, dumbfounded and still stark naked.

'Charles,' said Lucy, 'I've been trying for a long time now to find out more about Mr Geoffrey Greenwood – the man I'm supposed to have had an affair with, remember? – and then I started recalling things, like how you were supposed to get us a flat but were lucky enough to be given the free use of this one by a dear friend and client called Geoffrey Greenwood who was conveniently away abroad a lot, and how there was never a sign of anything to show that this was Geoffrey's place or that he'd ever been here, and then, how you came to be mistaken for him by Malcolm's investigator. So, after Malcolm had tried in vain to contact Greenwood, I carried on the search. I even wrote to the guy, but I never got a reply. I'd suspected for some time that he didn't exist, now I was sure I was right. And then, when I came by the desk today and asked the porter if Mr Greenwood was in, I was told, to my surprise, that he was expecting me and I'd find him in his flat. And who *did* I find in this flat? None other than you, Charles Bloody Brook.'

She turned to Eleanor. 'And you, Ellen dear, are you a friend of Geoffrey or Charles? I'd like to know because I've had a hot affair with one of them – the rat who does exist – and I've confessed to having an affair with the other one – the phantom who doesn't. Are you humping the rat or the phantom?'

Eleanor, shaken and bewildered, said, 'The name is Eleanor, not Ellen,' then picked up the rest of her clothes and moved towards the bathroom. As she did so, Lucy said, 'Oh, and did you know, Eleanor, this double agent's married and has two children?'

Eleanor turned, glanced at her, and stared at me as if expecting me to deny it all. I got up and walked towards her. 'Eleanor darling, please. I can explain.'

'You can explain?' She was in tears. 'What can *you* explain? I don't even know who you are.' She disappeared into the bathroom and closed the door.

Putting on my underpants, I shook my head at Lucy and said, 'What the hell do you think you're doing? Why are you being so bloody unfair, Lucy?'

'Unfair? Look who's talking about unfair. I don't know who she is or what she means to you, but I think she needs to know what you are. You lied to me, you bastard. You deceived me. Why did you tell me that bull-shit about someone called Geoffrey Greenwood and then let me confess to my husband that I was having an affair with him?'

She was distorting everything, but there was no point in arguing with her. What mattered was what she'd just done. We stood there glaring at each other. Then Eleanor came out of the bathroom fully dressed.

'Eleanor, please don't go. . . .' I said.

She cut me off. 'What do you suggest? That I stay for a *ménage à trois?*'

Lucy chuckled. 'Sounds good to me.'

Eleanor turned to her. 'You know something, Lucy? I've only just met you, but you're a first-class bitch.' And with that she walked out and slammed the door behind her. Now Lucy stood up.

'I'm going too, Charles. My marriage is finished and I'm having a nasty scrap with Malcolm. Your new ex-girlfriend's probably right about me – I *have* been a bitch this afternoon, but I don't regret it. I take the blame for getting involved with you and being found out, but I could have sorted my life out a lot better if you hadn't misled me, you snake. Goodbye.'

She closed the door only a little more gently than Eleanor had done.

I sat down on the bed again and put my head in my hands. What a crazy thing to have happened! The timing couldn't have been worse – and what irony that I'd told Clarke I was expecting others! But there was no going back on any of that now. The question was, where to from here? In one sense, Lucy had done my work for me; my relationship with Eleanor had been terminated, though in the most drastic, awful way. I needed to work out exactly what this meant, and what to do next.

The secret of Geoffrey's non-existence was now shared with both Eleanor and Lucy, but I still had to go ahead with my plan to get rid of Geoffrey. Was there anything either of them would or could do to frustrate that? I doubted it. They were both angry with me – Eleanor more so at this moment than Lucy, who must have gained quite a lot of satisfaction from the afternoon's events and deep-down knew as well as I did that she didn't really have a gripe against me; what was actually eating at her was still my rejection of her, quite obviously aggravated by the sight of me having sex with another woman, but neither of them had any inkling of my intentions or any real means of exposing me. Lucy had no idea of the deals I'd done in Geoffrey's name, and all Eleanor knew was what I'd told her about the trust, which meant nothing on its own. In fact, given what she'd just learned about me, she'd probably be thinking now that all that was a lie too. Besides, she wasn't the vindictive type and, even if she were, she'd have no reason to see me as anything other than a deceiver of women. I was sad about her, very sad – actually quite miserable – and not only because of the way it had happened. As difficult as it would have been parting as I'd planned to, it wouldn't have been so final. I realized now that at the back of my mind I'd been meaning to leave a door open between us. It had never really been a case of Marion or Eleanor, but a question of how I could still manage to keep them both in my life. Now that door was firmly and finally shut.

For the present, however, everything had to be dismissed from my mind but Geoffrey's forthcoming disappearance, which was becoming more and more of an imperative by the day. Time was short now, so I sat down at the desk and ran through my plan of action in detail.

35

I felt uneasy when I got back to the office. It wasn't just the emotional upset I'd suffered at Beverley Terrace, but I had a sense of having over-looked something important. I put my head into Jonathan's office.

'Hullo, Charles,' he said, warmly. 'How was the weekend in Cornwall?'

'Nice. Going back there on Wednesday.'

'With Marion again?'

'No, I'm afraid not. With Greenwood.'

Jonathan laughed. 'That's quite a change – from Marion to Greenwood.'

'Yes, I suppose it is, but this is business again. You know he wasn't with us in New York – had a bad car accident – and he wants to catch up on the whole deal and other things. But he's still recuperating, so he'd like to meet me at a seaside resort.'

'What's wrong with Brighton?'

'A lot – to him. Not quiet enough. And he wants sandy beaches, like the ones in South Africa.'

'I still haven't had the pleasure of meeting the man, remember?'

'Haven't you? Oh, well, I'll fix that next week, invite him to lunch.'

In the evening, at home, I told Marion that Greenwood had liked the idea of The Cuckoo's Nest and that we were planning to spend from Wednesday to Saturday there, though I could be back by Friday if our discussions went well.

'I envy you guys,' she said. 'It's such a lovely place.'

'Yes, isn't it?' I replied, absently. The overlooked factor that had been nagging me had suddenly hit me like a rocket. 'Marion darling, I'm sorry. I must go back to the office. I forgot about something important and it's bothering me.'

She frowned. 'Do you mean that? Or is it that other person of yours?'

'No, no. Nothing like that. I've done as I said I would – told her that it's all over.' I went over to her and kissed her cheek. 'That's a thing of the past, I promise you.'

'That's good. My cup runneth over.'

'*Our* cup, if you please. It's mine too.'

Instead of the office, I went to Beverley Terrace. In my deliberations about Eleanor, I'd forgotten all about her being Geoffrey's partner, the woman he lived with in London. When Geoffrey disappeared, she'd be notified, officially. How would she react now that she knew the truth? Probably with an annoyed, 'What do you mean? There's no such person. He's never existed and he can't disappear, or drown, or whatever. His real name's Charles Brook and he's a fraud. He uses the name Geoffrey Greenwood to seduce and deceive women'. It was hardly likely she'd simply listen to what they told her and say nothing.

What could I do about it? There was only one answer: I had to get to her somehow, tell her what I intended doing, and try to persuade her to go along with me, at least until everything had settled down. If she was willing to talk to me at all, she'd probably tell me to go to hell.

What, I asked myself, would have upset her most out of the things she'd heard from Lucy? That I was married, with kids, surely, and, of course, that

I'd lied to her so blatantly, especially about that. I must try and make her understand how it had been circumstances that had led me to maintain the Greenwood identity with her for as long as I had done, and convince her that I'd intended telling her the truth as soon as I could. She'd loved me deeply and sincerely, I was sure, and probably enough, I thought, to be open to some further contact with me once the initial shock of the afternoon's revelations had subsided. But I'd have to lie to her once more, tell her that my marriage was breaking up and that I still wanted to spend the rest of my life with her – that nothing had changed in fact, except that Lucy had pre-empted me by making the very disclosures I was about to make myself. I hated having to deceive her again like this, but there was just no other way. There'd be time later to make up something about why I couldn't leave Marion after all and, if need be, I'd have to carry on a secret affair with Eleanor until I was able to sort it all out. In fact, as I'd already conceded to myself, wasn't that what I really wanted? Marion as my wife again, and Eleanor as my lover? But right now, oh, what a mess! I simply had to recapture her confidence and secure her co-operation at all costs. It was far too late to think of changing course with Geoffrey.

I called the London flat on my mobile. The answering machine was on. I'd leave her a message, but not on this call; I had to work out exactly what I wanted to say, so that it had the desired impact: it must make her want to phone me back. So I wrote down a draft of the message, revised it, made a few more changes, rewrote the whole thing, and then committed it to memory to avoid making it sound as if I were reading it out. Then I rang the number again and left this message on the machine:

'Eleanor, darling, this is Charles. I really do love you. I *am* married, but I'm getting divorced. Geoffrey will be out of the way in a few days. Nothing's changed, I swear. Please call me on my mobile as soon as possible.'

I waited in the Beverley Terrace flat for over an hour before the phone rang. Eleanor's voice was subdued. 'Hullo?' she said.

'Eleanor darling, thank you for calling back. I know how you must be feeling, but it's very important that we talk about this – for both of us.'

'I can't see you now. That's out of the question.' Her tone was flat.

'I realize that. I also realize that you don't trust me. . . .'

'Trust you? I don't even know you.'

'You do, my love. You do. I'm still myself. Just hear me out, please.'

'What's this about doing away with Geoffrey? I don't understand what you mean.'

'That's one of the things I want to explain. Eleanor, you've known me as Geoffrey only because that's the name I was using to rent the flat – when we first met, remember?'

'Yes, but you never told me that it wasn't your name afterwards – after you'd seduced me,' she said accusingly. 'Wasn't that because you were married?'

'No. My marriage has been on the rocks for some time now. My wife and I haven't led a married life in ages and we're getting divorced.'

'That's what married men usually say to the women they seduce, isn't it?'

'Maybe. I don't know. But I didn't adopt the name Geoffrey Greenwood to mislead you. It was the name I'd used to rent the flat and—'

'Why did you have to rent a flat in a false name if your marriage was on the rocks as you say?'

'Lucy was worried about *her* marriage, that's why.'

'Oh, yes,' said Eleanor, speaking a little more animatedly now, 'Lucy. Now that you mention her, she wasn't too pleased with you either. You lied to her too.'

'Only about who Geoffrey Greenwood was, and there was a reason for that. And please don't let Lucy spoil what we have. She's very vindictive towards me because I rejected her, and she's got her own agenda.'

'Oh, Geoff – Charles, or whoever you are,' said Eleanor wearily, 'there's been so much lying I don't know what to think. I thought I knew and fell in love with a wonderful guy called Geoff. Now I discover he doesn't exist. Instead, there's some guy – married with kids – called Charles who's fucking me under false pretences.' She started sobbing and shouting into the phone. 'You're a bastard, you know? A rapist, actually. Isn't it rape to fuck a woman under false pretences? You're a lawyer, aren't you? You should know.'

'Darling Eleanor, you're very angry, justifiably, but if what we've had has meant anything to you, please don't throw it away until you're quite sure you know all the facts and you're certain that it's what you really want to do. We should meet. This is not a discussion for the phone.'

'Why not? Do you want time to concoct more lies?'

'No. Not at all. If I didn't care about you, I wouldn't have called you, or been speaking to you now.' I paused and she remained silent. 'You want to know what I meant about Geoffrey being out of the way. I've had to maintain the Geoffrey identity for all sorts of reasons – nothing to do with you –

and the time has come to discard it. I was going to tell you all this today, this afternoon – that's why I asked you to meet me. I wanted you to know everything. Then Lucy burst in, and that was that.'

'She told me all about you and her.'

'When? Not at the flat.'

'No, afterwards. We met up, and spoke.'

This surprised me. 'Oh,' I said. 'Well, don't forget, she's got an axe to grind.'

'Maybe. But where's all this leading?'

'Well, the imaginary Geoffrey's got to disappear, and I'm seeing to that in the next few days. It has to be convincing. I'll tell you why, but I can't now, on the phone. All I'm asking of you at this moment is that when you hear about his disappearance – from me, or the police, or anyone else – don't say anything about him not existing. It could do me tremendous harm if you did.'

'Why should I care about that? Harm is what you deserve.'

'Because of us, Eleanor darling. Nothing's changed, really. I'm still me, and you're still you, and we love each other, and if I can get you to trust me again, we'll have our whole lives before us.'

'And what if you can't get me to trust you again?'

'Then you'll have lost nothing. But you might be losing a lot by jumping to conclusions now.'

'From what I've heard today I wouldn't call it jumping to conclusions.'

'Well, you're doing just that, I assure you. And even if you believe you're not, why not wait and see?'

After a pause she said, 'So now you want me to start lying too? I must pretend I don't know there's no Geoffrey Greenwood. And what happens if I get found out?'

'Nothing. If you'd heard nothing today, that's exactly how you'd have reacted to the news. . . .'

'Yes,' she said acidly, 'I'd probably have been tearing my hair out with grief over a man who didn't exist.'

'No, you wouldn't. Because I'd have told you everything. Today. I wanted to make sure you knew all about Geoffrey Greenwood *before* you heard anything like that about him. Please, my love, it's very important you see this through with me.'

'I hate lying.'

'You won't have to lie. Just pretend you still believed what you knew this morning.'

Silence again, then she said, 'You say you're leaving your wife?'

'Yes.'

'Well, I must admit Lucy gave me that impression too. She told me things about – Marion, is that right?'

'Yes.'

'She said she'd been withdrawn, depressed for quite a long time.'

'Yes,' I replied, feeling disloyal towards Marion and angry with Lucy, who'd not been above taking advantage of Marion's depression in order to have an affair with her husband.

'I'd like to ask you something else,' said Eleanor.

'Of course. What is it?'

'This trust you spoke about – The Greenwood Trust? I suppose that was a pack of lies too.'

'Not at all. It's my money, legitimately mine. But I made it in Geoffrey's name, so I put it into a trust, with you and Geoffrey as the beneficiaries.'

'What about you? What will you get out of it?'

'I control it. It was really for you and me – when we got married. And I hope we still will.'

She sighed audibly. 'Oh, Geoff – Charles – if only I could believe you.'

'If you want proof – about the trust – I can let you have it. I can get the trust company to write to you confirming that you and Geoffrey are the only two named beneficiaries.'

'I'm not interested in the money. That's not why I'm asking about it. I'm just looking for *something* truthful about you. Then maybe I can start thinking about believing you again – though I'm still not sure I even know you.'

'Well then, I'll see you get a letter, as soon as possible.'

After a short silence, she said, 'You're right. We *will* need to talk this through fully, but not now. I can't promise you anything, Charles. Right now I don't like you very much, but I did love you as Geoffrey and I suppose it makes sense to give you a chance as yourself.' Now there was a longer silence. I thought she might have rung off when I heard her say, 'OK. I'll go along with you and not give anything away about Geoffrey when I hear of his – you said disappearance, didn't you?'

'Disappearance in the sea – presumed drowned. Off the Cornish coast.'

'When?'

'Within the next few days. Say, by the weekend.'

Another pause. 'Right, I'll promise you that much. And I'll promise to sit down and talk everything through with you. But that's all. Afterwards, we'll see – no, *I'll* see how I feel.'

'Good. Thank you. I love you, Eleanor darling.'

'Don't push it, Charles. I repeat, I still don't know you, and I don't know that I like hearing that from somebody I don't know.'

'OK. I won't say it again, until you want me to.'

'If ever,' she said. 'And if there is to be an 'ever', you're definitely leaving Marion?'

'Yes. Definitely. It's happening already.'

'OK. You'd better not be lying to me now.' A steely tone entered her voice, turning her into a stranger. 'If you are, I'll break you, Charles, and there's somebody I know who'll help me do that. Believe me. Right now, I've had enough. I'm taking a sleeping pill and going to bed – alone.'

'I understand.'

'I hope you do. Goodnight, Charles.'

'Goodnight, Eleanor – darling.'

36

Two days later, on Wednesday 10 September, I set off on my second journey in a week by road from Brighton to Cornwall, this time alone.

There were two suitcases in the boot of the car, my own and 'Geoffrey's'. Attached to the latter was a smart leather luggage-tag holder through the window of which peered the name 'G. R. Greenwood' and the address and telephone number of the St John's Wood flat. In Geoffrey's suitcase were the clothing and toiletries I'd bought for him. The boot also contained my laptop computer and my briefcase, inside which were two copies of the agreements in the Hall Computers deal.

The day before, Tuesday, I'd phoned Jeremy Lefarge and told him that Geoffrey Greenwood wanted a letter written to Eleanor Downing as soon as possible confirming her eligibility to benefit under The Greenwood Trust. In common with most trust managers, Jeremy would be accustomed to receiving such requests, as the wives and partners of wealthy men often needed reassurance that the trust mechanism was not being used as a ruse for depriving them of their expectations. Jeremy said he would comply immediately, but would like me to confirm the request in writing by fax and through the post, which I'd duly done.

I reached The Cuckoo's Nest just after 3.30 in the afternoon and took everything out of the boot other than Geoffrey's suitcase. In the lobby Martin Jones greeted me warmly. 'Where's your friend?' he asked. 'Mr Greenwood, is it not?'

'He's on his way down from London by rail. I'm meeting him at the station in Penzance this evening.'

'We can save you the trouble, you know. We have a car that meets guests there.'

'Thanks for the offer, but no. I've promised to be there myself and I'd feel remiss if I didn't. We'll probably have a bite to eat in Penzance and won't be getting back here until late. Can I check us both in now?' I said, pen poised to sign.

'Yes. That'll be fine. We have the two of you down as a party.'

'I should take his keys too, I suppose.'

'Yes, please. You remember the routine for late arrivals? Through the back door, with this key.' He indicated a key on one of the two sets he was handing me. 'Then up the stairs to the first floor, where your bedrooms are. I've given you gentlemen our two best rooms, numbers eight and nine. They're across the passage from each other. You're our only guests till the weekend.' He rang a bell on the desk.

'What's the weather forecast like, Mr Jones?'

'Martin's the name, please. The weather will be good, very good. It's been a bit cooler since you left us on Sunday, but sunny and warm is what they're forecasting for the next few days.'

'Good. My friend will be very pleased. He's looking forward to swimming.'

'Oh, I'm sure he'll be able to. Peter here will take your luggage and show you the two rooms.' A young man had appeared in response to the bell.

'Oh, thank you. My friend's bringing his own luggage with him. I'm sure we'll manage it comfortably between us.'

So far so good, I thought as I followed Peter up the main staircase and along the first-floor corridor. Peter showed me rooms eight and nine. They were much the same.

'This will do for me,' I said, surveying room nine. 'Mr Greenwood can have the other one.'

After thanking and tipping Peter, I lay down on the bed. There was one part of my plan which was still troubling me. I expected the police or the coastguard to want some proof of the missing man's identity, and it would look strange if none was found among his belongings at the hotel or at one of his two flats. To avoid that happening, I had to find a way of creating the impression that he'd brought his passport, driver's licence, credit cards and other personal items with him to Cornwall and that they'd disappeared with him. The problem was that people didn't usually take their wallets and ID documents into the water with them when they went swimming. I'd thought of a possible solution to this difficulty with which I wasn't entirely happy but to which I'd have to resort if nothing better came to mind.

On my arrival at the hotel I had set out on a course of action aimed at creating a series of impressions. I'd be making it seem that things were happening which weren't, and that someone was present who wasn't. It was a daunting undertaking, though it wouldn't matter too much if I made a minor mistake or two; unlike an illusionist performing on the stage, I was playing to an audience that was unaware it was witnessing a show. Nobody would have any reason to doubt the existence of Geoffrey, or to question his presence where the vestiges of it were in evidence, and the cessation of his supposed presence would then bear out my account of his disappearance.

After calling Marion and the office to report my safe arrival, I unpacked my suitcase, rang down to the desk, asked for a reminder call at 7.30, and dozed off on the bed. When it came, the call woke me from a deep sleep. 'Your wake-up call, Mr Brook,' said a familiar female voice. 'Nice to have you back.'

'Is that you, Jenny?'

'Yes, it is.'

'How are you?'

'Very well, thank you. And you, Mr Brook?'

'Fine, thanks, Jenny. Could somebody please find out the arrival time of a train for me?'

'Martin or Trudy's best for that. I'll get them to ring you back.'

'Thanks, Jenny.'

'See you around.'

'You, too,' I answered, not knowing why I was participating in this exchange when I'd so firmly resolved not to be distracted.

When Martin Jones called me a few minutes later, I asked him if he could find out the expected time of arrival in Penzance of the 15.33 from Paddington. He rang me back to say the train was running about fifteen minutes late and was expected at ten past nine.

I took a shower, dressed, and went down to the pub, where I ordered a gin and tonic – I'd be having no more than that, not just because I was driving but I needed to keep my wits about me. I noticed Jenny moving around with trays and things, then she noticed me and gave me a very friendly smile. I smiled back, but not as warmly. A grey-haired man standing a few feet away at the counter drew a little nearer and said, 'Quite a lass, that.'

'Yes, she is.'

'The talk is she likes men and the lucky ones get their bit of action with her. But I don't know how true it is. She's certainly a friendly girl, but sometimes people take friendliness as a sign of other things not meant. She's married to a local chap who travels and is away a lot, so that in itself leads to gossip.'

'Yes, I suppose it does.'

'You staying here?'

'Yes,' I replied. 'I'm meeting a business associate here. He's arriving tonight.'

'What business are you in, if I may ask?'

'I'm a solicitor. And you?'

'Oh, I'm a retired police officer. Cambridgeshire Constabulary. I live down this way now. It's the nicest part of Britain to retire to, I think. You from London?'

'Originally. Brighton and Hove now.'

After a brief silence I looked at my watch and said, 'I must be off now – have to fetch my client from the station in Penzance.'

'Well, it's been a pleasure,' said the man. 'My name's Grant, by the way, Claude Grant.' He reached out and shook my hand.

'Charles Brook.'

Getting into the car, I reflected that my brief discussion with Claude Grant had been useful because it had added another layer to the impression I was creating of Geoffrey's imminent arrival in Cornwall.

I got to the station early and bought a local newspaper, from which I checked the tide times for the next day. When the train from Paddington arrived, the platform got quite crowded and I went through the motions of looking for an arriving passenger – unnecessarily, because nobody was paying me the slightest attention. I mingled with the crowd leaving the station, then drove to a garage, where I filled the car and bought two chocolate bars and two soft drinks, paying for these with my credit card. From there, I drove to a car-park near the harbour, ate both chocolate bars, opened both soft-drink containers, drank one of the drinks, emptied the contents of the other container onto the ground, and threw both containers and chocolate wrappers into a nearby bin.

It was shortly after eleven when I got back to The Cuckoo's Nest. I parked near the back door, removed from the cubby hole the pair of driving gloves I kept there, put them on, got out of the car, said, 'I'll get it,' went round to the passenger's side of the car, opened the door, waited and then shut it, opened the boot, removed the suitcase, said, 'Over here,' unlocked the back door of the hotel, went up the staircase, unlocked the door of 'Geoffrey's' room, entered it, and shut the door. I then called out, 'Not bad, is it?' from within the room. After waiting a couple of minutes, I opened the door, emerged into the corridor, said 'Goodnight,' shut the door, leaving it unlocked, walked across to my room and opened the door, then holding it open removed my shoes, put them inside, shut the door without going in, moved silently across to Geoffrey's room again, and entered it.

Inside, still wearing the gloves, I quickly unpacked for Geoffrey, took off the bed cover, messed up the bed, flushed the toilet, ran the shower, wet the soap, squeezed some toothpaste onto the toothbrush, rinsed it off, drew the curtains, opened the door, shut the door quietly, locking it, crossed the corridor back to my own room, entered it, and took off the gloves. Letting out a deep sigh, I said to myself, 'Act One, done and completed.' I realized I was actually enjoying the charade, in a way.

Of course, I thought, all these elaborate movements and noises of mine could well have gone unobserved and unheard, seeing there were no other guests in the hotel, but I surely could not have been the only person on the premises. I had no idea where the Joneses slept, but if they or any of their staff were around, my efforts would not have been wasted. Whoever had overheard me must have been convinced that at least two people had entered the building and were occupying our rooms.

As for the gloves, I had decided, after some deliberation, to avoid leaving my own fingerprints all over Geoffrey's room. I couldn't imagine the police bothering too much with fingerprints after the event, but the precaution of wearing gloves was, I thought, just as easily taken as omitted. I would be coming back into the room in the morning, when I'd do some final wiping off of prints, just for good measure.

I set the alarm on my wristwatch for six o'clock and, despite the stress of the circumstances, fell asleep almost immediately.

37

It was 5.30 when I awoke of my own accord. I got up, stole across the corridor, and entered Geoffrey's room as soundlessly as I could. After checking once more to satisfy myself that everything looked as it should, I put up the 'Do Not Disturb' sign, closed the door, and returned to my own room, to emerge again at 7.30, dressed for a warm day at the seaside, which, true to the forecast, it had turned out to be.

Trudy Jones came up to me in the breakfast room. 'Where's your friend Mr Greenwood? We heard you arriving with him last night.'

So all my activity had not been in vain. 'He was exhausted and said he'd be lying in and missing breakfast.'

'We can always make him some sandwiches later.'

'Thank you, Mrs Jones. I'll mention that to him.'

'Trudy to you, please.'

'Thank you, Trudy.'

After breakfast I went upstairs to my own room for about ten minutes, put up the 'Do Not Disturb' sign, donned the gloves again, and went over to the other room, where I lay down on the rumpled bed until 9.30. I undressed, ran the shower again, flushed the toilet, removed from the wardrobe a T-shirt, a pair of underpants, a windcheater, a pair of trainers, and a pair of shorts. Then, using a cloth I'd brought with me, I wiped Geoffrey's toothbrush and razor as well as the door handles clean of prints, inspected the room again, and left it, carrying the clothes I'd taken from the wardrobe and turning the sign on the door around so that it read 'Please Make Up Room'. Back in my own room, I packed the clothes into a small knapsack I'd brought along in my suitcase. I dropped 'Geoffrey's' room keys into the knapsack, removed the gloves, put on my own windcheater, and left the room with the knapsack. Again, I turned the sign to 'Please Make Up Room'. I then made my way down the back stairs and out to the car through the back door, put the knapsack in the boot, walked round to the front of the hotel, entered the lobby, and approached Martin Jones at the desk.

'Lovely morning, eh, Mr Brook?' said Jones.

'Yes, it is. We've decided to go for a walk along the cliffs behind the beaches. Can we have a couple of beach towels, please? We may decide to take a dip in the sea along the way.'

Jones handed me two towels. 'Take care if you go swimming off those coves. You can find yourselves in deep water before you know it.'

I went out the way I'd come in, through the front entrance. When I got to the car, I looked around again and, seeing no-one about, got into the driver's seat, shut the driver's door, reached across to the door on the passenger's side, opened it, closed it again, started the car, and drove down the road to the car-park behind the main beach.

I parked the car at one end, alongside a clump of trees and bushes where the footpath began that led upwards behind the coves – the path I'd taken with Marion – with the driver's side of the vehicle facing the car-park and the main beach. Then I went through the motions, again, of pretending that two people were getting out of the car, one of them – myself – through the right front door and the other – my passenger – through the left, the latter ostensibly obscured from view by the car, trees and bushes. I opened and closed the passenger door, called out, 'Don't worry. I'll get it,' opened the driver's door, got out of the car, closed the door, went round to the boot, opened it, took out the knapsack, closed the boot, moved to the passenger's side of the vehicle, said loudly, 'This way, Geoff,' then walked into the thicket and from there joined the footpath. As I started up the hill, carrying the knapsack over my shoulder, I thought, that's Act Two, now for the big one.

From the cliff behind the fourth cove I took the narrow path down the steep slope towards the beach. As I did so, a helicopter came into view and seemed to be heading towards me when it veered off to the right and disappeared. I realized I'd omitted to consider the possibility of being seen from a helicopter, but nobody in it could have said with certainty that I'd been unaccompanied.

The cove looked deserted. When I reached the beach, I made my way to a rocky alcove along the cliff-face and, hidden from view in there, emptied the knapsack of its contents – Geoffrey's clothes and keys – and put them down on a rock, then took off all my own clothing and placed it on an adjoining rock together with one of the beach-towels. Next, I tucked the other towel around my waist and put Geoffrey's keys back into the knapsack together with some smaller rocks for ballast. Now I was ready for the main act, which I'd be performing, step by step, as if I were first Geoffrey and then myself. My concern was not so much with the observations of an unlikely spectator, but with adhering to a plausible timetable and sequence of events.

Playing the part of Geoffrey, I emerged from the alcove, the knapsack slung over my shoulder, and approached the water. After dropping the towel and putting it and the knapsack down on a small rock lapped by wavelets, I walked a short way into the sea and then, bracing myself against the cold, repeated what I'd done off the main beach a few days earlier: I crouched down and doing breaststroke swam a short distance away from the shore. This time, however, I got a horrible shock when I tried to stand again – I couldn't. Telling myself not to panic, I did a few strokes of crawl in the direction of the beach, and tried again. Now, thankfully, my feet touched the seabed, though the water was chest-high where I stood.

Relieved, I laughed aloud, reminding myself that the object was to drown Geoffrey, not myself. Then I crouched down and keeping my feet in touch with the bottom, began moving crab-like towards the bank of rocks bordering the cove to my right, as I faced the beach. The water grew choppy as I neared the rocks; then I suddenly felt a strong backwash and had to dig my feet into the sand to hold my ground. But the backwash soon subsided and I managed to reach the rocks with little difficulty. Once there, I used them as cover while I got out of the water and, still bent low, crept back to the alcove between the outer edge of the cove and the clumps of rocks that extended onto the beach. When I reached the alcove, I sat down on a rock, panting. Even had I been watched by a well-positioned, interested spectator, I was sure I'd done enough to avoid any manifestation of the swimmer's emergence from the sea. I carefully refrained from drying myself with the other towel – my own – and instead waited for the water on my body to evaporate.

As soon as I was dry, I got dressed in the alcove, then peered out of it and saw that, as expected, the incoming tide had washed the knapsack and Geoffrey's towel off the rock on which I'd left them. The disappearance of the knapsack was meant to explain the absence of a passport, credit card and other means of identification among Geoffrey's things – especially since his room keys would also be missing.

After waiting another ten minutes or so, I began playing the part of myself. I'd be saying afterwards that only Geoffrey, not I, had wanted to swim, that I'd waited at the back of the cove while Geoffrey went into the sea, that I'd watched Geoffrey begin swimming, that my attention had then been diverted, and that I may even have dozed off, but that I'd then become conscious of a lapse of time and the absence of any sign of Geoffrey in the sea or anywhere on land.

I now acted out what I'd have done next. Leaving the alcove, I gazed out to sea and made as if scouring the surface, from the shoreline outwards and then from left to right and back again. There was nothing to be seen other than the distant silhouette of a fishing vessel. Turning full circle, I surveyed the area all around me and looked into the alcove as if to check that Geoffrey's clothes were still there. Then, cupping my hands around my mouth, I called out Geoffrey's name, three times, facing a different direction with each shout. I'd be saying that by this time I'd become concerned, but not unduly worried, thinking Geoffrey might have come out of the water onto one of the other coves; but I'd continued my search – which I now did, jogging towards the water's edge and clambering up the nearest of the wet, slippery rocks there, calling out 'Geoff!' and 'Geoff-rey Green-wood!' Turning around again, I made as if to inspect the cove and the cliffsides around it once more. The only sign of life anywhere was a solitary soaring seabird.

I lifted my left hand to look at my watch, then ran back to the alcove, took out my mobile phone, and dialled 999. As expected, the phone gave a few rapid pips and the message 'No Service' appeared in the window. Pressing the dial button repeatedly, I ran towards the cliff-path and began ascending it, stopping briefly on the way up to catch my breath and try the call again. At the top I finally succeeded in making the connection.

My heart was beating so fast I could hardly say the words I'd so carefully rehearsed.

38

The speed of the response was remarkable. Within ten minutes of my call, a Sea King helicopter from RNAS Culdrose near Heston had begun raking the sea and the shoreline, an RNLI lifeboat was on its way from Sennen Cove, and two lifeguards from the main beach were at the scene with binoculars and other equipment. Five minutes later two police officers, one in plain clothes and the other in uniform, had arrived and were talking to me on the cliff-top, and a second helicopter, an air ambulance, had joined the search. Accompanied by the policemen, I descended the cliff-path and recounted my story to them again on the beach, pointing out where and how everything had happened – or at least as much of it as I could claim to have seen.

The uniformed officer made notes. They were polite and respectful, and when they were satisfied I had nothing more to tell them, said I should go back to the hotel and wait there for them.

'What do you think, Sergeant?' I asked the plain-clothes officer.

'Too early to say, sir. Don't get many drownings around this part of the coast – not swimmers anyway. Your friend could have drifted off to another cove, I suppose. Hard to say. If he did, coastguard will spot him soon enough. Better just wait and see. I wouldn't jump to any conclusions yet if I were you, sir. I'd say the odds are he'll show up.'

The two policemen arrived at the hotel a couple of minutes after I had. I'd decided to wait for them in the car, leaving it to them to tell the Joneses what had happened rather than having to do so myself, and we all entered the lobby together. The uniformed officer greeted Trudy, who was at the desk, told her there had been an accident, and asked if a room could be made available. Trudy offered them the use of the office, where they invited me to join them.

'We've already introduced ourselves to you, sir,' said the detective sergeant, 'but you might have missed our names. I'm DS Giggs and this is Constable Durrant. There's no sign of your friend yet, I'm afraid, so we can't disregard the possibility that he's been taken out to sea. His next-of-kin should be informed that he's gone missing. Can you give us his name and address please, as well as the same for his next-of-kin, if you have this information?'

I obliged, giving them Eleanor's name as next-of-kin and the address and telephone number of the London flat as those of both Geoffrey and Eleanor. 'They live together but they're not married. I'm Mr Greenwood's solicitor, by the way.' I omitted to mention that Geoffrey was from South Africa – deliberately, in case that led to contact with the police there – and offered to phone Eleanor myself. 'I think,' I said, 'she'll take the news better from someone she knows.'

'Of course, sir,' said DS Giggs.

'Do you think I could do so in private? It's not going to be easy for me.'

'Certainly. We'll leave you alone here so you can do so right away. But please tell her one of our colleagues in London will be in touch with her too – unless the gentleman shows up first, of course. It's police procedure.'

Eleanor would be at work. I rang her at the gallery.

'Eleanor, this is Charles Brook. I'm afraid I have some worrying news – about Geoffrey. He's gone missing. They're searching for him.'

'Really? How interesting.'

'We've been in Cornwall, as I think you know. Geoffrey went for a swim. I saw him in the sea but not what happened next. He might have been carried out by the current. They're searching for him now.'

'You've said that already. Is there any more?'

'I'm afraid not. The police will contact you. They may even come and see you.'

'Oh, no. Is that necessary? You've told me what's happened.'

'I know, but it's standard procedure.'

'Well, don't worry. I won't go back on my word. Is anyone listening to this, at your end?'

'No, I don't think so, but they might have been.'

'Sorry. I don't know how to do this kind of thing. Do you really love me, Charles? It's so strange to be calling you that.'

'Of course I do. I've told you nothing's changed.'

'Because I've been thinking, a lot, and I'm still very confused and feeling – well – kind of fragile.'

'I'm sure you are, but Eleanor, this is not the time or place. Please.'

'All right. I'll shut up now, but we do need to talk, Charles. Can you come and see me on your way back from Cornwall? It'll be the proper thing, won't it?'

'Yes, it will, and I will come. It's likely to be a couple of days. I'll ring again and let you know when.'

Someone tapped on the door, then Sergeant Giggs peered at me around it. 'Sorry, sir. We have to get on.'

I put the phone against my chest and said, 'Very distraught. Wants to know everything. Be finished in a minute.' Giggs nodded and disappeared behind the door.

'That was the police,' I said into the phone. ' I really must go now.'

'OK. I'll wait for your call.'

As I came out of the office, Giggs said, 'Just been onto coastguard. Still nothing.'

Martin and Trudy Jones were there. They looked at me sorrowfully and Trudy said, 'We're so awfully sorry about this. It's terrible.'

'Remember, I warned you there are no lifeguards there,' Martin put in. 'I never thought I'd be so right. I should have insisted you stick to the main beach.'

'Not at all. You're not to blame. We're both responsible adults.'

Giggs interrupted: 'Any idea where we'd find some ID for Mr Greenwood, sir?'

'What about his room?' I offered.

'Do you perhaps have his key?'

'No, I'm afraid not.'

'I can let you into the room,' said Martin Jones.

'Would you mind accompanying us?' Giggs looked at me. 'You might have an idea where he'd be likely to keep things.'

'Er, not really. But I'm happy to see if I can help.'

On the first floor, Martin unlocked the door to Geoffrey's room. A quick search by the two officers revealed no key or items of identification.

This was the time to mention the knapsack, I decided. 'I wonder,' I said. 'He had a knapsack with him – on the beach. Perhaps that's where he had those things.'

'On the beach, you say?' asked Giggs.

I made as if to be throwing my mind back. 'Yes; I remember him carrying it with him towards the water. He must have put it down somewhere.'

'Nothing like that's been found yet,' said Giggs. He turned to the constable. 'Get the duty sergeant to organize an immediate search for a knapsack. Can you describe it, Mr Brook?'

'I didn't examine it or anything, but it looked to me like an ordinary knapsack. Sort of greyish brown colour – no, khaki I'd say. About so big.' I made a square in the air with my hands.

The constable went off and Giggs said, 'Difficult this. Missing man, no identification – except, of course, your word, Mr Brook, which we don't doubt.'

'Sergeant,' I said, 'do you still need me now? I'd like to go to my room and have a lie-down. This has been tough.'

'Yes, of course. Just tell me though, sir, what will you be doing – I mean, about going back?'

'I'm not even thinking of that. I'm just hoping Geoffrey's OK. I'll stick around for as long as it takes.'

'Good, sir. That'll be helpful. Coastguard will keep us informed. And oh, we'll be needing to take a proper formal statement from you – unless, of course, Mr Greenwood shows up. Could you come to the Penzance police station – say, tomorrow morning?'

'Yes, of course.'

We were in the corridor now. I went up to the door to my room and inserted the key. It didn't fit. I tried again, unsuccessfully. Why, I wondered. This was definitely the room-key; the other two on the bunch were different. Then I looked at the metal tag. The imprint of the number eight stared back at me. I had Geoffrey's keys; I'd put the keys to number nine in the knapsack.

'What seems to be the trouble?' Martin asked, coming over. He took the keys from me and looked at the tag. 'These are the wrong keys,' he said, walking over to Geoffrey's door and opening it as if to make his point.

I was trying to stay calm. 'We must've got our keys mixed up this morning when we went out.'

'So it would seem,' said Giggs, frowning a little. 'Are you quite sure you don't have your own keys as well?'

I was. I knew exactly where my keys were: in the knapsack somewhere in the sea. But I felt in my pockets again, then replied, 'No – I mean yes, I'm sure.'

Giggs turned to Constable Durrant, who'd just returned from his errand. 'Call the desk sergeant again and tell him the search must include a set of hotel keys – like the one Mr Jones has got there, but with the number eight on the tag.'

'You couldn't have left them in your room, Mr Brook,' said Martin Jones, 'because your door would have been unlocked and the cleaning staff would have reported that. And I'm pretty sure your keys aren't at the front desk either. You didn't leave them there, did you?'

'No, I didn't. Perhaps they're in the car. I'll go down and take a look.'

Giggs said, 'Let's go down together.' He put out his hand. 'Meanwhile, Mr Jones, may I take that bunch of keys from you? We must take charge of the missing person's effects. I'm sure you won't mind. You do have duplicates, I take it?'

'Oh, yes, of course we do,' Martin replied.

The constable helped me search the car thoroughly; then Giggs said we ought to search my room too, just in case I *had* left it unlocked. This time Giggs himself participated.

When the futile search for the missing keys had ended, Giggs said, 'Please, gentlemen – Mr Brook, Mr Jones – let us know right away if the keys show up. And Mr Jones, may we leave the missing man's things in his room for the next day or two?'

'I think you must ask Mr Brook that question, Sergeant,' replied Martin. 'He booked the room till Saturday.'

'I've got no objection,' I said.

'Good,' said Giggs. 'As these are your premises, Mr Jones, I want you to know we're taking Mr Greenwood's belongings into police custody while we investigate his disappearance. We'll be wanting to post an officer outside the door of his room and use his key for access.'

'That wouldn't be very good for the hotel, Sergeant.'

'Martin,' I said, 'didn't you tell me you weren't expecting any more guests till Saturday afternoon? I'm happy to pay for the room till then. I think we owe it to Geoffrey to leave his things where they are at this stage.'

'Of course,' Martin replied unenthusiastically, 'as long as it's only till Saturday morning. We're expecting quite a few people from midday.'

'No, it won't be longer than that,' said Giggs. 'If Mr Greenwood hasn't shown up by then, other arrangements will have to be made.'

I entered my room with a spare key Martin had given me and sat down on the bed. Whew, I thought! Mission accomplished. The only jarring note had been the mix-up with the keys. How stupid I'd been to have put the wrong set into the knapsack! But had it mattered at all? It was quite feasible that a real Geoffrey and I could have swapped keys inadvertently – by, say, leaving both sets on the same seat, table, or rock and then picking up the wrong one; both *were* identical except for the numbers on the tags. But what if someone started adding things up? Like the fact that nobody at all had actually laid eyes on Geoffrey Greenwood, that all means of identifying him were missing, that I'd had his keys? Wouldn't someone think to question whether the man really existed, I asked myself, not for the first time? The answer remained the same: no, they wouldn't; people don't wonder about other people not existing; they wonder what they might be up to, or what's happened to them, but they don't suddenly think, hey, are they real? Not unless there's an obvious reason to do so, and in this case, I reassured myself, there wasn't.

As a whole, the experience had been far more stressful than I'd imagined it would be. Telling a false story to the police and the coastguard had proved more demanding than any of my earlier deceptions about Geoffrey. These were professionals whose job it was to be inquisitive, and I'd had to be on my guard all the way. And it wasn't over yet: I still had to make my written statement the next morning and keep up the act for at least another day or two.

The worst was over, though.

39

The search went on, the two helicopters working in tandem over the coast and the sea. I kept in touch with coastguard by phone and was told that all resources in the area had been alerted but that the longer the search went on the more pessimistic the searchers were growing; Geoffrey had not shown up anywhere on land and there was no report of his having been picked up by a vessel; the likelihood of his having survived was growing increasingly remote, especially since he would have been in cold water for several hours already.

The media were onto the story quickly. I received phone calls from two reporters and politely told them both that I had nothing to say to them because it was premature to assume Mr Greenwood had come to any harm. When pressed about the events of the morning, I simply said I'd made a full report to the police of everything I knew and suggested they approach them.

I spoke to Marion, and to Eleanor again. A policewoman had called at the gallery, given her a short, official report of the situation, and enquired whether she needed company or any kind of help, to which she'd replied, 'No thank you.' The officer had then asked her if she had a recent photograph of Geoffrey, and she'd said she didn't think so but could make a search for one and let the police know if she found anything. The woman had left her a contact telephone number and departed.

The Joneses were kind and considerate. Realizing I'd want to avoid curious people, they suggested I stay in my room and offered to serve me drinks and supper there. I accepted. At 9.30 in the evening there was a call from DS Giggs. 'I thought I'd just ring you personally, Mr Brook, to let you know there's still been no trace and the search has had to be called off for the day. But it will be resumed at first light. We're fearing the worst now, I'm afraid.'

'Thank you for that, Sergeant. I do realize the position, and I'm keeping Eleanor Downing informed.'

'Oh, good, sir. That was one of the reasons for this call – to be sure she was fully in the picture. Will you be coming in and making your statement in the morning?'

'Yes.'

'I'll be in all morning. It would be helpful if you could do the statement with me, as I know the case. Would, say, ten do for you?'

'That'll be fine.'

By early afternoon on the next day, Friday, I'd left Cornwall and was driving to London to see Eleanor. I'd told Giggs she was anxious to have my first-hand account of the incident, and he'd said I shouldn't delay my departure as there was no further need for my presence in Cornwall. There was no reason any more to avoid the London flat: I was going there as myself, and if Gragorin happened to show up I'd be happy to tell him about Geoffrey.

Making my formal statement had taken longer than I'd expected. I'd had no difficulty in recounting the 'events' of the previous morning again, but had felt uncomfortable throughout the process – especially when Giggs questioned me again about the confusion over the keys and about the knapsack, which hadn't been found yet.

After calling Eleanor and telling her to expect me at the flat in the evening, I'd rung Marion to let her know where I was going. 'I'll be staying overnight in London. I don't fancy driving on to Brighton right after the long journey from here.'

'You won't be spending the night with Greenwood's lady friend, I trust,' she said, jokingly – or perhaps not so jokingly.

'Of course not – nor with anyone else.'

'I was only kidding, Teddy. But seriously, I agree you should stop over. You'll be very tired.'

It was after nine when I found parking and walked around to the flat. There was no porter service at night and hence no risk of my being recognized as the missing Mr Greenwood. This time Eleanor was fully dressed when she let me in. She offered me a drink.

'I think,' she said, 'you'd better tell me everything now, from the beginning.'

I complied, starting with who I was and my marriage and the kids, and the way it had been with Marion (before her lapse), then telling her about my affair with Lucy and the renting of the flat, and ending with the staging of Geoffrey's disappearance. I mentioned having done some financial deals in Geoffrey's name, including one in New York which had led to the formation of the trust, but didn't go into any of the details. And I told her again that my marriage was over and that Marion and I were getting divorced.

She asked me questions as I went along, and when I'd finished said,

'Well, that certainly explains a lot, but it also leaves a lot for me to adjust to. I didn't want a relationship with a married man – even one with a broken marriage – and an affair with someone else's husband isn't what I want now.'

'It's not what I'm offering you, Eleanor darling. My marriage is really finished with.'

She looked at me thoughtfully. 'OK, let's say I accept that, but I still need a few more answers from you.'

'Go ahead.'

'First of all, do you swear that everything that went on between us was genuine – you weren't simply taking advantage of me?'

'Yes, I do. Absolutely.' That wasn't a lie, I thought.

'Then, if we *can* carry on where we left off, do you promise I'll be the person I thought I was when you were Geoffrey – the only woman in your life?'

'Yes, I promise.' That was a lie, a blatant one, but what choice did I have?

'All right. Now, I did get a letter from the trust company as you said, but tell me, Charles, did you really want me to be a beneficiary or were you just using my name as a convenience?'

Like a barrister leading a witness, she was prompting me to give her the answers she wanted to hear, and I realized how much I'd meant to her as Geoffrey and how desperately she wanted to hold on to that love of hers if she could.

'I did need a second beneficiary, but I chose you because I wanted it to be *our* trust, yours and mine.'

'Oh, Geoff – I mean Charles – I've already told you, it's not the trust that matters, only why you put me into it.' She frowned for a second, then smiled beautifully and asked, as if more of herself than of me, 'Can I believe you?'

Before I could answer she laughed out loud. 'This is ridiculous. It's like some sort of swearing-in – or even a marriage ceremony.'

Suddenly, she stood up, bent over me, and gave me a long open-mouthed kiss with her knee resting on the couch I was sitting on and one beautiful thigh emerging through the slit in her skirt. With which I succumbed, yet again.

We made love in the bedroom and I stayed there with her until half past three in the morning. When I left, I drove into the West End, and checked into a hotel on Portman Square. Five and a half hours later I was on my way home in the car.

40

Marion consoled me. 'You poor boy. What a terrible thing to happen, and while you were with him. Has there been any news?'

I shook my head. 'No. I'm sure it's over. He couldn't be alive.'

She helped me with my luggage. 'Where's *his* stuff?' she asked.

'Oh, the police have got that. They'll return it to his partner, I expect.'

'You mean the lady in London?'

'Yes.'

'How's she taking it? Badly, I suppose.'

'Terribly. They were very close.'

She made me tea and toast. 'Where did you stay last night?'

'At the Churchill. Got there quite late. It was a long drive – as you know – and she wanted to know everything, kept asking me questions, searching for little things that would give her hope.'

'What's she like, this – what's her name?'

Why was Marion so interested in Eleanor? 'Like a grieving widow,' I replied.

'And what *is* her name?'

'It's Eleanor – Eleanor Greenwood she called herself, but her official surname's Downing. Why do you want to know?'

'No special reason. It's like knowing the characters in a play or film – makes it easier to get the picture.'

At her suggestion, I spent the afternoon resting. Afterwards we went for a walk, with her arm tucked under mine, and had a drink together at a pub. She was transformed – no longer sulky and angry, just a loving wife and close companion.

Sitting alone in the conservatory on Sunday morning, I fortified my resolve to fulfil my promise to Marion. It was only when I was with Eleanor that I found myself drawn to her. It was as if she'd cast a spell over me that worked only in her presence. Away from her, I had no trouble with my commitment to my marriage; Marion and the kids were all I wanted around me. Eleanor must cease once and for all to be part of my life, and I must be strong and steadfast about that. I'd have to go and see her once or twice more, and then I could firmly and finally break up with her. By that time, official interest in Geoffrey's disappearance would have died down and I could make my excuses to her about why I couldn't go through with a divorce – I'd work them out, perhaps build them around the children – but one way or another there must be a clean break.

There were two incidental matters I'd have to sort out with Eleanor: the London flat and her interest in the trust. As for the former, I'd insist that she keep the contents and let me pay the rent for the next year or two. In regard to the latter, I'd arrange for her to get a cash distribution from the trust fund – a generous one; that would be not only fair, but desirable for the sake of appearances. I was ashamed of the way I'd just exploited her, but I'd had no alternative. How glibly I'd lied to her! In fact, how glibly and easily I was able to lie now, to everyone!

I wondered if I'd undergone a change of personality with the advent of Geoffrey. I'd been a decent, honest guy before then, I thought. No, I hadn't changed, I decided; I'd simply got onto that treadmill and hadn't been able to get off it since. After my very first deception – to Tolway Perry about Geoffrey being my client – all my lies and pretences had been responses to circumstances. And those included the lies I'd told Marion and Eleanor. Sustaining the illusion of a real, live Geoffrey Greenwood had become the foremost purpose of my life. Now that I'd disposed of Geoffrey, there was no need for that any more. I'd stopped the treadmill and I could get off it and cease lying, once and for all.

It was tragic, though, about Eleanor. Against my own will, I'd been terribly cruel to her, and I'd never get over that. Nor would I ever get over the loss of her.

Another fine day gave us the chance to take Emma and Paulie out again together. This time we walked down to Hove Park after lunch, put the children onto one of the coaches pulled by the miniature steam engine, and ran alongside the track all the way, waving at them and being waved back at. Then they went on the swings and slides, and we bought them ice creams – all to the accompaniment of much laughter and much hugging and kissing, a lot of it between Marion and me.

More absently than with real attention, I noticed on two or three occasions during the afternoon the nearby presence of a solitary elderly gentleman, white-haired and distinguished-looking, who was taking photographs in the park and seemed to be observing – and sharing vicariously – our enjoyment of the family experience.

Then, later, what had been a memorable day culminated in another romantic night in bed with my wife, and in the morning I held her close as she slept and very gently kissed her eyes, mouth, nose, and cheeks, while she stirred dreamily and cuddled closer to me. This, I reflected, was surely the only woman I'd ever truly loved.

41

'Gragorin,' said the familiar, gruff voice after the first ring.

'Mr Gragorin – George – this is Charles Brook. I have some news.'

'I know. I hear it already. Greenwood drowned.'

'Yes. It seems so,' I said.

'My bad luck. But I not sorry. He was bastard, big crook.'

'Now look here. . . .'

'Is true. He was never going to pay anything. But OK, he save me and my friends the trouble. Fuck him.' Gragorin grunted. 'I don't suppose he leave me any money in his will, hey?'

I pretended to miss the joke. 'I'm afraid not, or at least not that I know of.'

'If he did, you let me know. Meanwhile, fuck him – and you too. Goodbye.' There was no 'Mr Chips', suggesting the expression was used only when he thought he was calling the shots.

Well, that certainly seemed like 'Goodbye, Mr Chips' as far as Gragorin was concerned. I turned my attention to Jeremy Lefarge. Deciding that a measure of formality was warranted, I dictated the following letter, to be sent by fax as well as post:

Dear Jeremy,

The Greenwood Trust

It is with great regret that I have to inform you of the tragic disappearance of Geoffrey Greenwood off the Cornish coast last week. Although further news is awaited, he is feared dead.

He had told me he was planning to come and see you and would want me to accompany him, and I would probably have been calling you about now to make an appointment.

For the present there would seem to be no urgency to deal with the affairs of the Trust, nor indeed would I suggest that anything be done until the position has become clearer, but I shall keep you informed.

Please acknowledge receipt of this letter and call me should you wish to discuss anything.

Yours sincerely
Charles Brook.

Next, Conrad Reiman. Here a telephone call would be appropriate, but that would have to wait for a few hours until it was morning in New York.

I rang the desk sergeant in Penzance and was informed that there had been no further developments. Assuming the worst, I asked him, what were the chances of the body being washed ashore?

'That's difficult to say, sir. It may never be recovered at all, or it may appear anywhere along the coastline, or even on one of the islands. It could even come ashore in another country. We really can't say.'

My partners appeared at my office door. 'We're awfully sorry to hear about Greenwood, Charles,' said Jonathan. 'It must have been lousy for you.'

The ensuing conversation led predictably to the inevitable question – put by Barry – whether the firm would be handling the estate.

'No, we won't. He never made a will with me. I expect there's one in South Africa. But there won't be a deceased estate until his body shows up or a court presumes his death, which probably won't happen for years.'

'What about his property?' asked Jonathan. 'Won't someone have to do something about that in the meantime?'

'Well, that's not our affair. As far as I know, there are only odds and ends of his personal stuff over here. The big money – from the New York deal – is in trust in Guernsey, and that's in the hands of Citadel Trustees.'

'Won't you be working with them?'

'I imagine so. But there won't be any huge fees in that.'

The time had definitely come to get out of this partnership. I was determined not to let this greedy, inquisitive pair any further into Geoffrey's affairs – and not only because of the expense; I had to have absolute freedom to do as I pleased.

As soon as I was alone again, I rang Eleanor at work and was told she wasn't taking calls. 'Could you please tell her it's Charles Brook? I'm sure she'll speak to me.'

I held on, confidently expecting to hear her voice, but the same person came back on the line and said Eleanor was in a meeting and would return my call later. Although I wasn't asked for my number, I volunteered those of my mobile – which she already had, of course – and both my office numbers.

Then I phoned Marion, just to keep in touch, and after a brief chat with her ordered an expensive flower arrangement for delivery to her with a note saying, *To my wonderful wife, with all my love, from your Teddy.*

When there'd been no return call from Eleanor by 2.30, I tried her again, but got the same response: she was still tied up nd would ring me back.

At three o'clock I dialled Conrad Reiman's direct number in New York and got straight through to him. He hadn't heard the news and expressed his dismay and regret.

'He intended coming to see you from here, I believe,' I said, archly.

'I wasn't expecting him.'

'Really? He gave me the impression he had an appointment.'

'No, not at all.'

'Well, maybe I misunderstood him. He might have said he *would* be calling you. Anyhow, it doesn't matter much now, does it?'

'No, I guess not. Anyway, Charles, thank you for calling. It was thoughtful.'

A short while later Eleanor's secretary rang. She told me Eleanor had had to go out urgently and wouldn't be able to return my call after all. It didn't sound convincing, and it was now looking very much as if she was avoiding me. What did that mean? Probably no more than that she was having second thoughts about our relationship, which was understandable, I supposed, even after the warmth of our last meeting. Or was it?

I stood up and walked over to the window. From my vantage point on the second floor, I noticed a man I'd seen somewhere before – very recently – standing on the opposite pavement and looking up in my direction. I couldn't place him. He was elderly and looked distinguished and well-groomed, and he had white hair.

Marion phoned me at the office in the late afternoon to thank me for the flowers. She was bubbling over with delight and told me she loved me very much.

On my way home, I thought about Beverley Terrace. It was out of bounds to me now both as Geoffrey and as his solicitor. The contents of the flat were of little value, but something would have to be done about them. Had he been a real person living in South Africa, a court there would have appointed a curator to look after his affairs until his death could be presumed, and the appointee would have taken steps to find out about, and deal with, any assets of his in the UK. As it was, however, nothing was going to happen in South Africa, so I needed to take charge of the situation informally. I decided I'd write to the agents, Lawtons, saying I was handling Mr Greenwood's affairs, give them notice of the termination of the tenancy, ask for a final accounting, and tell them someone would be collecting his things. Then I'd arrange for one of the clerks in the firm to go the flat, pack up everything there, and take it to Oxfam or Age Concern. And I'd advise Eleanor to do the same with Geoffrey's clothing and effects in both Cornwall and London.

The next day I got a letter from her in the post. It was addressed to me at the office and the envelope was marked *Personal and Confidential*.

Dear Charles,

Please don't phone me. I don't wish to speak to you, and I'm sure you can guess why. I may write to you again for some answers, but probably not, as they will only be lies.

Eleanor.

P.S. The police came round this morning and told me they were calling off the search. Don't worry, I did not tell them the truth, although it was tempting. I'd have looked a fool to have done so, wouldn't I? You were very clever about that.

Bewildered, I read the letter again. What did she mean by 'you can guess why'? Whatever she meant, I told myself it was for the best; she'd saved me the trouble and pain of ending the relationship. And the postscript was reassuring: they'd given up on Geoffrey and her co-operation was complete. But I felt far from happy. In fact, I felt awful. This was definitely the end with her, and it struck me what all my vacillation had really been about: I'd been stalling, doing everything possible to find a way of keeping her in my life. Now it was too late; I'd lost control of the situation and she'd slammed the door on me. And to make it worse, I had no idea why. I forced myself to suppress the urge to try and do something about it. Eleanor was part of Geoffrey's life, and Geoffrey was no more. And I was committed to Marion. It was for the best, definitely.

Should I answer the letter? Probably not, but I had to let her know what I'd decided about the London flat and the distribution from the trust. On the other hand, was this the time to be telling her these things? At all costs, and despite my feelings, I *must* stay with my position and avoid dislodging her from hers. There'd be time, later, to be generous about the rent and the trust. The contents of the flat were another matter; she must be persuaded to accept them as her own, otherwise there could be complications. Resolutely, I picked up a pen and on the pad which I used for personal, handwritten communications wrote the date and then paused. How best to ensure the door remained shut? Tell her the truth, I decided.

> *Dear Eleanor,*
>
> *I don't understand your letter. But no matter – I don't mind calling it a day. I did mislead you, badly. I can't leave Marion. There'll be no divorce. I'm sorry about that. About the flat, please treat it as your own, including the contents. I'll see that you get my share of the rent for another six months in advance now. It's important to us both that you agree to keep all the contents, for legal reasons.*
>
> *Well, then, it's goodbye, I suppose, Eleanor darling. I will always remember you affectionately.*
>
> *Yours sincerely*
Charles

I read the letter through, inserted it in an envelope on which I wrote *Ms Eleanor Downing-Greenwood* and the address of the London flat, and put it in my out-tray for posting.

42

Over the next ten days I had spells of doubt about what I'd said in my letter to Eleanor, but what was done was done.

There'd been no reply from her by Friday of the following week, when Cindy announced that I had unexpected visitors, two police officers. This couldn't be about Geoffrey, I thought; it must concern one of my clients.

'Please tell them it's inconvenient now, Cindy. They should have made an appointment.'

Moments later she rang through to me again. 'They're very insistent, Charles. They say it's police business.'

'Can't they tell you what it's about? Perhaps someone else can deal with it.'

'I'll ask them.'

She came back to me seconds later. 'No, they say they have to speak to you personally.'

'Oh, very well then. Bring them in.'

Two men in grey suits were shown into my office. They introduced themselves as Detective Inspector May and Detective Sergeant Fuller of the Sussex Police. I gestured to two chairs, but they shook their heads and waited till Cindy had left the room.

'Charles Joseph Brook,' said DI May, looking at a piece of paper in his hand, 'I'm arresting you on suspicion of the murder of Geoffrey Robert Greenwood in Cornwall on the tenth or eleventh of September. You do not have to say anything. But it may harm your defence if you do not mention when questioned something which you later rely on in court. Anything you say may be given in evidence.'

43

It had to be some kind of practical joke.

I laughed. 'You're kidding. Who sent you guys?'

They both kept straight faces. If they were actors, they were bloody good ones. Eleanor must have sent them – who else? But why?

May said, 'I advise you to come with us, Mr Brook. It doesn't have to look like an arrest if you co-operate.' He gestured with his hand towards the door.

I suddenly very felt cold. They weren't actors; they were real police officers. But what the hell was going on? If it wasn't a joke, then it was a ludicrous mistake. In which case it would soon be sorted out. I'd better do as they say.

They followed me out of my office.

'I'll be out for a while,' I told Cindy on the way past her desk. 'I'll ring you if I'm delayed.'

They took me to the police station by car and from then on it was one ignominious humiliation after another – the formalities on my arrival, the photographing and fingerprinting, and being relieved of my possessions and shoved in a cell.

In my presence, Inspector May told the custody sergeant the reasons for the arrest. They suspected me, he said, of fatally shooting Geoffrey Robert Greenwood in a cove in Cornwall some time during the hours of darkness on the tenth and eleventh of September. The victim's body had been washed ashore and identified, and there was evidence placing me at the scene of the crime and of 'cover-up activities' by me the next day. There was also proof of motive. I'd never heard such nonsense.

I was told I'd be taken to Penzance for questioning the next morning. They let me call Marion, and she and Jonathan arrived and were allowed to see me briefly. I asked Jonathan, who seemed concerned and upset, to get me a competent criminal solicitor in Cornwall. Marion was distraught and bewildered. I assured them both the whole thing was a stupid mistake.

I spent the night in a cell, mostly awake, feeling cold, uncomfortable, and utterly miserable. Although it was reasonably clean and I had the cell to myself, there was a sickly dank smell to the place and every minute of my confinement to the bare harshness of its small interior was suffocating. I dozed off once or twice but was quickly roused by the awful, thudding reminder of where I was, then lay there on the hard bed shivering. I ate none of the food they brought me.

At 5.30 in the morning, I was led out of the cell and driven in the back of a police van to London, where I was handed over to two burly uniformed officers of the Devon and Cornwall Constabulary. In their custody I then made a seven-hour train journey from Paddington to Penzance followed by a five-minute ride in a van to the Penzance police station. The only conversation I had with the two policemen was about essentials like visits to the toilet and breaks for nourishment, all forms of which other than water I declined.

The custody sergeant in Penzance asked me if I was up to being questioned that afternoon. Although confused and exhausted, I said yes, I was. The sooner I could put the nightmare behind me the better. But the questioning didn't start until my solicitor had arrived from Bodmin over an hour later. Jonathan had managed to get me the services of Peter Cartwright, a young partner in a criminal practice there. Cartwright was a lanky fellow of about thirty with an untidy crop of blond hair. He and I were allowed to have a discussion before the interview began, but all I could tell him was that I hadn't killed anybody and was dumbfounded by the whole business.

I was questioned by a Detective Inspector Harrison, whom I'd not met before, and DS Giggs, whom I had. The statutory caution was read out to me once more before the questioning began. The reminder that it might harm my defence if I failed to mention something which I would later wish to rely on in court was ironic. What could possibly have been more relevant to a defence to a murder charge than the fact that the supposed victim had never existed? Having wrestled with that question for most of the last twenty-four hours, I'd decided it would be stupid to demolish the illusion of Geoffrey Greenwood just because of some silly mistake. They couldn't possibly have a case against me, so why blurt out the truth, get myself charged with criminal deception, and lose the Greenwood fortune?

The first part of the questioning was relatively straightforward. DS Giggs took me through my statement about the 'disappearance', asking me to reaffirm each fact as we went along. That done, Harrison invited me to reconfirm the statement as a whole – which I did – and enquired whether I wanted to add to it – which I declined to do. The interview was then adjourned for a break.

When it was resumed, Harrison said, 'Now, Mr Brook, we don't believe Mr Greenwood was with you at all that morning.'

'That's nonsense. Of course he was.'

'Then why was it that nobody laid eyes on him? He didn't appear for breakfast at the hotel. And you were seen walking alone on the cliff-paths.'

Peter Cartwright interrupted: 'By whom, Inspector?'

'I don't think I need to say, at this stage, Mr Cartwright. The point, Mr Brook, is that we do have witnesses, and having told you that, do you still stick to your story that Mr Greenwood was with you?'

'Yes, I do.' What else could I say, at this stage?

'Very well then. So let's ask you something else. Did you go to Porthderick on either of your recent visits to Cornwall?'

'Porthderick? Never heard of the place.'

'You may not know it by name, so I'll tell you where it is. It's a small fishing cove beyond the range of cliffs where you went walking that morning. There are a few small cottages there and some fishing boats. It can be reached by car – a ten-minute drive from The Cuckoo's Nest.'

'I've never been there.'

'But, Charles,' – there was something sinister in the sudden switch to my first name – 'you were seen leaving the cove at Porthderick around two o'clock in the morning on Thursday the eleventh of September – the very morning on which you later reported Mr Greenwood's alleged disappearance in the sea.'

'By whom, Inspector?' said Cartwright.

'Mr Cartwright, if you please,' replied Harrison. 'You're out of order.'

'I don't care whether he's in or out of order, Inspector,' I said. 'I wasn't there. And whoever says I was is lying or mistaken.'

'Where were you at that time, then?'

'In my room at The Cuckoo's Nest.'

'Is there anyone who can confirm that?'

'Yes, I'm sure that Martin and Trudy Jones will.'

'We've spoken to them. They say they heard you and Mr Greenwood arrive at the hotel shortly after eleven, but you could both have gone out again. You had back-door keys and could come and go as you wished.'

'I did not go out again. Nor did Geoffrey, as far as I know. And if he did, he couldn't have gone very far without a car.'

Giggs then questioned me about my having been in possession of the wrong set of room keys after Geoffrey's disappearance. I told him I had nothing to add to what I'd already said about that.

'You mean,' said Harrison, 'that you believed you and Greenwood had mistakenly changed keys?'

'Yes.'

'When and where do you think that could have happened?'

'In the car maybe. On the beach. Anywhere. I don't know.'

'You see, Charles, we think there's a much more likely explanation. After you killed Greenwood that night, you had to pretend he was still alive until you could stage his drowning the next morning. So you took charge of his belongings, including his keys – to get you into his hotel room so you could make it look and sound as if he'd spent the whole night there. You probably also dumped his passport et cetera somewhere – maybe in the sea – where they couldn't be found. What do you say to all that?'

'It's rubbish – pure conjecture.'

'So you deny it?'

'Of course I do.'

'Very well, Charles. Now, are you aware that Mr Greenwood's body has been recovered and that he died from a gunshot wound?'

'What? I *am* unaware of that, and I don't believe it.'

'Exactly what do you not believe?'

'Well, you may have found such a body – I really wouldn't know – but it can't possibly be Geoffrey Greenwood's.'

'Why not?'

'Well, unless he was picked up by a boat, then shot dead, and thrown back in the sea. But how likely is that?'

'I agree. In fact, as I've just said, we suspect it was the other way around – that he'd already been shot dead, the night before, by you. You see, Charles, that body has been identified as his – conclusively.'

'How?'

'By his partner, Eleanor Downing-Greenwood, as she calls herself.'

'What?' This was madness. Eleanor saying somebody's body was Geoffrey's? Impossible. 'I don't believe that.'

'Well, it's true. Why shouldn't it be?'

I stifled the temptation to tell Harrison precisely why. 'Because she'd have to be crazy to do something like that. If Geoffrey Greenwood's dead – as he probably is – he must have drowned or been eaten by sharks, or whatever. That body must belong to someone else.'

'So you're saying she's lying?'

'If she says the body of someone who was shot dead belongs to Geoffrey Greenwood – yes, she is lying.'

'And the DNA traces? Are they lying too?'

'What DNA traces?'

'There are positive matchings between the dead body's DNA and traces found on some of Mr Greenwood's personal items.'

'Whatever damned body you're talking about is definitely not Greenwood's body,' I said. 'I don't know very much about DNA, but I'm sure of that.'

Harrison and Giggs exchanged glances. 'OK,' said Harrison. 'So you've told us Eleanor's either a liar or crazy, or both. And that the same goes for our other witnesses. And that there can't be any DNA matchings. Now, what do you have to say to this? Room eight at The Cuckoo's Nest – Geoffrey Greenwood's room, eh?' – he looked at me and I nodded – 'was examined for fingerprints the day after he disappeared. That was done so that we'd have a means of identifying Greenwood's body if it ever showed up, because we had no photographs or ID documents to work with. Then, when the body which is now in the mortuary appeared on the scene, it turned out that the dead man's prints had been all over the room.' Harrison raised his eyebrows and tilted his head at me questioningly.

'What?' was all I could say. Was I unwittingly taking part in some kind of nonsense play where everyone else knew the plot and their lines but I didn't? Someone was framing me for an impossible crime – and making a damned good job of it. Here I was, listening to a police officer telling me that the imaginary person that I myself had made up had not only a body but DNA and fingerprints, and had been shot dead and identified by Eleanor, and that it all hung together, and that everything pointed to this figment of my imagination having been murdered by me.

'Geoffrey Greenwood did occupy that room, did he not,' Harrison asked me, 'from about eleven that night until anything up to one or one-thirty?'

I stared at him and frowned. It was a trick question. 'He did occupy that room, Inspector, but not only for a few hours – for the whole night, from eleven until the morning.'

'Yes, you would say that, wouldn't you? Anyway, we seem to agree he was there long enough to leave fingerprints. And those just happen to match the corpse's prints. What do you say to that?'

I was thinking fast. The dead man – whoever he really was – must have been in room eight at some time. But when? It couldn't have been long before that fateful night, for two reasons: one, the police thought the prints were Geoffrey's, so they must have been quite fresh; two, the dead man was shot dead in the vicinity.

'He couldn't have been the only person who was in that room,' I told Harrison. 'Those prints belong to someone else and you people should be making enquiries about the previous occupants. One of them may be missing.'

'Why? Taken on their own, the prints could certainly belong to someone else, as you say, but we're not relying on them alone. What they do is corroborate the DNA evidence and Ms Downing-Greenwood's iden-tification of the body. And by the way, the DNA traces come from personal articles of Mr Greenwood's – stuff *he* brought into the room that wasn't there before.'

I shook my head. This nonsense nightmare kept getting worse and worse, and more and more incredible.

'Mr Brook shakes his head,' said Harrison into the record. 'Right then, let's move on, shall we?'

'Just a minute, Inspector,' I said. 'Are you telling me that traces of DNA from Geoffrey's clothing came from the corpse that you've got?'

'Yes. Not only clothing though. Other items of his, too.'

I shook my head again. 'This is . . . it must be . . . someone's trying to frame me.'

'Who, Charles?'

'I've no idea.'

After a brief pause, Harrison said, 'Very well then. As I said, let's get on.'

He and Giggs then questioned me in turn about the deals I'd done for Geoffrey and about the Guernsey trust. Here, they were clearly out of their depth, but they had got to know about the trust, the size of the trust fund, and the extent of my authority from Greenwood. Eleanor must have told them some of that and given them the name and address of Citadel Trustees in Guernsey from Jeremy's letter to her. But would Jeremy have divulged the confidential details of the trust's affairs? Probably not without a court order, but perhaps they'd got one, and besides, the same information was available from my office file.

'We're advised,' said Harrison, 'that with Greenwood out of the way, you're in a position to control the trust fund for your own benefit. Is that so?'

'Definitely not. I'm not one of the beneficiaries. And it's quite normal for someone in Geoffrey Greenwood's circumstances to empower his solicitor in his absence.'

Obviously not equipped to argue the matter, Harrison retorted, 'Well, we'll see about that. Now tell me something else, Charles: how well do you know Eleanor?'

'Not very well. I met her through Geoffrey and knew her as his companion.'

'Did you ever spend any time alone with her?'

'Hardly that I remember. Perhaps once or twice. I did go and see her after Geoffrey disappeared.'

'Mr Brook, I'd like you to listen to a tape-recording please.' It seemed we were back to my surname now. 'It comes from the telephone answering machine in the flat in which Mr Greenwood and Ms Downing lived.'

Putting a tape cassette into a recording device that was connected to the larger piece of equipment which was being used to record the interview, Harrison declared for the record, 'DI Harrison places the casette logged as Item B1 in the case file into a second recording device and will now play the tape to the prisoner.'

I listened, with growing alarm, to the recording of the message I'd left for Eleanor after Lucy's intrusion at Beverley Terrace. What I'd said about Geoffrey being out of the way sounded awful. Yet another blow, this one of my own doing. The playback was followed by a short silence, broken by Harrison. 'Did you leave that message?'

'Yes.'

'Please explain it to us. What did it mean, and why did you leave it?'

My mind was racing. Was *this* the time to come out with the truth about Geoffrey? It seemed the more I persevered with my resolve not to do so, the worse off I was getting as a murder suspect. The tape could only have come from Eleanor, who must have made a statement about it and was clearly doing her best to get me charged with Geoffrey's murder. I'd never have believed her capable of such terrible vindictiveness. She couldn't have been acting alone; someone else – her father, almost certainly – must have been behind it. But wasn't she taking a dangerous chance? How could she – or they – be so sure I wouldn't own up to having created Geoffrey, especially after being arrested for his supposed murder? It didn't add up. Did she – or they – know something I didn't? I'd have to think it through properly once I was alone again and had the time. Meanwhile, I had to answer Harrison's question and go back on what I'd just told him.

'What I said a few minutes ago was not true – about my relationship with Eleanor. She and I had a brief affair. I saw her a few times when Geoffrey was away. She was in love with me and wanted me to leave my wife.'

'And what about you? Were you in love with her?'

'At one stage, yes, I thought I was. I was infatuated with her.'

'I see. You told her you were getting divorced. Was that true?'

'At the time, yes, it was. But the situation was changing from day to day. My wife and I were heading for a divorce, but then we became reconciled. And there were the children – we have two small kids. She – my wife, that is – and I had been very close once, and I love my kids, so it was all very complicated – and Eleanor was one of the complications.'

'What did you mean when you told Eleanor that Geoffrey would be out of the way in a few days?'

'I was referring to a business trip he was taking.'

'But why did you use the words "out of the way"?'

'I meant that he'd be away and we – she and I – would be able to meet and talk things over.'

'Surely she knew herself that he'd be going away? You didn't have to tell her something like that.'

'I wasn't telling her he was going away, only that his intended absence would give us an opportunity to meet for a proper discussion.'

'What did you mean by telling her, 'Nothing's changed'?'

'Inspector, you must understand. When I got involved with Eleanor, it was very intense and we made each other promises. As I've said, my marriage had broken down. And Eleanor intended leaving Geoffrey for me. Then, Marion started having therapy and things improved at home, and I was confused. There were days when I wanted Eleanor more than my marriage, which was how I must have felt when I made that call.'

'Well, Eleanor has told us a rather different story,' said Harrison. 'She says you were in love with her, but the feeling wasn't mutual. In fact, she didn't fancy you at all. That you kept pestering her and she'd stopped talking to you by the time you left this message because you'd come to see her and offered to share the trust fund with her if she left Geoffrey for you. You even mentioned the eventuality of Geoffrey's death in a way that suggested to her he might be in danger.'

Cartwright intervened. 'Inspector, did she say whether she'd ever told Greenwood about any of this?'

'Yes. She says that at first she avoided saying anything to him, for fear of upsetting his relationship with his legal adviser, but afterwards she told him everything.'

'How did he react?'

Harrison grinned at Cartwright. 'Now who's asking the questions? Never mind, I'll tell you. He told her not to worry; he'd take care of the matter.'

'What she's told you is totally untrue,' I said, marvelling at the absurdity of Eleanor making up stories about what Geoffrey had said and intended doing.

Harrison looked at some notes, then at Giggs. 'Right then, gentlemen,' he said. 'At this point I think we can adjourn overnight.'

The adjournment formalities completed, I had another short meeting with Cartwright, who told me he thought the police were intent on charging me with Greenwood's murder.

'What about bail if they do?' I asked him.

'Oh, you'll get that. You have a right to bail – in theory, anyway – and there are no valid grounds for refusing it in your case. The amount will be substantial, though, and you'll need good sureties.' After a short pause, he said, 'Charles, you're really adamant about that not being Greenwood's body, and I can understand why. But would you like to see it, just to be sure? In the mortuary, I mean?'

Would I like to? Definitely not. Should I, for the sake of appearances? No. If I did, I'd be pretending that Geoffrey could have had a body, which I might yet want to deny.

'No,' I said. 'There'd be no point to it, and I'd be suggesting I had doubts about my own story, wouldn't I?'

'At this stage, yes, I agree. But you may need to later, when we give notice that we want to contest the identity of the dead man.'

'Can they compel me to view the body now, while I'm in detention?'

'No. I don't believe they can.'

'What if they ask me if I'd like to see it?'

'I doubt they'll do that, but if they do, simply say that you'll need to take advice on the question, and we can then discuss it further, in private.'

44

What ensued was another miserable night in police custody, though I had the cell to myself once again and did manage a few hours' sleep, out of sheer exhaustion. For the rest, I used the opportunity to do some serious thinking. I had to concede that, from their point of view, the police had every reason to suspect that I'd killed Geoffrey. If, as they believed, he was already dead when I reported his disappearance in the sea, my conduct was inexplicable except as a cover-up. Had the body not been identified as Geoffrey's, I wouldn't have been arrested. Ergo, if I could prove that the body was somebody else's, I'd be off the hook. The hotel's guest register would reveal who'd occupied room eight during the week, say, before it had been Geoffrey's room. If it turned out that any such occupant had gone missing, I'd be getting somewhere. Cartwright must go into that.

Eleanor would never have identified the body unless she'd known her evidence would be corroborated by the fingerprint and DNA reports. Her father had probably had access to the forensic evidence through his police connections. But why, I wondered once more, had they been so sure I wouldn't divulge the truth about Geoffrey? Then it struck me – they didn't have to be. It didn't matter to them what I told the police about Geoffrey; all they needed to be sure of was that I couldn't *prove* Geoffrey had never existed. Surely I hadn't made such a good job of my pretence about Geoffrey that I couldn't go back on it myself? But whether that was so or not wouldn't matter if the real identity of the dead man could be established. Meanwhile, what was I to tell Harrison in the morning?

Certainly not the truth – not until I was left with no choice, and anything could happen before that point was reached: I hadn't been charged yet, and might not be, and if I was, the prosecution might be dropped before there was a trial, for one reason or another – that was the way with litigation – but once having blurted out the truth, I'd be stuck with it and all the consequences of my deceptions. And if I *were* prosecuted and tried for Geoffrey's murder, I'd have committed myself irretrievably to a defence which I might not be able to sustain.

No. All I could do at this stage was persist in my version of what had happened to Geoffrey, get Cartwright moving with enquiries about the last occupant of room eight, and convince myself that, whatever occurred next, I could never possibly be convicted of an entirely illusory crime.

Cartwright was the first to speak when the interview was resumed in the morning. 'Inspector, is there anything else on that tape that might be of interest to us?'

Harrison looked a little abashed. 'I'm afraid I don't know.' He turned to DS Giggs.

'The tape's still going to the lab, sir,' said Giggs, obviously embarrassed. 'I don't believe anybody's played it through yet. We were shown where to locate this particular message only.'

'Very well,' said Harrison, looking very much as if it was not very well at all. 'Mr Cartwright, all I can say at this stage is that this tape, as a whole, will, as you know, have to be disclosed to the defence, one way or the other, if your client is charged, of course.'

'I agree with that, Inspector,' replied Cartwright, 'but seeing one part of the tape has been played to my client in this interview, it seems only fair and proper that he be allowed to listen to the rest of it too.'

'Do you mean here and now, Mr Cartwright?'

'Yes, I do.'

DS Giggs intervened. 'Does your client have any reason to believe there might be something else on this tape that could be relevant to our enquiries?'

Cartwright looked at me. I shook my head.

'No, but I think he'd still like to hear it.'

Then I suddenly remembered something that could have been on the same tape – one of Gragorin's messages for Geoffrey. I'd picked it up by telephone at around noon on the day of Lucy's disastrous intrusion at Beverley Terrace, and my message for Eleanor had been left later the same day. Gragorin's message wasn't at all relevant to what was going on now, but it could reinforce the illusion of a real Geoffrey Greenwood, which might not suit me very well. So I looked across at Cartwright and frowned. He took the hint.

'On reflection, Inspector, I think it might be more practical if you were simply to let me have a copy of the tape in the next few days. My client and I could then listen to it in our own time without holding up this interview.'

'That sounds like a sensible suggestion,' said Harrison. 'I see no reason why we shouldn't do that, Mr Cartwright.' He read this arrangement into the record and, moving on, went over some of the ground we'd traversed the day before, tidying up bits and pieces. Eventually, he asked me solemnly if there was anything else I'd like to say.

'No,' I said.

Harrison stared up at the ceiling and said, almost casually, 'Charles Brook, we intend charging you with the murder of Geoffrey Robert Greenwood unless you can now tell us anything to change our view. On the evidence we have, you had cogent motives for the crime: you believed that Mr Greenwood's death would leave you clear not only to pursue your unwanted advances towards his partner, Eleanor Downing, but to gain control of some fifteen million dollars of shares and cash in the trust he had set up. I put it to you that you got Mr Greenwood to join you in Cornwall so that you could kill him here and then pretend that he had drowned. After meeting him at the station, you filled your car in Penzance and shared a snack with him – chocolates and soft drinks you bought at the garage shop. At the hotel, you helped him move his things into his room. A couple of hours later you drove with him to a lonely cove in Porthderick for a nude swim in the moonlight.' He looked at me impishly. 'Was there perhaps a gay aspect to your relationship with him?'

'Inspector,' Cartwright interjected angrily, 'you've got no basis for that kind of speculation.'

'OK, Mr Cartwright. I withdraw that bit. Anyhow, to continue. As he entered the water, you shot at him two or three times, killing him with a bullet in the back. He fell into the water and his body was taken out by the tide. You disposed of the gun, possibly in the ocean, as well as all his means of identification. In the morning, you went through the motions of accompanying him on a walk which, you claimed, had ended with him stripping, going into the sea, and disappearing, but there is clear evidence that nobody at all accompanied you that morning and that your version of what happened to him was entirely false.' Harrison paused, then said, 'Well, Mr Brook, what do you say to all that?'

Put like that, the case against me sounded ominously impressive, even though it was largely circumstantial. If I were convicted of such a cold-blooded, premeditated murder, I could expect a life sentence. The key to everything now was the identity of the body.

'I deny it all,' was the answer I gave Harrison.

45

I was formally charged with Geoffrey's murder that afternoon and held in custody for four more days. During that time I appeared in the Penzance magistrate's court and then, three days later, was taken to Bodmin to attend a preliminary hearing in the crown court, where I was represented by Edgar Yeats, a Cornish criminal barrister engaged by Peter Cartwright, who applied for me to be released on bail, successfully. Marion and – to my astonishment and silent, apologetic gratitude – my partner Jonathan stood as my sureties jointly and severally for an amount of £150,000. The bail conditions prohibited me from interfering with prosecution witnesses, obliged me to surrender my passport to the police and to report in person at a police station every second day, and confined me to East Sussex, West Sussex, and Cornwall, and journeys between those counties.

The four additional days and nights which I spent in a cell were somehow slightly less depressing than the first two had been, which left me musing cynically that I must be getting used to incarceration. I was pleasantly surprised by the relative ease with which I got bail, but Yeats had confidently repeated Cartwright's earlier advice on the subject and then gone on to prove its validity.

Cartwright had visited me in my cell twice. During one of these visits, I told him I was convinced the dead man had stayed in room eight. 'If he'd been an employee of the hotel, he'd have been missed soon enough,' I pointed out. 'The police won't check it out, but why can't we, Peter? All we have to do is look at the hotel register and then try and trace what's happened to everyone who occupied room eight during, say, the preceding week. If it turns out any one of them's gone missing, we hit the jackpot.'

'I've got no problem with that, Charles. I'll get someone onto it right away.'

'Thanks. Is there anything else we can do to try and find out whose corpse that really is?'

'Well . . . police forces and coroners do sometimes advertise for help with identifying dead bodies. There's a missing persons website which features likenesses and descriptions of unidentified dead people and invites the public to come forward if they recognize them. I really have no idea whether the website would run a feature like that on our instructions, but I'd think not – I imagine the police or the coroner would have to OK it, or even do the instructing – and I don't know how co-operative the police or the prosecution are going to be, given the strength of the ID evidence they already have. We might need a court order, *if* we can get one. But you know, Charles, I don't want to go off half-cocked on publicity. It'll be far better to discuss everything fully with counsel first. The body'll keep in the meantime – it's being well refrigerated. All we need do is notify the coroner that we don't want it released to anyone yet. However, I think there is one other line worth pursuing. Teeth. They never lie. What do you know about Greenwood's dental records, if anything? I suppose they'd be in South Africa, would they?'

I didn't want any enquiries to be made about Geoffrey in South Africa, even futile ones, but no harm could come from a vain search for dental records in the UK. 'I'd guess so. But he did say something to me not long ago about going to see a dentist while he was in this country.'

'Did he mention a name or a place or anything?'

'Not that I can remember.'

'Well, I could make some enquiries from the professional body here. Should I do that?'

'Yes. Why not?'

'And what about South Africa?'

'Why don't you leave that to me?' I ventured. 'You know, I was born there and I've never lost touch with the country. I've got useful contacts out there and I know how things work. I also have to keep an eye on the cost factor' – I grinned at him – 'and this is something I can handle myself.' I couldn't tell him I'd be doing nothing other than reporting to him in due course that no dental records of Geoffrey's had been located in South Africa.

'Fine.'

*

I had another meeting with Cartwright after my release – in Bodmin – shortly before flying home with Marion and Jonathan from Newquay to Gatwick. Jonathan was present at my request.

Cartwright reported that he'd checked the guest register at the Cuckoo and spoken to Trudy Jones. Room eight had been occupied twice before during the week preceding the fateful night. An elderly couple called Bradley had stayed there on the Friday and Saturday nights – when Marion and I had been at the Cuckoo – and they'd been traced to their home in Leeds, where they'd been found to be alive and well and highly enthusiastic about their visit to Cornwall. The other occupant – the last before Geoffrey Greenwood – had been a man by the name of Harold Tyler, who'd slept there on the Monday night. Trudy had remembered him well. He had given his permanent address as being in Wellington, New Zealand, and had stayed only one night, checking out the next morning and leaving on foot, with his backpack, just as he'd arrived the previous day. He hadn't made an advance booking and wasn't asked for any further or forwarding address. The Cuckoo didn't ask for guest's passports or other identity documents; they had very few foreign guests. Tyler had paid the bill in cash. Cartwright was instructing a firm of lawyers in Wellington to make enquiries about him there. A Cornish firm of private investigators had also been hired to try and trace Tyler's movements after he'd left the Cuckoo.

Cartwright then recommended engaging a forensic expert to check the DNA tests that had been carried out, find out all the related facts, and report back, and said he knew the ideal person for the task. I authorized him to go ahead.

'So much for the ID,' said Cartwright. 'Now about your defence, Charles, I'm going to be frank with you. I'm very unhappy with your version of what happened to Greenwood. I'm not accusing you of lying, but the police say the dead man was killed during that night. If so. . . .'

'Hold on a moment, Peter,' said Jonathan. 'That body was in the sea for days if not weeks. You can't pinpoint the time of death under those conditions. I know that from some of the criminal work I did years ago. The medical evidence would have to be very approximate. I'm talking about days, not hours.'

'Good point,' said Peter, 'but remember, Charles, Harrison said something about a witness who saw you at Porth— whatever the place was, that night. That means they think the shooting took place there. They must have something to go on, like people who heard shots or saw things. I strongly suggest that until we know what their evidence actually is, we assume they can prove that the dead guy was shot during that night. And since the body's been identified as Greenwood's, no jury is going to believe that he accompanied you on an excursion the next morning. You'll need to be able to produce somebody or something convincing to prove he was still alive then.'

'It all gets back to the identity of the body,' I said.

'Yes, it seems so. Anyhow, I don't want to discuss it in detail now – there'll be time for that – but I advise you to do a lot of thinking before we meet again. We really need to be sure of all our facts before I brief counsel – assuming you want me to carry on as your solicitor.'

I did. Very much. Cartwright had impressed me greatly and I liked him. 'Of course I do. When will you be wanting to brief counsel?'

'Before your next appearance – at the plea and directions hearing here in Bodmin. And we'll know pretty soon when that will be. I'd like to retain Yeats, if you agree, and import a criminal silk from London to lead your defence. Do you know anyone you'd like to bring in, or would you prefer me to come back to you with a recommendation?'

'Please recommend someone. And yes, please keep Yeats.'

We then discussed some of the practicalities, including costs. This was going to be an extremely expensive business, none of the funding for which could come from Geoffrey Greenwood's supposed resources. But I'd manage to finance it – I'd have to – and I'd get it all back out of the trust once I'd got out of this mess, if I did. Fortunately, there was enough equity in the house to support a substantial remortgage. Marion would have no problem with that, though she might well have had but for our reconciliation. Sitting next to her on the flight home, I started thinking again about coming out with the truth about Geoffrey. The murder charge was looking much more formidable now, and if there was to be a trade-off, I'd rather be convicted of deception than murder. Either way, I'd lose the $15 million.

My secret had become too hot to handle on my own. It was time to share it with someone who could help me. I looked across the aisle where Jonathan sat reading a magazine.

46

Penzance had been abuzz over my arrest, which was enjoying a fair measure of prominence in the national media, and there must have been quite a lot of excited talk in and around the Royal Penzance Hotel about my wife's presence there. Marion had been putting up with the strain admirably, and neither she nor Jonathan had thought for a moment of leaving Penzance until my bail application had been dealt with.

I'd never have believed that my partner Jonathan Amery could become my greatest ally in a crisis, but he had. The fellow's commitment to my cause and his display of allegiance and friendship had been amazing. How badly I'd misread him! He had deserted his practice, his family, and everything else in his own life for the past week and was seemingly willing to continue doing so for as long as necessary.

When we landed at Gatwick, I invited him to come over to my house in the evening, which he did.

'I can't tell you how much I appreciate everything you've been doing, Jon,' I told him as I poured us drinks. 'I'm overwhelmed and deeply grateful. I'd hate to think where I'd have been without you.'

'Say no more. We're partners and friends. And Barry's in this all the way too, you know.'

'That's good to know. I'm grateful to him too.'

'You've got things to tell me, Charles, haven't you?'

'About Geoffrey Greenwood, you mean?'

'Yes. Was there really such a person?'

I hesitated, taking a sip of my drink. 'What makes you think there wasn't?'

'Well, I've been wondering – about all sorts of things. Like the fact that no one in the firm ever met him, or even spoke to him on a phone. As I said to you once, it was as if you were keeping him to yourself. I don't believe you're capable of a cold-blooded murder, so I couldn't understand why you'd want to pretend that Greenwood got drowned off that beach – unless you'd invented him and needed to get rid of him for some reason.' He lowered his head and looked at me with knitted eyebrows. 'Well, come on, Charles, am I right or not?'

I hesitated again. Somehow, I wanted to cling to the illusion a little longer, but I couldn't afford to. 'Yes, you are, Jon. Geoffrey Greenwood never existed. I made him up. It wasn't to mislead you or Barry, I assure you.' Hadn't I once said something similar to Eleanor in that bygone age before my arrest?

Jonathan was staring into his glass. After a short silence he said, 'But you did mislead us, Charles, didn't you? You even wrote in his New Client Particulars that you'd verified his identity, and there's a photocopy of a passport in his file certified by you. Did you forge that?'

'Well, you could say I did, but that document wasn't created to deceive you and Barry. It was a copy of something I put together later in New York, when I needed an ID document for the trust I was forming for him, and when I got back from there I simply closed the loop by putting a copy in the file. When I invented Geoffrey, it was for entirely personal reasons – I needed a name to put on a tenancy agreement, nothing more.'

'So you rented that flat yourself? And that money in the client account was yours?' Was there an unpleasant edge to his tone, I wondered.

'Yes – to both questions.'

'Why? Were you having an affair or something?'

'Yes, I was. Marion and I were having trouble and well . . . I'd rather not go into all that. It's not relevant any more. But I'll tell you the rest.' I did so, carefully avoiding the sensitive details of my personal relationships. When I was finished, he raised his glass to me and said, 'Cheers! Charles my friend, you've just told me the most incredible story I've ever heard, and I believe every word of it.'

'Thanks, but it hasn't done me much good, has it?'

'Well, I wouldn't say that, Charlie boy. You've still got fifteen million dollars in Guernsey, haven't you?'

'I can whistle it goodbye one way or the other – by getting myself convicted of Geoffrey's murder or by revealing the truth about him.'

'Maybe, but the money's less important than your freedom, surely. And hell, you won't be jailed for *life* for your deceptions. You can't possibly risk getting a life sentence for murder, so you have to think seriously about telling the truth. A judge might not take such a harsh view of your deceptions if you explained everything as you just have to me. And I hate to say it but I think you're in deep trouble on the murder charge unless you can prove the real identity of that body or the fact that Greenwood never had a body.'

'Well, I strongly suspect the body belongs to that Tyler chap. Otherwise how did its prints get into that room? Hopefully, we'll hear that he's gone missing.'

'Yes, but you'd still have to prove the body's his, not Greenwood's, and how would you do that?'

'Teeth would be one way. If he's got any dental records in New Zealand and they match the teeth of the corpse. . . .'

'That's a possibility. But what if that all leads to a dead end? Shouldn't you be getting evidence to prove that Geoffrey Greenwood never existed?'

'How do you prove a negative, Jon? I expect that's why Eleanor and her father – I'm sure he's behind her – took it for granted I'd never be able to establish the truth.'

'I don't agree, Charles. An imaginary character can never become a credible human being. There are far too many aspects to the lives and affairs of real people for that to happen. And if enough of those elements are missing, they must add up to something like positive proof, mustn't they? There'll be no evidence of Greenwood ever having had a home in South Africa, or a place of work, or a family or any friends. And no record anywhere of his ever having been issued with a passport or a driving licence or a credit card, or having had a bank account or an account with a store, or been a passenger on an airline or a member of a frequent flyers' club, or any other club for that matter, or having been a director of a company, or gone to any school, or had a doctor or a dentist? And so on and so on.'

'Well, you're not entirely right about the passport – what about my forgeries? There are two documents certified by me to be true extracts from his passport, one in his file at the office – as you've just mentioned – and the other with his trustees in Guernsey. I'd have to explain them, wouldn't I? Confess to forgery, which you'll now say is better than being convicted of murder. But the point is, would I be believed? Forgery's a form of lying, so my credibility would be in question either way.'

'It was a Zimbabwean passport, wasn't it? Well, your confession could be tested quite easily in the official records there.'

'The official records in Zimbabwe are in a mess, Jon. Take my word for it, that's why I chose the country. And anyway, as for the rest of the missing elements you mention, you can't stop at South Africa, Britain and Zimbabwe. You have to do the impossible – eliminate every single element everywhere.'

'Charles, the prosecution has to prove its case beyond a reasonable doubt. All you need do is raise a reasonable doubt about whether Greenwood actually existed.'

'How can I ever do that, Jon, when there's a dead body? If we can't prove the body belongs to Tyler, or someone else who's not Greenwood, then

Eleanor's evidence and the DNA and fingerprints will stand. So the prosecution will have established that the body is Greenwood's. Even if we'd excluded all the other attributes of a real person, as you say, there'd still be the bloody body. Imaginary people don't have bodies, Jon.'

Jonathan stroked his chin thoughtfully, then nodded. 'Yup. Good point. We go around in a circle, don't we? Though I still want to think about that a bit more. But then, what about another tack? You've told me you were known and recognized as Greenwood by various people, like the caretaker at that block, Beverley whatever. . . .'

'Terrace.'

'Terrace, thank you. And the porters at the other flat, in London. And the cleaning lady at Beverley Terrace. And the lady you first had an affair with as yourself – Lucy was it? Well, she didn't know you as Greenwood, but she found out he didn't exist and she might be able to say how she did that. What about all that evidence?'

'Well, for one thing, people are always impersonating other people, but that doesn't mean the other people don't exist, does it? I could have been impersonating the real Geoffrey Greenwood.'

'But it wasn't like that, Charles, was it? You weren't so much impersonating Greenwood as being him. If there was a real Greenwood, why didn't *he* ever put in an appearance anywhere? I think we must get statements from all the people who knew you as Greenwood and see where that takes us.'

'You speak as if you're going to get personally involved in all this, Jon.'

'Of course I am. You're facing a bloody murder charge and there's no one else you can turn to. So yes, I'm getting involved. In fact, I'm planning to run this side of the show. You can't. Now tell me, who would you say are the people who'd have known you as Greenwood? Besides Eleanor, of course.'

'You've already mentioned most of them, if not all. There's Clarke at Beverley Terrace. He'd be the best, I think. Then there's Maria, the Spanish cleaning lady who did my flat there. Then the two daytime porters at the St John's Wood flats - there wasn't a night porter. And Lucy. I can't think of anyone else for the moment, actually. But even if all of them – other than Lucy, of course – were to say they knew me as Geoffrey Greenwood, wouldn't we simply come up against the damn body again?'

'Yes, but we'd have a base from which to start challenging Eleanor's evidence and the forensics, especially if we backed it up with that other negative evidence we've been talking about. You can't just lie down and die, Charles. Juries can be persuaded. The fact is that Geoffrey Greenwood never existed, and courts of law are there to find out the facts.'

'OK then, Jon. How do you propose we go about this?'

We worked out a plan of action. We'd approach Clarke first, accompanied by an independent witness, and let him acknowledge me as Greenwood; then we'd take a written statement from him, on the spot. We should be prepared, Jonathan pointed out, for the likelihood that Clarke – who'd probably have learned of the alleged murder – would be shocked to see Greenwood alive and would react accordingly, but if so, we both agreed, it would be all to the good. Maria, the cleaning lady, would be our next target, to be handled similarly.

As for the porters in London, a different approach was necessary in view of the travel restrictions under my bail conditions, so Jonathan would engage a firm of investigators to call on them with a photograph of me. If that met with a positive response, we could consider our next move.

Lucy was an unknown quantity. We agreed that, given the background, it wouldn't be wise for her to be approached by anyone other than me personally.

We also talked about building up a dossier of 'negative evidence' about Geoffrey, but only after we'd got statements from one or two witnesses who were willing to swear they knew me as Geoffrey Greenwood.

Before we broke up for the night, Jonathan asked me how much of the Greenwood story Marion knew.

'None of it, yet,' I replied.

'You'll have to tell her, Charles. Perhaps not every little thing, but most of it. You can't go on concealing it from her now.'

'I know. She hasn't asked me any questions yet – probably just leaving the timing to me – but I do plan to talk to her, as soon as possible. Perhaps even tonight.'

47

I went upstairs as soon as Jonathan had left and found Marion waiting for me in the bedroom. There'd been no chance for us to have a proper discussion in Cornwall and she'd been busy with the children and her mother when we'd got home earlier; then Jonathan had arrived.

I kissed her on the cheek and said, 'I've got some explaining to do, haven't I?'

'Yes, you have, Teddy.'

'How much do you want to know?'

'As much as you think I need to.'

It was a tactful response which indicated that she was expecting to hear things she wouldn't like and would prefer me not to go into them too deeply, for both our sakes. So I gave her a fairly brief account of how I'd come to invent Geoffrey Greenwood and what had happened since I'd done so, leaving out a lot of the detail and being as sensitive and considerate as possible about my two extramarital relationships. She listened silently and attentively without interrupting me, right to the end, when I tried to explain why I'd found it necessary to continue misleading her about certain things even after we'd begun to repair our marriage – like Geoffrey being a real person, and there having been nothing between me and Eleanor, and my never having had an affair with Lucy.

At the end of it all we were both silent, for two or three minutes, during which she stared across the room with tears in her eyes. Then suddenly, she spoke, with great venom – but not about me. 'The bitch. The dirty little bloody bitch. My dear friend, Lucy Cole. Smiling sweetly at me while shagging my husband behind my back. I could strangle her.'

'I was as much to blame as she was,' I said.

She glared at me. 'Don't you dare protect her. And you're wrong about that anyway. You had every reason to be unfaithful to me. She didn't. Anyway, I don't want us to waste this precious time talking about her.'

'I agree. What do you want to say to me then?'

She stared ahead at nothing, then said, 'The first thing I want to say is thank you, Charles, for telling me all this. It must have been a very hard thing to do. And as I've just said, I don't blame you for being unfaithful when our marriage was on the rocks. I also understand why you couldn't be candid with me about some things. But I had no idea you could be as – how shall I put it? – inventive as you were.'

'You mean devious, Marion, don't you?'

She hesitated. 'Yes, I suppose so. As I've said, I realize there were times when you had to lie, but it seems to me there were others when you needn't but did.'

'My unnecessary deceptions.'

'What was that?'

'Just something about untruthfulness I've thought about. People speak of white lies – harmless deceptions if you like. I kept telling myself that my deceptions were justified, not because they were innocuous – some of them weren't and I knew it – but because they were necessary. As you've just said, there were times when I had to lie. The first was when I decided to put up a fight over the option in the Beverley Terrace lease. The only way I could do that was to deceive the other side into believing Geoffrey existed. It was a necessary deception. And everything that followed from then on was down to that first, necessary lie. If it's my unnecessary deceptions that trouble you, that's fine. I can't think of any lie I told which wasn't a necessary one.'

'Hmm. That's interesting, if a bit contrived, don't you think? You know, I'm not sure that lying is ever justifiable. But I'm not here to judge you. What matters to me is where we go from here. I must be able to trust you implicitly from now on. Can I do that? No more lies between us, please – necessary or unnecessary, white or black. I want to be able to believe whatever you tell me. Can you promise me I'll be able to do that?'

She'd forgiven me – for everything. What a generous person she was! If that was her only demand, I had every reason to be grateful. I reached out and took both her hands in mine. 'Marion, my darling, my dearest love. Thank you, thank you for your understanding. I love you. And yes, I do make you that promise, with all my heart.'

And I meant it.

Jonathan and Barry came over the next evening, Saturday, to discuss my role in the practice pending my trial. They both assured me I was welcome, as far as they were concerned, to carry on as if nothing had happened, coming to work daily, seeing clients, and so on. But it was obvious they were just saying the right things, so I thanked them and suggested it might be better all round if I kept away from the office, at this stage at least, and worked from home. I expressed my doubts about the willingness of any client to consult a lawyer suspected of murdering another of his clients, but said that if there were any such people, they could come and see me at home.

Jonathan stayed behind after Barry had left.

'He doesn't know the truth about Greenwood, does he?' I asked him.

'You mean Barry? No, I don't think so. At least I haven't told him. Do you want him to know?'

'Not especially. But if it puts you in an awkward position. . . .'

'It does, to be honest. It's difficult for me to do what I'm doing with you on the firm's time without bringing him into the picture. He could also be a useful member of the team, you know.'

I considered this. Barry had every right to know as much as Jonathan did. Both were my partners and they were both standing by me. And if my defence turned out to be that Geoffrey had never existed, there'd no longer be any secret to keep from Barry.

'Very well, Jon,' I said. 'Tell him.'

'OK, I'll do that. Now, about seeing those witnesses at the flats, I've spoken to Ivan Shreeves at Black and Ellison and they're happy to make a clerk available to us at no charge.'

'That's good of them. How much did you tell Ivan?'

'Well, he knew about you, of course – I mean about the prosecution. Everybody does. But I gave him no idea what evidence we were trying to get. He just said they'd be happy to help and to wish you well.'

'Nice of him. Tell him it's appreciated. When do you think we should start?'

When Jonathan arrived at the house on Monday afternoon, he had with him a young woman whom he introduced to me as Lisa Jackson of Black and Ellison who'd be accompanying us as an observer. I thanked Lisa for her willingness to help and we all got into Jonathan's car.

There was a strange man at the desk when we arrived at Beverley Terrace. He enquired if he could help us and I asked him where Mr Clarke was.

'I'm afraid he's no longer with us, sir.'

'You mean he's left?'

'More than that. He's left this world, passed away, last week. Seems he'd had a stroke recently and then had another massive one that took him.'

I couldn't believe what I was hearing. It was as if fate had developed a twisted sense of humour and was doing everything possible to harm and frustrate me. I'd had every confidence in Clarke becoming my champion by identifying me unequivocally as Geoffrey Greenwood, the man who'd come to view the flat and then rented and occupied it. But now that spark of hope had been snuffed out, along with Clarke himself.

'Is there anything I can do for you gentlemen – and lady? My name is Horton, Felix Horton, and I'm the new caretaker and porter.'

I felt like saying, 'Yes, please. Would you kindly call me Mr Greenwood and come to court to tell my accusers that that's who I'm known as around here?' But it was Jonathan who spoke.

'Mr Horton, we're solicitors. Mr Clarke would have been a witness in a case we're handling. I'm afraid I'm not at liberty to discuss the case with you, but there is another witness whom we'd like to see if possible – if she's here. She's a cleaning lady by the name of Maria.'

'Ah, Maria. Yes, she's here,' said Horton. 'In fact, here she comes.'

Maria emerged from the lift and was walking towards us, carrying a handbag and looking as if she had finished her work for the day. I was about to greet her when Jonathan restrained me with a touch of his hand.

'Good afternoon, Maria,' said Horton. 'These good people would like to speak with you.'

She stopped and looked at us, screwing up her face at the sight of me but saying nothing.

'Hullo, Maria,' I said, deciding that it was now appropriate to address her. The hoped-for 'Hullo, Mr Greenwood' was not forthcoming. Instead, she just continued looking at me and said, 'Yes?'

'You do remember me, don't you, Maria?'

'Maybe. I no sure.'

'I have a flat here – upstairs, on the third floor. Flat thirty-four. You clean it for me.'

She screwed up her face again. 'Yes. I do some flats. Thirty-four yes.'

Jonathan chimed in. 'Maria, excuse me asking. Do you wear glasses at all?' She was not wearing any at the moment.

'No, never. My eyes, they perfect. Why you ask?'

I wasn't altogether surprised by her failure to acknowledge me by name. She'd had little direct contact with me; I'd seldom been around when she was cleaning the flat and she'd been paid by Clarke on my behalf, not by me. But I had expected that she'd at least have recognized me as the tenant of one of the flats she cleaned.

Jonathan took the bull by the horns. 'Do you know this man?' he asked her, gesturing with his hand towards me.

'He say he is tenant here – number thirty-four. If he is tenant for thirty-four I know him.'

Jonathan made a further, desperate sally. 'Maria, do you know Mr Greenwood?'

For a second or two it seemed as if he'd struck gold, because she glanced at me before answering. Then she said, 'I see name of Greenwood on letters. Mr Clarke he sometimes give me letters to take up to flats. But I no remember now which flat is Greenwood.' At this point she gave the whole endeavour the kiss of death by looking straight at me and asking, 'You looking for Mr Greenwood?'

The mission to Beverley Terrace had been a dismal failure.

Lucy was the next target. I rang her mobile number.

'Lucy Cole,' she answered.

'Hullo, Lucy.'

'Charles!' She sounded surprised. 'Where are you?'

'At home. Have you heard—'

'Yes, of course. It's all over the place. Have they let you out?'

'Yes. I'm on bail.'

'I see. Well, did you do it?' Lucy wasn't one to beat about the bush.

'Lucy, you know I didn't do it. I couldn't have, and you know why.'

After a short silence she said, 'What are you saying, Charles? I know I once thought there was no Greenwood, but when I heard he'd drowned and later that you'd been accused of murdering him, I was sure I'd been wrong and assumed you'd only been impersonating a real person to your new girlfriend, Eleanor. Are you now telling me I was right all along?'

'Yes, Lucy. Greenwood did not exist.'

'But Charles, if that's true, how on earth can you be accused of his murder?'

'That's why I'm calling you. I desperately need your help. Lucy, would you be prepared to testify for me and tell them everything you found out about Greenwood? They're convinced there was such a person.'

'But I've read that they've got his body. How do you explain that?'

'It was falsely identified.'

After a brief silence, Lucy said, 'What on earth can I possibly say about all of that? I'm totally confused now. And besides, Charles, Malcolm and I are together again. We're reconciled and he's forgiven me for my 'affair' with Greenwood. Can you imagine what would happen if I now declared that the man had never existed? Forget it, Charles.'

Yet another dead end, I thought, though it hadn't been one I'd been pinning any great hope on. Lucy had never actually known the truth about Geoffrey as a fact. What she could have testified to – had she been willing – were the things she'd seen and heard at first hand which had subsequently led her to conclude that there'd never been such a person. In a way, all she could have done was add to the weight of the negative evidence about Geoffrey Greenwood. It would have been useful to have her on board as a witness, but by no means crucial.

'I understand your position, Lucy, and I'm glad to hear about you and Malcolm. But I think I should tell you that Marion knows about us – you and me. I'm sorry, but I had no choice: this ridiculous murder charge has created havoc with my life and forced me to say things I'd never have revealed. . . .'

'What's she going to do about it, Charles? Is she going to tell Malcolm?'

'I don't know what she's going to do, but I very much doubt she'll tell Malcolm anything. She is very angry with you, and she may or may not confront you. But if I were you, I'd just stay out of her way.'

'Well, thanks a lot, Charles. You've turned out to be a prince. I'm sure you didn't murder anyone, but I really hope they put you away.'

The phone went dead.

So that left the porters in London. Jonathan had arranged with private investigators for each of the two men to be approached, shown a photograph of me, and asked if he recognized the likeness on it. If one or both of them answered, 'Yes, I do. That's Mr Greenwood,' that might just be something to build on.

48

I kept thinking about Eleanor. She'd had every right to be angry with me. I'd used her and treated her very badly, albeit reluctantly and by force of circumstances, but even under the influence of a vengeful father, her retribution was beyond justification. I'd never have believed her capable of such extreme severity. She'd gone out of her way to put me behind bars for the rest of my life. 'Hell hath no fury like a woman scorned.' How true! Though not of Eleanor, surely?

But it hadn't been as simple as that, as I would learn in due course. While I was desperately seeking a way out of my predicament, Eleanor wasn't just sitting back and enjoying my plight; she was deeply troubled and very unhappy. With the benefit of hindsight, I am now able to describe her thoughts and feelings as they were at the time.

Without her father around to stoke its fire, Eleanor's anger had subsided and she was now nursing both a deep sense of guilt and a nagging anxiety. Her guilt stemmed from the knowledge that, as much of a bastard as she believed I was, what I had done to her wasn't murder and I didn't deserve to spend the rest of my life in prison for it. Her anxiety was about whether her identification of that awful mess of a corpse as Geoffrey Greenwood was going to stand up, despite her father's unshakeable confidence that it was.

Yes, Raymond Downing had been a deputy chief constable, and he knew a great deal about criminal law and the criminal courts, and he had excellent connections all over the land, and he had her best interests at heart, and yes, he was probably right to have warned her that if she didn't identify the body in the face of all the evidence, she herself could come under suspicion for having conspired with me to murder Geoffrey Greenwood, but there were other respects in which he could well have been wrong. She did not, for instance, share his conviction that the true identity of the dead man would never emerge.

'Come on, Ellie,' he'd said, 'who's going to think of linking that body to some missing person when it's already been identified as Greenwood's visually and forensically? And how on earth is Brook going to prove that Greenwood never existed when his dead body is lying in the mortuary?'

It had all made sense to her at the time, but that was because she'd been blinded by her own fury and Raymond's irresistible forcefulness. Left to her own devices, she'd never have done it – and she very nearly hadn't. In fact, it had only been at the very last moment, when she'd actually looked at the dead man's face and felt so utterly sickened by the whole business that she'd heard herself sobbing and blurting out those words that she'd never be able to retract: 'Yes. Yes, that's him. That's Geoffrey Greenwood,' as if they hadn't been hers at all but those of some other woman standing behind her who was truly in mourning for the poor creature lying on that cold slab.

She recalled how that journey of hers had begun, the journey that had ended with her utterance of those words. How Detective Inspector Harrison from Penzance had arrived at the flat with a WPC and told her about the body that had been washed ashore, and about the medical report supporting the possibility that death could have occurred at or about the time of Geoffrey's supposed disappearance, and then about the dead man having been shot in the back. And how she'd longed to be able to tell Harrison the truth about Geoffrey Greenwood, but she couldn't because of what had gone before. Even so, she now reflected, if only she had done that! Whatever trouble she'd have got into for having misled the police in the first place would have been nothing compared to what she was going through now – and would still have to go through if her identification were to be overturned.

What she'd actually done instead was protest that the body couldn't have been 'her' Geoffrey's because he couldn't possibly have been shot, but Harrison had urged her – in her own interests, he'd said, and even if only to put the matter to rest in her own mind – to come down to Penzance and make quite sure that it wasn't Geoffrey's body.

In the middle of it all her father, who'd been staying with her, had shown up and introduced himself to the two officers, and Harrison and his young colleague had been so impressed and overawed to find themselves in the company of a retired senior officer of his high rank that they'd allowed him to take over the proceedings from there and to extract from Harrison some confidential information about the investigation, more particularly that the police had been able to match fingerprints found in Geoffrey's hotel room a day or two after his disappearance with those of the corpse, and that DNA tests were being run on traces taken from personal items in the room belonging to Geoffrey. Questioned by Raymond, Harrison had admitted to him that I would be under suspicion if the body turned out to be Geoffrey's.

Her father had called her aside and advised her to do as the inspector asked, if only to be faithful to the role she was playing as Geoffrey's partner. She'd then agreed to go down to Penzance in the next day or two and had asked Raymond to accompany her.

After the two officers had left, her father had phoned his old friend and colleague, former Chief Superintendent Claude Grant, who'd served under Raymond and had since retired to Penzance, to find out more of what was going on. Grant happened to be well up with developments, having become the friend and confidant of the chief superintendent in Penzance, and had put Raymond even more fully in the picture. And when she and Raymond had arrived in Penzance, Claude Grant had told them about the positive provisional DNA matchings, which had astonished them both.

She was due at the mortuary the next morning, and she and her father had spent most of the night discussing what she should do when she got there and trying to guess how the DNA results had come about. Clearly, the fingerprints pointed to the dead man having recently occupied Geoffrey's hotel room, but the DNA was inexplicable, unless, as Raymond pointed out, he'd left some of his things in the room or someone had planted them there after the event. Raymond had urged her to identify the body as Geoffrey's and she'd resisted. But his arguments were persuasive and in the end she found herself weakening. He told her that, according to Grant, the police were convinced that the body was Geoffrey's and were expecting her to confirm the fact. They'd be suspicious, her father said, if she didn't, and might well think that she and I had been in it together, especially since I controlled the Guernsey trust and she was the sole surviving named beneficiary. And he spoke about revenge and how it was an essential need of the human condition, and how she'd never have peace of mind again without it.

He'd asked her to sleep on it, but she hadn't. She'd dismissed it from her mind, hoping that somehow it would all go away. And then it had happened, in the cold, harsh light of the mortuary, when she saw the body and mourned for her lover, Geoffrey, whom I, Charles Brook, had so cruelly created for her and then so selfishly destroyed.

Afterwards, she'd moved as if in a dream, unwilling to face the reality of what she'd done, and when Raymond had advised her to tell Inspector Harrison about the tape, she'd tamely complied and made a statement about it. And Harrison had arranged for someone from the Metropolitan Police to come and fetch it from her at the flat when she got back to London.

She wondered now how it would have turned out had she not divulged everything to Raymond in the first place. After she and I had been together for the last time on that Friday night, she'd decided that she needed some reliable independent proof of what I'd told her about the state of my marriage and my impending divorce before she could finally take me back as myself instead of Geoffrey. So she'd gone to Cambridge on the Saturday morning and told him everything – the whole story of her relationship with the man she thought was Geoffrey Greenwood, and how she'd found out my real identity, and what had happened after that. She'd brought the tape with her and she'd played to Raymond the recording of the phone message I had left her on the answering machine at the London flat after she'd stormed out on me at Beverley Terrace.

Raymond had then offered her his own services as an experienced detective and, after he'd made some phone calls to Brighton and Hove, they'd travelled together to Brighton in his car, which he'd exchanged on their arrival there for a surveillance vehicle borrowed from its current owner, a former CID officer who was now working as a private investigator in Sussex, together with some ancillary equipment, including a camera, binoculars, and some electronic listening devices. They'd then driven to Hove and parked the vehicle across the street from my home. She'd been present only because Raymond had needed her to point me out, seeing she had no photograph of me. Raymond had wanted her to return to London once she'd done so because he intended to continue the investigation on his own over the next couple of days.

They'd been sitting there for about an hour when I appeared, and she could still feel that awful sense of disbelief and shock when she saw me emerging from the house in the company of an attractive dark-haired woman who could only have been my wife, and the two of us walking off together, hugging and holding onto each other and smiling and laughing as only lovers did. When we had disappeared around the corner, Raymond had patted her hand and said, 'Sorry, Ellie,' and then driven her to Brighton station, where she'd taken the train.

Raymond had spent much of the Saturday night parked outside my home, making observations and picking up sounds with the aid of the equipment, then followed the family to the park the next day, Sunday, and continued his observations on the Monday. I'd not have been aware I was being watched, though I might occasionally have noticed the proximity of a white-haired elderly gentleman with a camera.

When Raymond reported to her on the Monday evening, he did so very gently and considerately, because the news he brought her could not have been worse. I had been proved to be an abject liar; I was living the life of a happily married family man, clearly in love – and sharing a bedroom – with Marion. I'd spent the whole weekend in her company and there'd been no sign at all of any tension or disharmony between us. On the contrary, I'd sent Marion a huge flower arrangement with a note telling her of my great love for her which Raymond had managed to read surrep-titiously because the flowers had been left outside the front door while she was out. Raymond had a collection of photographs and tape recordings to bear out the results of his investigation, but she hadn't wanted to see or hear any of them. As her father had suspected, I had deceived her, not once but twice, and the second time I had simply exploited her, purpose-fully and ruthlessly.

Raymond had helped her compose a dismissive, but dignified, letter to me, and my reply a few days later had been the final insult – a contemptible admission of all my deceit.

Her feelings towards me had since mellowed. She'd come to realize that much of what I'd done could have been due to the circumstances in which I'd found myself, and that perhaps some of what I'd told her had been true. It was impossible that a loving relationship such as ours had been entirely one-sided. And now that she'd had her retribution, there was room in her for compassion and forgiveness. The fact was that she missed me – as Geoffrey, that is.

It was time, she decided, to leave the flat we'd shared; living there was compounding her misery. She needed to be in an environment which was not permeated with Charles-alias-Geoffrey, and she hated the idea that she was still being subsidized by me. Raymond argued that I'd had no right to the money I'd given her for the rent and the furnishings, but that didn't convince her. She'd have moved out by now but for her father's advice to the contrary; he believed it would look better if she stayed where she was until the trial was over.

Her distress was compounded by the grotesque situation in which her identification of the body had put her. She'd been told that the body would be released to her once all issues concerning its identity were out of the way, which might however take some time. Released to her? The corpse of a total stranger? Raymond had told her not to worry, that all it meant was that she'd have to take responsibility for some kind of funeral. But the whole idea was utterly repugnant. It was as if she'd not merely identified an unknown body, but acquired it.

And then there was her growing concern about a successful challenge to her identification of the body. It was all very well her father asserting that the body itself proved that Geoffrey had existed; she'd thought a lot about that and it seemed to her like begging the question. To her mind, all my lawyers needed to do was produce one reasonably substantial piece of evidence that Geoffrey Greenwood had not existed and that would start a process that could well lead to her being prosecuted for perjury or perverting the course of justice or something like that.

She hoped that her conversations with the two porters in the St John's Wood block had reduced slightly the chances of that happening. She'd told them that they might be approached by people representing the fiend who had murdered Mr Greenwood and that she'd be gravely disappointed should either of them be inclined to co-operate with such people in any way or answer any of their questions, even the most straightforward ones, such as how well they had known Mr Greenwood and what he looked like. In response they'd both assured her earnestly that she could rely on them not to disappoint her. Fortunately, they were both very well disposed towards her.

The other fact that was contributing to her discomfort was that Raymond kept saying things which implied that he was expecting her to lay claim to the trust fund once I had been convicted of the 'murder'. Although he hadn't expressed these expectations in so many words, he did seem to be working on her. She had never wanted to benefit financially from her relationship with me when she'd known me as Geoffrey, and she had no intention of doing so now.

49

The tide hadn't turned. Jonathan rang me to report that the approach to the porters in London had been unsuccessful. One of the two men had apparently looked at the photograph and said, 'No, I don't,' in reply to the question, 'Do you recognize this man?' while the other had simply been evasive, saying that he didn't want to get involved and was no good at remembering faces. The investigators reported having sensed that the porters were both being deliberately uncooperative. It seemed very much as if Eleanor had got to them.

'We need to talk,' said Jonathan over the phone. 'Are you free right now?'

'Free? Of course I'm free – now – though it doesn't seem as if I'll be for much longer. You're welcome to come over, Jon.'

Well, that was that, I reflected, in terms of producing witnesses who could say they knew me as Geoffrey. My dilemma was no longer whether to reveal the truth about Geoffrey, but how the hell to prove it if I did. The negative evidence route was still open, but without witnesses to say they knew me as Geoffrey all the negative evidence we could muster would founder against the fact of an identified corpse. My hopes now rested on establishing that the dead man was Tyler, and on that score there'd been nothing further yet from Cartwright. My despair was deepening and my morale collapsing. Was I really going to spend the rest of my life in gaol? I'd often in the past tried to imagine what it must be like to be a long-term prisoner: the confinement; the restrictions; the spartan, violent, smelly, masculine conditions; sadistic wardens; psychopathic, sexually deprived fellow-inmates; unbearable separation from loved ones; and unmitigated loneliness and humiliation. Surely it couldn't happen to me?

When Jonathan arrived, I was feeling too desolate and depleted to pay any real attention to what he started telling me. It had to do with The Greenwood Trust, a total irrelevance given that my impending conviction for having caused the imaginary Geoffrey Greenwood's death would disqualify me forever from getting anywhere near the trust fund. But after a while Jonathan thrust his face into my line of sight and spoke loudly and slowly, stressing each word. 'Charles, you must please listen to me. What I'm saying is important.' He paused to be sure that he had my attention, then continued, 'You haven't been tried yet and you could get off, you know. In case that happens, you must protect your interests.'

'Against what?'

'Well, Eleanor Downing for one thing. She's the only surviving named beneficiary and I wouldn't put it past her or her father to have been in touch with the trustees by now.'

'I'm quite sure, Jon, that the trust company won't pay anything out to Eleanor or anyone else at this stage, not till the trial's over anyhow. But what are you suggesting?'

'That's exactly why I'm talking to you about this, Charles. Barry and I have discussed the matter and we're willing to help, but we're not sure how. You understand these offshore things far better than we do.'

I considered what he was saying and decided it made sense. 'Well, I suppose you chaps could front for me. You could contact the trust company and say that the firm is dealing with Geoffrey's affairs, and that I'm not involved, at least pending my trial. You could even perhaps hint vaguely at family interests abroad. Then ask them to give you an assurance that they won't deal with the trust fund or make any distributions without referring back to you.'

'Will they do that?'

'Almost certainly not, but they'll probably tell you that they don't *intend* making any distributions. That won't bind them, but the practical effect would be the same.'

'Very well then. Who's the person to contact?'

'Jeremy Lefarge at Citadel in Guernsey. It's all in the file.'

'I know Lefarge. You referred me to him once, remember?'

'Not really, but if you say so. Please deal with it, Jonathan.'

'OK, Charles. You seem really down today. Don't give in yet, please.

There's still a long way to go and who knows? You may well come out on top, in which case all that lovely lolly is going to come in very handy for you, Marion, and the kids.'

'If only it were so.'

'Now, I didn't come over just to talk about the trust. We must discuss your defence, Charles.'

'What defence?'

'Come on, man. That's just what I mean. You're going under without a fight.'

'Well, have you got any ideas?'

He began speaking about negative evidence again – getting as much of it as possible, and how we could go about it and what it would cost, and the possibility that in the process we might just unearth something that could lead us on to something else which would become positive proof of Greenwood's non-existence. I listened half-heartedly and when he was finished said, 'Don't be offended, Jon, but I don't think we're getting anywhere with this. We agreed last time we discussed all this that negative evidence alone wasn't enough, not without witnesses that I was Geoffrey. And to me that remains the case. Tyler's the one hope I've got left now. But I'll think about everything you've just been saying.'

'Peter Cartwright said there was a time factor, remember. There's this plea and directions thing that's going to come up and he wants to brief counsel.'

'I know, Jon. Give me a few days and I'll get back to you. And thanks again for everything.'

'All right then, let's leave it at that. I'm available whenever you're ready. Meanwhile I'll get in touch with Lefarge.'

After he'd left I sat where I was, staring out of the window at nothing. Then the phone rang. It was Peter Cartwright.

'I've heard from Wellington, Charles, and I'm afraid it's not good news.'

My heart sank. 'Tyler's alive and well, I suppose.'

'No, that's not it. He doesn't exist.'

'What? What did you just say?'

'There's no such person.'

'*What?*'

Now I was really hearing things. It was plain that I'd gone absolutely crazy. I already knew that the person who the police thought had been murdered didn't exist; now my lawyer was telling me that the person who I thought was murdered didn't exist either.

'There's no such person as Harold Tyler in Wellington,' Peter went on, 'and there's no such address as the one he gave the hotel. Well, there *is* a Harold Tyler in Wellington, but he's seven years old and he's never been to Britain. And they've checked out all the other Tylers in Wellington and none of them's missing.'

'He checked in under a false name,' I said.

'And address. Yes, that much seems clear. Now, the guys there have extended their enquiries to finding out who in Wellington may have gone missing while on an overseas trip – more particularly, a solitary traveller fitting Tyler's description – but he may not have come from Wellington at all, or even from New Zealand. When I spoke to Trudy Jones at the Cuckoo she told me his accent was more Australian than New Zealand, and that she knew the difference because she had family in both countries. The next step might be to use a missing persons service – or more than one – here and in the Antipodes and get them to advertise, in the media and on the web. But it's going to be bloody expensive.'

'I don't care, Peter. We've got to do everything we can to find out who this guy really was and what's happened to him. I'm surer now than ever that he was the dead man. Someone travelling about under a false name is quite likely to have had enemies.'

'Yes, perhaps. Very well then, I'll keep the ball rolling. But I need you down here again, Charles. That's the main reason for this call. We have to meet again, in Penzance which is where the prosecution are putting their case together, since most of the evidence is there.'

'When do you want me?'

'As soon as possible. I want to brief counsel now – Yeats, and the silk as well. Are you sure you can fund all this?'

'Yes, I'll manage, even if it breaks me. Don't worry about that. Is this to be another general chat or what?'

'Well, it's mainly to get everything nice and clear in our own minds before we instruct counsel. I'm talking about your defence. I hope you've got one.'

'Of course I have.'

We agreed to meet three days later at the offices of Peter's Penzance correspondents.

'Any chance of my being allowed to drive to Cornwall in my own car?' I asked him. 'I'm really not in the mood for company, or for the hustle and bustle of crowded railway stations or airports.'

'As far as I'm concerned, you don't need anybody's permission. Your bail conditions permit you to travel between Sussex and Cornwall – as long as you keep reporting to the police, but I think we should tell the prosecution service you're coming anyway, and how you'll be travelling. Meanwhile, there've been other developments you should know about. The prosecution have made some formal and some informal disclosures. First, I've got the copy of the tape, and I've listened to it. I'll play it to you when we meet. There's an interesting item on it besides your message for Eleanor – a message left for Greenwood by somebody called Gragorin' – he pronounced the name 'Gra-go-reen,' accentuating each syllable. 'It's a very strange one. Sounds as if the guy was threatening Greenwood. Anyway, you'll hear it when you get here.'

'I know about—' I stopped myself in mid-sentence; I wasn't supposed to know about that message. 'I mean I know something about that situation. I dealt with—'

'Don't let's go into any of that now, please, Charles. You'll tell me all about it when we meet. Now, what else was there? Yes, I've managed to get some informal advance notice of the evidence against you. There's the DNA report, which is no longer provisional. Dr Blunt, our expert, says it seems sound, though there are one or two points he wants to raise with us. I told him we'll be wanting to see him with counsel and to hold back his report in the meantime. Then there's the statement of this witness who claims to have seen you at the scene of the crime. It's a young woman, name of Jenny Cooper, who works at the Cuckoo and says she recognized you because you'd stayed there. She also says a few not so nice things about you having tried to get off with her at the hotel.'

'What? The little bitch – she's lying, twice over.'

'And then, of course, there's Eleanor's statement, which you may like even less. These two women don't seem very fond of you.'

That wasn't news as far as Eleanor was concerned, but Jenny? What on earth was she up to?

'Charles, now listen to me, please,' Peter continued. 'I'm going to need clear instructions from you on Thursday.'

'You'll get them,' I said, without the slightest idea what I was going to tell him.

50

I drove down to Cornwall on the Wednesday, the prosecution having offered no objection to my coming alone by car, provided that I reported to the police in Hove before leaving and to the Penzance police within an hour of arriving there and that I followed the same procedure on the return journey. For the rest, my bail conditions were to apply. Marion and I had agreed that she shouldn't keep coming to Cornwall with me; it was too disruptive, especially for the children.

I'd made a booking at the Royal Penzance Hotel. Happily, my arrival there attracted no particular attention and I was received by the hotel staff as courteously and respectfully as if my notoriety had not preceded me – which I guessed it had.

At half past two I placed a lunch order with room service and after about twenty minutes a young woman arrived with the tray. She thanked me when I tipped her and then said, in an Irish accent, as casually and politely as if she were commenting on the weather, 'Jenny needs to speak with you, sir.'

'What's that?' I was sure I'd misheard her.

'It's what I'm saying, sir. My name's Marjorie – Marjorie O'Brien. I used to work with Jen at the Cuckoo, but now I'm employed here. She's desperate to talk with you.'

'You mean Jenny from The Cuckoo's Nest?'

'Yes, sir. I do mean her. We're friends.'

'What does she want of me?'

'She'll be telling you that herself, I'm sure.'

'I dare not talk to her. I'd be locked up if I did.'

'That's what she said herself, sir, but it can be arranged so nobody'll know.'

'How did she find out I'd be here?'

'Oh, someone in the know told her. She's had trouble, serious trouble, and she thinks yourself and herself can help each other. If you'd not ordered room service, I'd have found another way of giving you her message.'

What could Jenny possibly want of me? I didn't trust her one bit. She'd lied about me and was up to something. Perhaps she wanted to tell me about it. Or was this some kind of trap? She was a witness for the prose-cution. Whoever was trying to get me convicted of murder might be using her as bait to get me to break my bail conditions. On the other hand, if it was true that she was desperate, then I was even more so. Here I was, on the day before I was due to meet my solicitor, and I still didn't know what I was going to tell him. At this stage, I was ready to clutch at straws. I decided I had to take the gamble.

'OK, Marjorie, when and where does she want to meet me?'

'Do you have a car?'

'Yes.'

'Good. D'you know how to get to The Cuckoo's Nest from Penzance?'

'Yes, I do.'

'Well, if you drive up the road that winds past the Cuckoo, she'll wait for you along the roadside a little way beyond the hotel. You can pick her up and she'll tell you where to go from there. There's a secluded spot higher up that road where you'll not be seen.'

I remembered the area from the reconnaissance I'd carried out up that hill during the weekend with Marion. 'When?' I asked Marjorie.

'Pick any time from' – she looked at her wristwatch – 'say five thirty, and I'll get the message to her.'

I thought for a moment. It shouldn't be in broad daylight. 'Let's say six o'clock. How's that?'

'Great. I'll tell her.' Marjorie was staring at me. 'You don't look like a killer to me, if I may say so.'

'I'm not one, Marjorie, I assure you.'

It was so dark by the time I drove up the hill past The Cuckoo's Nest that I was hoping I wouldn't miss Jenny by the roadside. There'd been no sign of any vehicle tailing me and the road behind me seemed clear of traffic now. About a quarter of a mile beyond the Cuckoo my headlights caught a figure in a raincoat standing on a bend. As I slowed down, the person raised an arm and waved. I stopped the car, lowered the front passenger window, and peered through it. Jenny peered back at me, said, 'Hi', and got into the car.

'Drive on,' she instructed me. Under her directions, I continued up the winding road for about a mile and then turned right onto a dirt track that soon widened into a clearing.

'Park just beyond that clump of trees,' she said, pointing.

'How safe is this?' I asked her, as I pulled up the handbrake and turned off the engine.

'It's fine. Nobody ever comes here after dark.'

'Well, Jenny? What's this about?' I turned to look at her. Despite the darkness I could see her well enough to be shocked by her appearance – her lips were bloated and her face seemed somehow distorted.

'I'm so glad you've come, Mr Brook. And I want to say sorry. I'm really sorry. I never meant you any harm.'

Surely she hadn't brought me here just to apologize? 'Well, whatever you meant, you've certainly done me a lot of harm,' I said bitterly.

'But I want to undo it. Really. That's why I'm here – well, one of the reasons. You see, something's been done to me – something awful – and it's made me very angry with some people, and very sorry about you. And I want to fix both things, with your help. I think maybe we can help each other – well, you being a lawyer, and me needing legal advice, and you facing prison for a murder you didn't do, and everything needing to be put right, in a way—'

'Jenny, it sounds like there's a lot you need to tell me. Why don't you just start at the beginning?'

51

The dead man's name was John Richardson, Jenny told me, though she had known him as Harold Tyler, the name under which he'd checked into the Cuckoo. She'd met him in the hotel bar while serving there on the evening of his arrival, and spent about five hours in his company later that night after going off duty. They'd been for a walk on the beach; then she'd invited him home, where they'd become lovers. He told her he was from New Zealand and was hiking around Britain alone. At her suggestion, he checked out of the hotel in the morning and moved in with her for the next few days.

She'd been married for three years and lived with her husband, William (Bill) Cooper, in a cottage in Porthderick, a tiny village which lay just beyond the stretch of cliffs and beaches on which I'd staged Geoffrey's disappearance. The cottage, which stood between a fishing cove and a copse, belonged to Bill, who'd been away at the time and was not expected back for at least two weeks. She'd lied to Tyler that she was single and lived with her father who was on an extended business trip up-country.

'Bill *is* old enough to be my father, Mr Brook,' she said, 'and we never had much of a marriage, so it wasn't really far from the truth, what I told Harold. You see, I never fancied my husband as a man, if you know what I mean – it was what you'd call a marriage of convenience. He's a bit of a runt, Bill, and quite an ugly one at that, but he made me an offer and we did a deal. I met him when I was working in a pub in Penzance and he took a fancy to me, chatting me up and whispering in my ear and telling me how beautiful I was and what he could give me and do for me if I came to live with him. He said all he wanted was a beautiful woman to go with his cottage and his two cars. I found out afterwards that only one of the cars belonged to him – the small Fiat. The other one, a big Merc, belonged to his bosses. He drove it for them, on long trips to London and beyond, and they let him take it home between trips. He kept it in a lock-up not far from the cottage.

'You know, I never had a home before, Mr Brook. Never knew my parents. I grew up in an orphanage in Devon, run by nuns, and went to the convent school there. Then I left school at sixteen and travelled about, all around Devon and Cornwall, working as a cleaner and barmaid and such-like. So I quite fancied the idea of living like a lady in this chap's cottage, but the trouble was I'd have to live with him and that didn't appeal to me much, and I knew he'd get tired of me one day and chuck me out. So in a joke I told him I'd come and live with him if he married me and gave me his Fiat car as a wedding present. I never dreamed he'd agree, but he did – though not to give me the car as my own, just let me use it as if it was mine – and also he said he'd pay for driving lessons for me. Well, that was fine with me, so we got married and I moved in with him.

'It was OK for a while at first, 'specially seeing he was away on his trips a lot, but he turned out to be a miserable bastard, bullying and teasing me and using me as if I was his servant. And claiming his rights as my husband – if you know what I mean – in a rough, selfish kind of way, as if I wasn't a woman but some sort of bag or something. At least he was always quick about it. But he was just a nasty little man in every way, so nasty that I named him 'Nasty' in my own mind, and even to his face once or twice. That was because he was always calling me nasty names. His favourite was 'whore' – usually 'bloody whore' or 'fucking whore' –

because he knew I appealed to men and he was very jealous about that and never trusted me.'

'And was he right not to?' I asked her.

She managed a smile. 'Of course he was, Mr Brook. But he started it. He called me a whore for no reason, so I thought I might as well live up to the name – not selling my body for money, I mean, just having a bit of company from time to time. How could I live with a nasty runt like him and put up with his bullying and name-calling and not have a little fun when he went away? I was lonely and I worked in places where there were men – nice, good-looking ones, and well bred, like yourself, if you don't mind me saying so. Harold looked a lot like you, you know. You were both my type: tall, slim, blue eyes, well-spoken. I love blue eyes in a man, they really turn me on. And I'd spend a bit of time with the ones I liked best, if they were willing, as they usually were – not you though, I'm bound to say, though I think you might have been if . . . Anyway, it wasn't all the time, just two or maybe three times a year, and they had to be really nice. Which Harold was, gentle in a manly way.'

'Is that why you went on working after you married Bill? Because you were lonely?'

'Well, yes and no. I needed the money. Nasty would give me an allowance to pay for food and drink and the upkeep of the cottage, but nothing for myself, not even for clothes. And I wanted to be my own person.'

'You mean independent?'

'Yes, independent.'

'Did you take all these men home with you? I mean like you did Harold?'

'No. Not usually. It was risky, but with Harold I really didn't expect Nasty back. He'd gone on a trip just a day or two before you arrived at the Cuckoo and when he left he said he'd be away for three weeks or longer. And he'd never before come back sooner than he said.'

'Jenny, are you saying Bill came back to the cottage unexpectedly when you were with Harold?'

'Yes, that's just what happened.' She took a long, trembling breath, then continued, 'Harold moved in with me on the Tuesday – I had the day off and we spent it together. He stayed the night. On the Wednesday I was off during the day but I had a night shift at the Cuckoo. When I got back, Harold was in bed, so I got undressed and joined him there. We had some fun and then I fell asleep, next to him, both of us in our birthday suits.'

'And Bill came home?'

'Yes. He woke us up. I heard the porch swing-door open and close, then the bedroom door, and then his voice. 'Hullo, Sleeping Beauty. Prince Charming's back.' I was sick with fright. And then Harold mumbled something, sort of half-asleep, and the light went on and there was Nasty, standing and staring at us, with me and Harold both sitting up in the bed. Then Nasty started bellowing and screaming, calling me a fucking whore, as usual, and Harold a fucking bastard. All of a sudden he left the room, and I jumped out of bed, and Harold did the same, on the other side. But then Nasty was back, with a handgun. He kept two of them in the cottage, a pistol and a revolver – both illegal. Used to brag about his guns and kept showing them to me. "This is a semi-automatic pistol, Jenny. Take a good look at it. This is what I'll kill you with if I ever find you with another man. Or maybe it'll be this one, the revolver. See the difference, Jenny?" And so on.'

'Are you going to tell me he shot Harold?'

'Yes, he did, with the pistol. But not then, not in the bedroom. He pointed the gun at me first and then at Harold. Then Harold crouched down behind the bed and Nasty moved to the side to keep him in sight. But Harold made a dash for the kitchen and I heard something smash in there, then a yell. Nasty dashed out after him, and I chased after Nasty and tried to grab him, from behind, to stop him, but I couldn't. Harold ran out the back door into the wood behind the cottage, with Nasty behind him and then me. On my way out, I saw blood on the kitchen floor and a broken bottle base and pieces of glass. Harold had knocked a bottle off the kitchen table and cut his foot.'

Jenny paused and drew a deep breath, then continued, 'Well, there was Harold, stumbling away with Nasty chasing him and me chasing Nasty. Then I heard a shot and I knew Nasty had fired at Harold. But he must have missed because I could still see Harold in the moonlight, stumbling between the trees, but Nasty had gained on him and I saw him stop and take aim, and I tried to reach him but couldn't. And then there was another shot and Harold's arms went up in the air and he fell forwards against a tree trunk, then over onto the ground. By now I'd caught up with Nasty and I pushed him aside and ran to where Harold was lying. There was blood on the ground and he wasn't moving. I'd done some first-aid at school, so I bent down and felt his neck for a pulse. There wasn't one, so I turned his head sideways to see if he was breathing, and he wasn't. Nasty had shot Harold in the back and killed him.

'So there I was, starkers, with the naked dead body of the chap I'd been sleeping with. And there was Nasty, standing and looking at me with the gun in his hand. I was sure he was going to shoot me too, but instead he just dropped the gun on the ground. I started screaming at him, 'You bloody mad bastard! You've killed him, you crazy bastard!' Then I stopped yelling and started thinking about everything and getting scared. Here we were, Nasty and me, with a dead body on our hands, and there was bound to be trouble, not just for Nasty but for me too.'

'Why for you? You didn't shoot Harold.'

'I was all mixed up. I'd been the cause of it all, hadn't I? And anyway, I just had the feeling that if we got rid of the body and cleaned up all over, it would all go away and nobody would ever know about it. I didn't want the police coming round, whatever happened. Afterwards I realized I'd probably been wrong about that, but by then it was too late – I was already a . . . what's the word for it? Someone who helps a criminal.'

'Accessory.'

'That's it. Because I helped Nasty get rid of the body. I told him to fetch his wheelbarrow and helped him lift Harold onto it – he was a big, heavy chap and it wasn't easy – and together we wheeled the barrow to Nasty's boat at the top of the cove and rolled the body into the boat. Then Nasty took the boat out and dumped the body in the sea a bit of a way offshore. I told him to dump the gun too, but not near where he dropped the body, and he took it with him in the boat.'

'Why did you take control like that, Jenny?'

'Well, you see, Nasty caved in. He went limp and quiet. I guess it hit him that he'd just killed somebody and he was scared. So I had to take over.'

'What else did you do?'

'Well, when Nasty went out with the boat, I walked back up to the cottage and put on some clothes and cleaned up in there, 'specially the blood and the broken glass, and stripped the bed and changed the sheet. Then Nasty came back and started calling me names again and telling me to get out of his house. I shouted back at him, and he slapped my face and I put my knee into his privates, and he fell down on the floor crying and moaning. I left him there and made myself a mug of coffee in the kitchen, and when I looked again he was gone. I didn't know where he was, but I lay down on the bed in the small room – that's the child's room next to the bedroom, though we've got no kids. I couldn't sleep, and then I heard him come in and I went to speak to him. I told him I'd been thinking and that we'd better stop fighting and stick together until everything settled down, and I'd sleep in the small room meanwhile. And that we must go outside at sunrise and look for bloodstains and the cartridges from the two bullets he'd fired, and make sure there were no more signs of what had happened.'

'And what did he do?'

'Oh, he just stood there, all grumpy and pulling faces. But he did listen to what I was saying. Then he asked me who my 'fucker' was, and I told him it was none of his business and he needn't worry, I'd get rid of the chap's things. When it got light, I couldn't find Nasty again, so I went outside and walked out the back door through the trees, trying to follow where Harold ran and covering over anything that looked like a bloodstain with the soles of my shoes and making sure everything looked OK. But I didn't try and find the cartridges, because I thought that was for him to do. He came back around midday and I reminded him about the cartridges, but he just said, 'OK,' and swore at me again. Just then a Navy chopper flew by, quite low, and I said something about them looking for Harold's body, and Bill said, "It's got nothing to do with that. There's a bloke who's drowned and they're looking for him. He was staying at the Cuckoo." I thought it might be you or your friend.'

'What did you do about Harold's things?'

'Well, I packed everything of his into his backpack. I knew I must get rid of it but I wasn't sure how best to do that and I wanted to wait till the next day when the hubbub about the drowning had died down. Then, on the Friday morning I went off to work at the Cuckoo – I'd volunteered for cleaning duty – and Trudy Jones told me about Mr Greenwood. There was a young copper posted outside his room, number eight, and I got talking to him, very friendly-like, if you know what I mean. And then I got an idea. You'd just checked out and there were no other guests due that day.'

'That's right.'

'Yes, well, after a while I told Trudy I was feeling poorly and she let me go home. I drove back to the cottage and went through the backpack. In Harold's wallet I found some British money and some foreign notes too, which I put aside. The British notes I put into my purse – Harold wouldn't be needing them any more. I also found his passport, which I looked at and there was Harold's picture but not his name. The name in the passport was John Richardson and it was an Australian passport. I put the passport and the foreign money into a Sainsbury's shopping bag. One thing I didn't want was to be found with a photo of a murdered man. There's an open fireplace in the cottage, so I shoved the shopping bag in the fireplace to burn later. Which I did that night. All the rest of the stuff – his clothes, a hairbrush, toothbrush, razor, and some tubes and things – I put into two large black bin-bags. I first checked each piece of clothing to be sure there were no labels or such-like with a name or address on them – there weren't any, but there was an airline luggage sticker on the backpack which I tore off and chucked in the fireplace too. The wallet went into the backpack, which I took down to the cellar where we kept our own suitcases and stuff. Then I packed the bin-bags in the boot of my car and drove back to the Cuckoo.'

A small bell which had been tinkling in a distant part of my brain suddenly began ringing loudly. 'Don't tell me, Jenny, that you put that stuff in Greenwood's hotel room?'

She nodded. 'That's just what I did. Well, not the bin-bags themselves, only what was in them – Harold's clothes and brushes and razor and so on. I just mixed them in with Greenwood's things – except I removed some of Greenwood's things where it'd look funny if he had two, like the toothbrush and the razor and such-like.'

'How did you get into the room? It was under police guard.'

'I'll tell you. First I told Trudy I felt better and wanted to carry on. There wasn't much cleaning to do, but the regular cleaning girls both had the Friday off and she was glad to have my help. I did your room, then came out with the cleaning trolley and told my friend the young copper something about getting into trouble if I couldn't get into the room he was guarding to clear up something or another – I can't remember exactly what I said, but I invited him to come in with me, sort-of making promises with my eyes. Then, when we were in the room, I came onto him – like I did with you that day, remember? – and we started hugging and kissing, then I pretended to get all alarmed and told him I'd forgotten the owner's wife was coming to check on me and he'd better get back to his post and I'd be out in a few minutes. Well, he scampered out of that room like he was on fire, and I quickly did what I had to in there. It took me about five or six minutes, and when I came out Denis – that was the copper's name – was all fretting and worried, and why had I taken so long. I just whispered in his ear and said I'd make it up to him, because I wanted to keep in touch with him. Being a policeman, he might get to know things like if anyone was missing Harold or if his body got washed up or something.'

'Why on earth would you want to put Harold's things in Greenwood's room?'

'Well, there was quite a bit of the stuff and I'd have needed to make a bonfire to burn it properly, which people might notice. And this was all personal stuff of Harold's which I dared not keep in the cellar like the backpack and the wallet, which had no name or initials or anything on them and could have been Bill's or mine. So I remembered that room eight had been Harold's and since Greenwood seemed to be dead too, I thought it would be an idea to put all their stuff together. If the police or anyone ever noticed the difference between Harold's clothes and Greenwood's, they'd simply think Harold had left some things in the room when he checked out.'

'But the room had been cleaned after he left, hadn't it?'

'Yes, but sometimes cleaners don't clear away properly. And anyhow, it was the only way I could think of to get rid of the stuff safely. The important thing was it would be out of my hands, and Nasty's.'

So, I thought, that explains the DNA traces. Oh, poor misguided Jenny! But she wasn't so misguided in her statement to the police, I remembered.

'Jenny, what about that statement you made about seeing me at the murder scene that night, and how I'd tried to get off with you at the Cuckoo? That wasn't very nice, was it?'

'No, Mr Brook. It wasn't. In fact, it was evil. That's why I've been apologizing to you. I had to make that statement because Denis was keeping me in the picture and the body'd showed up by then and he said there was talk at the police station that it could belong to Mr Greenwood and if it did you could be in trouble. And he told me that the Jordans, an elderly couple who lived in our village, had heard gunshots coming from the wood that night and reported it, and he asked me if I hadn't heard them too because I lived right by the wood. So I said yes, come to think of it I did, but I'd thought they were firecrackers or something, and he said I should go into the police station in Penzance and tell them about it as soon as possible. Well, I did that and two plainclothes officers took a statement from me. They wanted to know if my husband had heard the shots too and I said he hadn't been at home at the time. Then they asked if I'd seen anyone, and I thought this was the chance to point the police away from me and—'

'And that's when you decided to put me right in the shit, Jenny? And to lay it on thick too, with that nonsense about me coming onto you at the Cuckoo.'

She hung her head. 'Yes. I'm so sorry about that. I really am. It was horrible of me.' She put her hand over mine. 'Can you possibly forgive me, Charles?'

I pulled my hand away. 'Forgive you? How can I? And don't you call me Charles! I don't like you very much at this moment, Jenny Cooper. Maybe your Mr Nasty was right when he called you names. I feel like doing that myself now. Didn't you realize you could be putting me away for the rest of my life, or most of it?'

She didn't answer, and I sat there, trying to quell my anger. This self-centred, thoughtless little vixen had seen fit to frame me for murder and all she could do now was apologize. It was outrageous. It had, admittedly, required other ingredients to produce the stew I was in – among them my own stupid determination to make a stage show out of Geoffrey's disappearance, the unfortunate timing of that show, and Eleanor's vindictiveness – but Jenny's exploitation of me had been deplorable. And I doubted the sincerity of her apology and protestations, since she still clearly had an agenda of her own, concerning which I was now to hear more.

She'd started crying into the sleeve of her blouse. 'I am truly sorry, Mr Brook,' she sobbed. 'But it's not only about that. I'm crying because something terrible's happened to me. It's awful and I don't know how to tell you about it, but I have to. I must. You see, it was two nights ago. . . .'

52

She had awoken from a deep sleep to the sound of Nasty's voice and the glare of the overhead light.

Blinking, she made him out, standing over the bed. Oh, how she despised him! And there was someone with him. Someone much bigger, dwarfing him. An immense, grotesque stranger, with a crop of ginger hair and a bloated, ruddy, boyish face, who was staring wide-eyed at her.

Nasty pulled the bedclothes off her, exposing her naked body. She moved to retrieve them, but the stranger reached out and snatched them away.

'Nice, hey, Bobby boy? What did I tell you?' said Nasty. Then to her, 'Now, whore, I know how much you like company in your bed, so I've brought someone to try out your wares.' He turned to the stranger. 'OK, Bobby, she's all yours.'

A deep chill of terror and revulsion gripped her and she scrambled to get up, but both men moved quickly, pinning her to the bed, Nasty holding her down at the ankles and the one called Bobby depressing her upper chest with his forearm. Screaming, she punched wildly at his broad neck and shoulders, but his massive frame was suddenly on top of her and the awful stench of his breath in her face. She turned her head to escape it, then had to gasp and gulp for air as her chest was crushed beneath his great weight. She felt her knees being prised apart by his powerful limbs, and a vile, hot, gigantic thing began probing the space between her legs. Then there was nothing but the searing pain of his forced entry into her resistant dryness and the agony of his accelerating thrusts as he bored into her and ripped her apart.

Grunting, Bobby raced to a climax, gave a shrill bark, and slid off her with a low growl.

She choked and coughed as she sucked the air back into her lungs, then lay motionless, breathing deeply and trying to muster the will and energy to get up. But her respite was short-lived.

'Hold her down for me, Bobby,' she heard Nasty say. And now it was he who was on top of her, pushing himself into her where the pain was worst, lustfully, as if her body were new to him and the spoils of Bobby's rough cruelty his to take.

Too weak to move, she'd have let him have his way even without Bobby's restraints, and when he'd finished and got off her, she turned onto her side and lay there curled up, battered and sobbing. Then she heard his hateful voice again. 'Right, filthy bitch of a whore, now justice is done, I want you to piss off once and for all. Me and Bobby are leaving now, but I'll be back in the morning. Make sure you get yourself and your things out of here before then. And only *your* things. Leave the car and all your keys behind, and never come back again, ever.'

She didn't turn around or look up, but listened numbly to the sounds of their departure, and after they'd gone she sobbed aloud, shuddered a few times, and then, shivering, pulled the covers up over her head.

She struggled to tell the story, stumbling over her words and lapsing into tears again at the end of it, but she told it vividly and in detail, as if it was important to her that I know all about it – but more probably, I thought, because that was the way it was stuck in her memory. When she'd finished, she looked at me with wet eyes so pathetically that I couldn't help putting my arm around her and letting her rest her head on my shoulder. She'd done an awful thing to me, but something abominable had been done to her.

'Why didn't you go to the police?' I said. 'What about your friend the constable?'

She gave me the typically pitiable answer of the rape victim. 'I was too ashamed. And even if I did go to the police, you know how these things work – the woman always gets the blame and the men get off. Nasty would say I'm a whore and that I sleep around, and that I seduced Bobby. I found out afterwards that Bobby's retarded – he's a huge man, but he's got the brain of a small child.'

'Who told you that?'

'The nursing sister who tended me afterwards.'

'At the hospital?'

'No. After they'd gone – Nasty and his big fat pig of a friend – I struggled out of bed, put on a coat and shoes, and dragged myself to the phone booth up the road – there's no phone in the cottage because Nasty's got a mobile – and I rang my friend Marjorie, the one who sent you here, and she came around with a nursing sister she knows well, name of Ruth, in the nurse's car. Ruth brought bandages and medical stuff and she examined me and tended me where it hurt and cleaned me up and gave me pills for the pain. Then they both helped me pack up my things and took me round to Marjorie's. That's where I've been staying since. Ruth kept saying I should go to the hospital, but I refused. I was scared they'd take a statement from me or call the police. Then Ruth told me about Bobby – they knew him at the hospital – and said she'd see he was dealt with, confidentially, by the people responsible for him. He's in some sort of home most of the time, though they do let him out. She also asked me if I was on the pill and was relieved when I told her I couldn't fall pregnant – there's something wrong with my tubes – and she said I shouldn't worry about catching anything from Bobby because this was probably the only time he'd ever had sex. Nasty had put him up to it. Anyway, Ruth and Marjorie swore to me they wouldn't tell a soul about what had happened, other than Ruth reporting the matter to Bobby's carers without giving away my name.'

'What did Bill mean when he said he'd warned you before to get out?'

'He had. You see, at first, after he'd killed Harold, he went along with what I'd said about sticking together, but afterwards he got all cocky and sure that nobody would ever find out what had happened. And we kept arguing whenever he was around. Then one day he said he was going up-country again and that he was sick and tired of keeping a whore in his house, and that I must take my things and piss off before he got back, or else there'd be big trouble when he did. I didn't take him seriously because he was always bullying and threatening me. I intended leaving him and finding out about a divorce, but I wanted this thing with Harold put behind us first.'

'So this awful rape happened when you'd been alone in the cottage and he'd just got back from his latest trip?'

'Yes. That was the way he showed up – with this horrible Bobby creature. I've no idea where he got hold of him, but he must have promised him goodies and then told him he'd let him fuck me because I was his wife and I belonged to him or something like that. It's not difficult to work out. And in his nasty, twisted way, he clearly enjoyed the whole thing even more than Bobby did.' She paused. 'Well, that's enough about them. Regarding the police, I did speak to Denis, that's how I heard you were coming down and where you'd be staying, but I didn't tell him about the rape. I just couldn't. And I knew he'd make me report it, and the last thing I wanted was the police getting involved and finding out about Harold. But I'm determined to make Nasty suffer and I think maybe I can, with your help, but I'm not sure how. I despise him more now than ever before and I want him locked up forever. I hate Bobby too and I'll never forget what he did to me, but as Ruth said, Nasty put him up to it – he didn't have a mind of his own.'

'What is it that you want, Jenny?'

'I want Nasty to sit for life for murdering Harold – I mean John Richardson – but I don't want to have to say what actually happened. For two reasons. One, I don't want to be . . . what's the word?'

'Implicated?'

'Yes, implicated. And two, I also don't want to have to admit I had a man in my bed. As it is, people around here talk about me, but they can't prove anything. If I go to the police or to court and I have to say how Harold came to be in my bedroom naked and tell the truth about how he got there, it'll become public and everyone will call me a whore, not just Nasty. And the police won't understand, neither will a judge or jury, and they'll all have sympathy for my fucking husband and he'll get off. . . .'

'No, he wouldn't get off, Jenny. Men can't kill their wives' lovers in this country and get off scot-free, but he might get a lighter sentence. You want to put him away for life, and that's what he deserves, as much for what he did to you as for shooting Harold, but I understand your feelings and your fears. . . .'

She sat up and touched my hand. 'Wait, there's one thing I haven't told you. The gun, the one Bill shot Harold with. He's still got it. I saw it in the cottage the other day, with the revolver. It's still there, in his drawer that locks. He doesn't always lock it, and he hadn't, so I looked.'

'It needn't be that one. He might have got another one like it.'

'How? You know it's against the law.'

'Maybe where he got the first one.'

She shook her head. 'No. The more I think about it, it would be just like Nasty not to ditch that gun in the sea. Illegal handguns aren't easy to get hold of and he's mean as mustard. He was pretty sure he wasn't going to get caught, 'specially after you were charged.'

'Well, that could be helpful. Now, tell me, Jenny, what did you find out about Harold Tyler-alias-John Richardson when you were with him?'

'Not much. He said he was divorced and had no kids, that's all, but he was probably lying, like with his name and him being from New Zealand.'

'Did you notice an address in the passport or anything to say where it was issued?'

'No, I didn't.'

Well, so that's it, I thought. Jenny had filled in all the gaps, other than a few that only Eleanor could plug, but I had a pretty shrewd idea of the latter's contribution to the unwitting collaboration that had led to my arrest. Eleanor and Jenny had managed between them to nail me to a cross without ever having communicated with or even known each other. And although what Jenny had told me would provide a lot of ammunition with which to fight my cause, most of it wouldn't be available to me as evidence unless she actually testified for me, which she could hardly do without divulging the very things she was so determined not to reveal. At least I now knew the name of the dead man, but what I really needed was a means of making the best possible use of everything I'd just learned.

'How do you think I can help you, Jenny?'

'Well, you are a lawyer. And you're in trouble right now, as far as I know. And I think, if we can work together, we must be able to help each other. Greenwood's disappearance has got all mixed up with Harold's murder and maybe there's a way of separating them so you can get off and the truth can come out about who Harold was and how he died. To me it's like we have to make something up together.'

I was paying careful attention to what she was saying. Although she sounded confused, she was actually making good sense. What she was telling me was that she wanted her husband convicted of her lover's murder, that she was prepared to lie – again – to get that result, that she thought I could advise her how to do so, and that she was willing to act in any way that would help me too.

'Jenny,' I said, 'do you mind if I step outside for a while and do some quiet thinking?'

'No, of course not. I'd like to get out of the car myself and have a stretch.'

It was chilly outside but I was wearing a warm anorak. I moved off about twenty paces from the car, then squatted under a clump of trees, my mind churning. Ten minutes later, I was back in the car. By then Jenny had resumed her seat too.

'Jenny,' I said, 'that Jordan couple you told me about. Did the police confirm they'd actually made a statement about hearing shots that night?'

'No, they didn't - I mean the Jordans. They went to the police but no statement was taken from them. That's what the officers who took my statement told me. The Jordans had been the whole reason why I'd gone in to make a statement, but when I'd made it, I mentioned the Jordans and the officers told me they'd sent the Jordans away because they were both so hard of hearing they couldn't hear any of the questions put to them, so the police tested them with various sounds and decided no court would believe they'd actually heard anything that night, even gunfire. It seems they were also very confused about the time, and even the date. Mrs Jordan thought she'd heard the shots during the daytime. The officers thanked me for coming and making my statement and said my evidence would be important and I'd make a good witness.'

'That's all very good, Jenny, because now I think we can do something together, possibly.' I stared straight into her eyes and took her hand. 'Tell me, Jenny, are you sure – quite, quite sure – that you're not mistaken about who was killed by Bill, and about when it happened?'

53

It was after midnight when I eventually dropped Jenny off near The Cuckoo's Nest. We'd been together for over six hours and our discourse had turned out to be the most positive and constructive thing that had happened to me since my arrest. By the end of it, we'd become firm allies in the same cause.

Peter Cartwright was late the next morning, having been delayed by an accident on the road from Bodmin, so it was after 10.30 when our meeting got under way. While waiting for him, I wondered how Jenny was getting on at the police station, the plan having been for her to get there as early as possible. Despite having had hardly any sleep, I was feeling alert and full of energy. I now had both a purpose and a direction in which to pursue it.

'Well, Charles,' said Peter, 'have you thought about your defence?'

'Yes, I have, Peter. I didn't kill Geoffrey Greenwood and everything I told the police is true.'

'Are you saying Greenwood was still alive that morning?'

'He most certainly was.'

'Then you're still saying he wasn't shot and that's not his body?'

'Well, I'm not so sure about that any more. You see, Peter, I've been thinking. I was convinced he'd drowned. But you know, we all make assumptions, especially about what must have happened after we'd last seen something. We assume the natural order of events has taken place. Someone who was last seen swimming in the sea doesn't normally die of a bullet wound, so we dismiss that possibility. In my case, it was much more feasible that Eleanor was lying and the DNA and fingerprint evidence were wrong. But since then, I've realized it was my assumptions that may have been wrong. Peter, I must see that body, as soon as possible.'

Peter looked thoughtful. 'I'm sure that can be arranged. What you're saying now is, if the body's not Greenwood's, then we must pursue the identity issue, but if it is, then we need to reconsider everything.'

'Yes, that's more or less right.'

'But have you got any ideas about how we find out what happened to him? Remember, Charles, the coastguard carried out a full-scale search for the chap on land and at sea, with helicopters and boats, and *they* found nothing. Which is why the CPS have concluded you killed him. Well, they also claim they can prove he was killed the night before, in which case your story can't be true.'

'Exactly what evidence have they got for that, Peter?'

'Well, they haven't given me everything yet, but it sounds to me they're relying on that Jenny Cooper. As your partner Jonathan pointed out, time of death of a body that's been in the sea is tricky. I suppose they'll lead medical evidence to prove a time window within which the fellow could have been killed – probably days – then call Jenny to pinpoint the time and place, and to say she saw you there.'

'So, they'll be relying on Jenny's testimony to prove the guy died that night? In other words, without Jenny they couldn't say my story was false?'

'Yes. But Jenny is going to pinpoint the time, and if she stands up to cross-examination they're OK on that. But even if she doesn't testify or she's disbelieved, you're going to have a problem, Charles, because you were the last person to see Greenwood alive and your version of what happened to him isn't consistent with a death by shooting, as you yourself have just said. Your only salvation would be to prove what actually happened to him, or at least produce sufficient evidence of some kind to raise a reasonable doubt in your favour. And you can't do that. Which takes us back to square one.'

There was a knock on the door and a young woman opened it. 'Mr Cartwright,' she said, 'there's an urgent call for you from a Mr Neville Dodds of the Crown Prosecution Service. Do you want to take it?'

'Very well. Put him through here, will you?' Peter turned to me. 'This might have something to do with your case, Charles. Dodds is the chap who's working on it for the CPS here in Penzance.'

When the phone rang, he said, 'How are you, Neville?' then listened for several minutes, in silence except for the occasional 'Yes'. 'Very well, I'll come over there right away.'

He smiled broadly at me as he put the phone down. 'Charles, there's been a development. Jenny's changed her story and they want to tell me about it.'

54

Peter having promised to call me as soon as he'd finished with Dodds, I went back to my hotel room. I hadn't expected things to move so fast, but Jenny's spontaneous change of evidence must have made a huge impact on the prosecution if they wanted to talk to my solicitor so soon. Of course, it wasn't as much her statement as ours – hers and mine – with most of the creative stuff coming from me.

I'd realized while sitting in the car with her that the way to avoid being convicted of the murder of Geoffrey Greenwood was to incriminate somebody else – and who better than her husband, 'Nasty' Bill Cooper, the person actually responsible for the corpse identified as Geoffrey's. Just as a vengeful Eleanor and a confused Jenny had between them succeeded in turning John Richardson's body and his death into those of Geoffrey, so might I, with the aid of a now vengeful and contrite Jenny – turn Richardson's killer into Geoffrey's. The fact that Nasty Bill didn't know whom he'd killed would also help.

When I'd told Jenny what I had in mind, she'd embraced the idea enthusiastically, and we'd spent the next few hours working out her story, then going through it together several times and ironing out the details, after which she'd rehearsed it with my assistance, three or four times, until we were both as satisfied as we could be with what she'd be saying and how she would tell it.

Of course, had I been able to find out all about John Richardson and then prove it was his body, I'd not have needed any such plan, but that was a long shot with every prospect of failure, and it would have taken time. I had no idea where in Australia he came from, and John Richardson might not have been his real name at all – he seemed like the kind of person who could easily have been carrying a forged passport. I had to strike while the iron was hot and Jenny still in her present frame of mind.

Peter rang me at the hotel just after 2.30. 'Charles? Stay where you are. I'm coming over right away.'

Four minutes later I opened the door to his grinning face. 'Boy, have I got news for you!' he declared as he entered the room. He opened his briefcase and took out a folder. 'I want you to read something, Charles, in a few minutes. First, to fill you in, I met Dodds with the chief super. Dodds told me that Jenny Cooper had shown up at the police station early this morning saying she wanted to change her statement. He and Harrison interviewed her and took a new statement from her. Within fifteen minutes after they'd finished, the CPS had made three decisions. One, Jenny was to be taken to a safe haven and given police protection. Two, the murder investigation was to be reopened. And three, you and I were to be put in the picture immediately, hence Dodds's phone call to me.'

'Why? I mean why should they have to put us in the picture?'

'Well, if Jenny's story is corroborated by forensic and other evidence, you're off the hook, sir. In which case they'll need you as a prosecution witness. And besides, they have to tell you they're reopening the murder investigation.'

'Oh, this is marvellous, Peter.'

'Yes, isn't it? And there's more. Detectives and forensic people were sent to the site even before the interview with Jenny was finished. And when it was, Harrison took her off there so she could show them where and how everything happened. They're all over the place there now. . . .'

'Where is this site, Peter?'

'Where Jenny previously said she'd seen you. Porthderick. It's where she lived until a few days ago. In a cottage with her husband. The shooting took place in a copse behind the cottage. But wait. While I'm sitting there with Dodds and Chief Superintendent Hague, Harrison phones in and tells the super they've found a pistol in the cottage which they think may be the murder weapon.'

It was all falling into place beautifully. Surely my nightmare was ending now. Jenny had been right: Nasty Bill had been too mean to dump the gun. 'So they told you what Jenny said in her new statement?' I asked Peter.

'They did better than that.' Peter reached into his briefcase for a file. 'I give you' – he paused for dramatic effect – 'a copy of Jenny Cooper's brand-new statement.' He handed me a document of several pages.

'How come they gave you this? We're not entitled to it yet, are we?'

'No, but we will be. So I just asked for it, and got it.'

'Have you read it?'

'I've had a dash through it, but I want to read it properly right now and I suggest you do the same. Shall we?'

I nodded and started reading.

55

The words were clearly not Jenny's own, but those of Dodds or Harrison – probably the former – based on what she told them.

After the opening formalities, the statement went on:

This statement consisting of six pages, signed by me, is true to the best of my knowledge and belief and I make it knowing that, if it is tendered in evidence, I shall be liable to prosecution if I have wilfully stated in it anything which I know to be false or do not believe to be true.

I am employed by the hotel establishment known as The Cuckoo's Nest in Porthcurran, Cornwall, and until three days ago, 25th October, I resided at Cottage Number 3, Fisher's Walk, Porthderick, Cornwall, with my husband, William George Cooper ('Bill'). On the 5th October of this year I made and signed a statement as to what I had heard and seen outside my home on the night of the 10th to 11th September. That statement ('my first statement') was untrue. I made it under circumstances to be described in this statement and I now retract it. The statement which I now make sets out the truth as I know and believe it to be and as I would have told it but for the aforesaid circumstances.

Bill was employed as a driver and spent a lot of time away from home up-country. He would often stay away for a week or more and sometimes for several weeks at a time. He had come home following one such trip on the night of the 10th to 11th of September, then gone out again early the next morning. At about half past eleven that morning, the 11th, I was busy in the kitchen when I heard the noise of helicopters flying around. I went outside and walked down to the cove in front of the cottage. A helicopter which had been hovering above the cliffs to my right moved away and disappeared. It was a warm day and I walked onto the small beach at the bottom of the cove. Suddenly, I noticed a human body lying in the shallows a few yards away from me. I got a fright because I thought it was a corpse, then I saw the person move, as if trying to stand up but not being able to do so. I went nearer and saw it was a naked man. There was slime all over his body and he was shivering and shaking with cold. Realizing he needed help I approached him and helped him to his feet. His body and limbs were slippery, but I managed to get him to lean against me and put his arm around my neck, and slowly, step by step, I helped him limp with me up the cove and into the cottage. As we proceeded, I kept looking up to the sky for the helicopters, because I thought they could be searching for him and I wanted to attract their attention, but they were out of sight now. There was nobody else about.

Once in the cottage, I helped the man into the bathroom, where I sat him down on the closed toilet seat and ran a hot bath for him. I gave him water to drink from the mug we kept in the bathroom. He drank two mugfuls and seemed to gain strength. Then I helped him into the bath and showed him a towel he should use. He kept his hand over his privates and I told him not to be embarrassed, that I wasn't offended by his nakedness. He kept saying, 'Thank you. Thank you,' then sitting in the bath he said, 'I drowned, you know. I went for a swim and I drowned.' I said, 'Nonsense. You didn't drown. You're still alive.' I asked him if he was hurt, and he said yes, he was sore all over, and I noticed there were bruises on his body. The water quickly became filthy, so I let it run out and then ran a fresh lot of water while he sat in the bath.

Then I told him I had to go up the road to the phone booth to ring for help. There is no phone in the cottage. I asked him if he'd be all right and said he could get out of the bath whenever he wanted and go into the bedroom and lie down on the bed until I got back, that I wouldn't be long and was sure they'd send an ambulance for him right away.

My clothes were filthy with the slime from his body and I wanted to change into clean ones, but I thought it was more urgent to go and call 999. So I left the cottage by the back door and walked out through the side gate. I'd only gone a few steps up the road when I heard someone shouting loudly inside the cottage. It was a man's voice. Then I realized it was my husband Bill, who must have come in through the front porch and found the stranger in the house. I turned around and dashed back. As I got to the back door, the stranger came outside from the kitchen, limping and hopping and looking strained and desperate. Then Bill almost ran straight into me and nearly knocked me over. He had a gun in his hand and was screaming and swearing at the stranger. Bill pushed me out of the way, but my presence had delayed him for a few seconds and the stranger was already in the copse behind the cottage. I shouted at Bill, trying to explain what had happened, but the helicopter noise had started again and he didn't hear me. The chopper making the noise was nearby, but not right over us, though the people in it would probably not have been able to see what was going on in the copse even though it was overhead, because of the density of the treetops. Then I watched with horror as Bill raised the pistol and took aim. He fired a shot, then another ten or fifteen seconds later. The shots were barely audible above the noise. I saw the stranger lurch forward onto a tree-trunk and roll over to the ground. I dashed past Bill and ran to where the stranger was lying. Blood was coming from his mouth and body and he was lying perfectly still. I bent down and felt his neck for a pulse, but there was none. Then I put my face down near his mouth. He wasn't breathing. Bill had killed him.

I turned around to find Bill standing over me, pointing the pistol at me. The noise of the helicopter was receding. He started shouting and swearing at me, wanting to know who my 'fucker' was. I shouted back that he was not my 'fucker' but a man who was drowning and had come ashore. After a while, he began paying attention to what I was saying and started to look worried. He then said something like, 'Oh hell, that must be the man they're looking for. They were talking about it in Penzance.' Then he asked me to tell him exactly what had happened, and I did so. 'Where the hell were you when I came in?' he said. I explained that too and told him I would hardly have sex with a man in our home, especially when he might walk in at any moment. He stood there thinking, still with the gun in his hand, then he said he'd have to kill me, because I was the only witness to what had happened, but I could save my skin if I helped him dispose of the body. If I did, then we'd be in it together, otherwise he'd have to kill me to stop me going to the police. Having seen how cold-blood-edly he had killed the stranger, I knew he was capable of doing the same to me. I had been afraid of him for years, but now even more so. He had always bullied me and never really loved me. I had been wanting to leave him for a long time, but was scared he would come after me. He treated me as if I belonged to him, like one of his possessions. And it was true I was the only witness to the shooting. So I decided not to try and argue with him but just do as he said.

There was a ditch near the body, so we rolled the body into it and covered it over with sand and leaves and sticks and stones. Bill did not let me out of his sight for a moment, and he kept the gun in his hand or pocket all the time. He made me sit with him in the copse until well after nightfall, keeping a watch on the body – though we did go back together briefly once, to fetch food and water from the kitchen. While we were there, we heard the noises of helicopters and boats continuing the search. Choppers flew overhead several times, but they moved on. After dark there were searchlights in the distance, but not in our direction. Eventually, when there was no more noise and no more lights, Bill and I put the body into a wheelbarrow and then into the Bill's boat, which he kept at the top of the cove. Bill then took the boat out and dumped the body in the sea.

When he came back, he told me that I didn't need watching any more because I was right in it with him now. He meant I was implicated in his crime and I believed it, but he said that anyway we'd both be safe with the body back in the sea as nobody would have any idea that Greenwood had ever come ashore.

When we had first gone back into the kitchen, there had been broken glass and blood all over the floor. Bill told me the stranger had knocked a bottle off the table and trod on it, cutting his foot. Before going to bed that night, I washed the kitchen floor, cleared away the broken glass, cleaned up the bathroom, and washed the towel Greenwood had used. The search had been resumed, so Bill and I agreed not to do any cleaning up outside yet. Bill said he would look for the cartridges from his gun later, after they had given up the search.

A couple of days later he went off on another trip. While he was away I heard at work that a dead body had been washed up somewhere nearby and that the person had been shot. I knew it must be Greenwood. Bill returned on Monday the 5th October and asked me if I knew a lawyer called Charles Brook who had stayed at The Cuckoo's Nest. When I answered yes I did, he asked if I would recognize the man if I saw him and I said yes again. Then he said I could do us both a big favour, that he had it on good authority that the police suspected Charles Brook of shooting Greenwood on the night before he was supposed to have disappeared in the sea, and we could 'nail him' and make sure he got convicted. If I didn't do as he said, he would kill me. He didn't need me any more, and he was sick and tired of me anyway. He told me that if I wanted to stay alive I must go to the police station in Penzance and make a statement about that night. I was to say that I had been alone at home that night and had woken up to the sound of gunshots coming from the direction of the cove and had then looked out of the window and seen Charles Brook outside leaving the cove. I was to mention that I recognized Brook because he had once tried to get off with me while staying at The Cuckoo's Nest. (It was true that I knew Mr Brook had stayed at The Cuckoo's Nest, but it was untrue that I had seen him that night and that he had ever flirted with me.) I told Bill I was unhappy about making a false statement like that to the police, but he said, 'Very well. Then you die,' and went to get a gun. He'd had two of them – a pistol and a revolver – and I noticed it was a pistol, just like the one he had shot Greenwood with, which surprised me because he had told me he had dumped his pistol in the sea with Greenwood's body. But I was not altogether surprised because he was mean and valued his guns, which were illegal as far as I knew. It occurred to me that if he did kill me he would not have anybody to help him get rid of my body, but I was not prepared to gamble my life on that, so I reluctantly agreed to do as he said and we went through the statement I was to make and rehearsed it several times. The result was my first statement, which I repeat was untrue and have now retracted.

Some time after making that statement I heard of the arrest of Mr Charles Brook for the murder of Mr Greenwood. I started feeling bad about what I had done and the way I had lied about Mr Brook. I kept thinking about it and getting increasingly upset with myself. Meanwhile, Bill continued to berate me and three days ago, on Sunday the 25th October, he came home and beat me up very badly. I decided then and there that I had had enough and that I should leave him and go to the police, ask them for protection, and tell them everything. So I packed my things, left the cottage, and moved in with a friend.

I have hence made this further statement and been given police protection. It is my intention to divorce my husband.

Jenny had done well – exceedingly well.

56

Peter and I discussed Jenny's statement. We agreed that if it was true there ought to be plenty of evidence to corroborate it.

Despite all her diligent washing and cleaning, the dead man's DNA would probably be found on the kitchen floor and possibly in the barrow and the boat. His fingerprints could still be in the cottage too. From what Peter had already learned, the fatal bullet had lodged in the deceased's chest and the pistol found in the cottage was of the same calibre. Whether it was the actual weapon would depend on the ballistics. Additional ballistic evidence could also come from the cartridges that would probably be found in the wood – if Cooper hadn't already found and disposed of them.

'The point for me, Charles,' said Peter, 'is that even if Jenny's story is not corroborated, the prosecution won't find it easy to continue prosecuting you. Without her original evidence, there's nothing to disprove your story of Greenwood's disappearance. The eye-witness evidence Inspector Harrison was talking about when he questioned you – you remember, about people saying you were alone that morning – would be of no value on its own, especially because nobody can be really sure of having seen one person alone under those circumstances. At worst for you, there must now be a reasonable doubt of your guilt, because Jenny's story *may* be true. In other words, the corroboration is really required to convict Bill Cooper, not to discharge you. I think the CPS has no choice – they must drop your prosecution.'

I couldn't help agreeing with his analysis, which I liked very much. 'What do we do now, Peter?'

'Oh, I think we should both stick around till tomorrow and see what happens. If they don't come back to us by lunchtime, I'll go back to Bodmin. I don't want to waste too much of my time, and your money. But I'll be in constant touch with Dodds. As for you, you might as well do the same – go back to Brighton, I mean – but don't decide that just yet.'

He then invited me to join him for dinner in Mousehole that evening. I accepted and enjoyed the occasion, particularly because it seemed to mark my imminent readmission to normal society. Nobody in the restaurant appeared to know who I was or care that I was there.

During the afternoon I'd rung Marion and Jonathan to bring them up to date. All I told Marion was that a material witness had changed her evidence as a result of which there was now every chance of the indictment being withdrawn. She said she was delighted to hear the good news and would be holding thumbs. To Jonathan I said much the same, but identified the witness and told him I didn't want to say any more on the phone. He responded enthusiastically and said he was looking forward to hearing more. He also asked if there was anything he could do to help the process, to which I replied, 'Thanks, Jon, but not at the moment.'

I called Marion again from the hotel before going to bed and we had a long chat, about almost everything other than the case, and she told me how much happier and more relaxed I sounded. After putting the light out, I lay awake for a long time, on edge, vacillating between excited anticipation and an inexplicable sense of anxiety. Jenny's statement had been perfect; she had left nothing out and had not slipped up on any of the detail. Of course, most of it had been true. The exceptions had been the identity of the victim and the time he was killed, both vital to my cause. And yes, she'd also succeeded in avoiding having to confess to the circumstances in which Bill had actually found her and to the fact that she'd acted of her own accord both in helping him cover up the crime and in making that atrocious first statement of hers.

57

Peter rang me at the hotel just after 11.30 the next morning and in an excited voice said, 'It's marvellous news, Charles. They're discontinuing the prosecution. How about that?'

A great wave of relief came over me.

'The formalities will take a few days,' Peter went on. 'Meanwhile, you're still on bail and must continue to report.'

'Thank you for all your good work, Peter. Can I go home now?'

'Yes, of course, but first meet me for a snack in the hotel bar in fifteen minutes. There's more to tell.'

I used the time to phone Marion and Jonathan again. Marion was overjoyed and urged me to come home quickly so we could celebrate. Jonathan was out of the office, so I left him a message saying there was great news and I was coming home.

Over beers and sandwiches in the hotel bar, Peter told me that he'd just seen Dodds again. 'First,' he said, 'the police have found two guns in the cottage – a semi-automatic pistol and a revolver. The pistol's the one that interests them, of course. There was a bullet in the barrel and a magazine inside the gun with three bullets missing from it, indicating that two shots had been fired since the gun had been loaded. The only fingerprints found on the gun were those of Bill Cooper. They're waiting for the ballistics report, but they're pretty confident this is the weapon that killed Greenwood. All possible doubts will be removed if the markings on the bullet found in the body match those in the barrel.'

Peter paused. 'So much for the weapon. Now, the dead man's fingerprints have been found inside the cottage, and DNA testing is being done on samples taken from various places, including the kitchen, the barrow, and the boat. Bill Cooper was arrested yesterday and is still being questioned. He's doing badly, according to Dodds. They're definitely going to charge him. How's that?'

'Tremendous,' I said, 'and thank you again, Peter, for everything you've done. You've been great.'

I drove home that afternoon filled with relief, joy, and incredulity. I couldn't believe that the English legal system had actually conferred on the imaginary Geoffrey Greenwood the status of a real human being and would probably be incarcerating a real human being for killing him. I had no qualms about the injustice of it, because after what Nasty Bill Cooper had done to his wife, he deserved no better. Besides, it had been a matter of him or me.

The next day Peter phoned me at home to say that the ballistics report had confirmed that the bullet found in the corpse had been fired from Cooper's pistol; two cartridges found in the wood had also been tested and proved to have come from the same weapon; and there were more than enough positive DNA matchings to bear out Jenny's story and confirm the identity of the victim.

I had resolved to let no one – not even Jonathan or Marion – into the secret of my collaboration with Jenny. It was much too dangerous to share. As it happened, I found Marion not only totally lacking in curiosity about what had brought about the dramatic change in my fortunes, but positively unwilling to discuss the subject. All she wanted to know was whether it was really all behind us, and I assured her it was, but for the need for me to testify for the prosecution in the trial of a man who'd actually murdered someone. I refrained from mentioning that the victim was mistakenly believed to have been Geoffrey Greenwood, sensing she wouldn't want to know that. Her ostrich-like attitude suggested that she would deliberately ignore the publicity and everything else she might hear or read about the case and might never, therefore, get to know about that anomaly – or, if she did, would cast it out of her mind. At worst, there'd always be time for an explanation when the issue arose. All that said, she was a very intelligent person and may well have guessed I'd had to lie – yet again – to get out of the mess my earlier lies had put me into, but if so she'd almost certainly have preferred not to hear it from me as a fact.

Jonathan, on the other hand, had been very inquisitive, but I pretended I didn't know what was in Jenny's statement other than that she'd incriminated her husband for killing a man whom everyone assumed was Greenwood.

'Astounding!' He smiled at me. 'You're an amazingly lucky chap, Charles Brook. Or did Jenny lie for you?'

I frowned. 'What are you suggesting? That she and I worked out her story together?'

'Of course not. You weren't in contact with her, and couldn't have been.'

'Just fortunate, I suppose, as you say. I certainly needed some luck, didn't I?'

Jonathan shook his head. 'Don't worry, Charles. I respect your need to keep your own secrets.'

He was no fool, my partner. Just a very good friend.

58

Raymond Downing, predictably, was livid when Claude Grant told him what had happened. He protested vociferously about the stupidity of the CPS and the Devon and Cornwall police, and claimed that I'd had managed to pull the wool over everyone's eyes. He asked Claude to ring Eleanor and break the news to her, saying he wasn't up to it himself.

Eleanor, it transpired, had a very different reaction. She thanked Claude for the information and sat back with an overwhelming sense of relief. By now, she so regretted what she'd done and was so concerned about her own situation that she had been hoping for something to happen – anything – that would get her out of it all. Her bitterness towards me had evaporated and, to her own surprise, she found herself missing me and longing to be back in my arms, in the bed in which she lay, being made love to. That, of course, she reminded herself, could never happen again. She felt cold, and very lonely.

John Richardson's body was released to her and she was informed that she could go ahead with the funeral arrangements. This she did by engaging a firm of undertakers to arrange a small, simple cremation service, which was not publicized and was attended only by her and the undertakers' people. She found the whole business difficult, distasteful, and disturbing, the last because she kept thinking about those unknown people somewhere – perhaps a wife, a lover, children, parents – who were missing the dead man and would never know what had happened to him or be able to mourn his death and attend his funeral. She felt as if she'd stolen him from his loved ones.

I received this letter from her:

Dear Charles

I want you to know that I thought of inviting you to Geoffrey's funeral, but couldn't. There were several reasons why I did not think it would be appropriate. You will realize what they were.

Secondly, I presume you are in charge of Geoffrey's affairs once again. That being so, you should know that I have decided to move out of the London flat.

I have also decided that I do not want anything at all from the Greenwood Trust and would like my name removed from the list of beneficiaries. Could you possibly see to that?

I look forward to hearing from you.

Yours sincerely
Eleanor

When I read the letter, I was impressed with Eleanor's ability to adhere to the script. The message that she didn't want any of the trust fund was welcome, not because it would have any direct financial implications – she couldn't have got anything out of the trust without my co-operation anyway – but because it meant there could never be any kind of interference from her or her father in the affairs of the trust.

Seeing that I'd just arranged to go and see Jeremy Lefarge in Guernsey, I decided I'd take Eleanor's letter with me so that her request could be complied with. I didn't intend rushing anything with the trust; I now had all the time in the world to put into effect one or more of several ideas I had about how to gain access to what was in it. In fact, I'd prepared a letter of wishes for that purpose before going to Cornwall to stage the disappearance; it was still in the file and bore Geoffrey's signature. Which reminded me: I must get the file back from Jonathan. I'd invite Marion to come along to Guernsey and we could spend a couple of pleasant days together there.

To my own surprise, I was disappointed that there had been nothing personal in Eleanor's letter. She could not, of course, have expressed remorse for what she'd done – certainly not in a letter, if she'd have wanted to at all – but just a hint of warmth would have been welcome. On the other hand, how could there possibly be any warmth at all between two people who had done so much damage to each other?

So I wrote back to her in the same vein, saying little more than was necessary to remind her that she should treat the contents of the London flat as hers and to assure her that her request to be excluded as a trust beneficiary would be passed on to the trustees.

59

Marion's response to the news that I was going to Guernsey was by no means enthusiastic. 'Oh, Teddy,' she said, 'I was hoping it wouldn't come to this – well, not at least until we'd talked the whole thing through. It's all too fresh still, for us both.'

'What do you mean?'

'You must know I've found it tremendously difficult coming to terms with everything you've told me—'

'You mean the untruthfulness, my – er – duplicity?'

'Yes, but not only that. My first priority was to stand by you during your ordeal, but I was hoping that somehow, when that was behind us, we'd see eye to eye about where we'd go from there.'

'And don't we?'

'Well, no. Not really. I was hoping not to have to explain any of this. It's not just your duplicity as you call it; it's this whole Greenwood business. Your affair with Lucy I understand, she and I were to blame for that, but this Eleanor person, you lived with her as man and wife. You shared a flat with her. She replaced me.'

'That's not true—'

'Oh, Charles, it's not an objective matter; it's how I feel about it. I can't help my feelings. What you had with her was much more than an affair. You must surely concede that.'

'Yes, it's true she meant more to me than Lucy, but she never meant anything like you do to me and have always done.'

'Always?'

'Well, it was tough going when you weren't yourself and had withdrawn from me. But I did still love you. And it was I who broke up with Eleanor, you know.'

'I thought Lucy broke it up.'

'Yes, but I was about to myself and—'

'Look, I really don't want to know the details of your relationship with this woman. What matters to me is that we're able to go forward together. I want everything to do with your Greenwood experience banished from our lives – blacked out, erased, deleted – as if the whole business never happened.'

'But that's so already. It's all behind us now. The imaginary Geoffrey is no longer, and I'm not being tried for his murder, so I've no need to lie or deceive anyone, least of all you. And Eleanor Downing is out of my life altogether.'

'But the Greenwood money's not.'

'Of course it's not. It's there for the taking. What do you expect me to do? Abandon it?'

'Yes, Charles. That's exactly what I'm suggesting.'

'What?' Was she being serious? 'Marion darling, this is fifteen million dollars. And it's not money I stole or anything.'

'I'm not sure I agree with that, but that's not the point. The point is that it's part of this fucking bloody Greenwood business of yours. Can't you understand that? For heaven's sake, Charles!'

She fell silent, and so did I. This was insane; I had to get her to see reason. Then, in as conciliatory and rational a tone as I could manage, I said, 'Please listen to me, my darling wife. There is nothing in my life more precious than you and the kids, and this money is there for us all, to give us a better life.'

She lowered her head and gritted her teeth. 'That – is – not – the – point.'

I sighed. 'Look, I have to go to Guernsey. If you don't want to come. . . .'

'Oh, I'll come, if it's to be there with you when you abandon the money. And when you've done that, however you do that kind of thing, I'll be delighted to have a holiday there with you.'

There was another silence, which I broke. 'Marion dear,' I said gently, 'I'm going to Guernsey, and it won't be to abandon the trust fund. If you're not coming, I'll just go for one day, as soon as possible. I must. What you ask of me is out of the question; in fact, it's madness. I implore you, Marion my love, while I'm away, think about all this. You're too sensible and intelligent to throw away a fortune. And when I come back, we'll talk again.'

She turned her head away tearfully and did not reply.

'Please, please, Marion. All I ask is that you think about it.'

For about two minutes she sat there and said nothing, then she whispered, barely audibly, 'Very well, Teddy dear, I will think about it, I promise you.'

'Good. Then let's leave it at that, shall we?'

I looked at her and she nodded once, slowly.

60

Jeremy Lefarge greeted me warmly. 'How are you, Charles? Good to see you again. So all the bother's behind you now, is it?' He poured us both coffee.

'Yes, I'm glad to say. They've got the real culprit now.'

'I believe so. Still, it must have been hell for you. Are you here on some new business then?'

'No, not at all. It's about the Greenwood Trust. I thought I'd come over personally for an update.'

'Well, it was all done, as you'll be aware – a while ago in fact. So it's just what you might call the dregs now. Hardly worth your making the trip here.'

'The dregs?'

'Well, the hundred thousand that's left.'

'Left where?'

'In the trust.'

Bewildered, and beginning to worry, I said, 'Not a good joke, Jeremy. I'm a bit too battered for that kind of thing, I'm afraid.'

Jeremy frowned at me across the table. 'You mean you don't know?'

'Know what?' I asked, suddenly growing cold. 'I've got no idea what you're talking about.'

'We transferred the whole of the trust fund except for a hundred thousand dollars to an account in Panama, on instructions.'

'Whose instructions?'

'Geoffrey Greenwood's, of course.'

61

I stared at Jeremy in disbelief. 'What do you mean?'

'Well, Greenwood had changed everything before he died. He'd signed a letter of wishes.' Jeremy took a document out of the folder in front of him and handed it to me. 'You'd better take a look at this.'

I recognized the document at once; it was a photocopy of the letter of wishes I'd drawn up and signed as Geoffrey before going to Cornwall to stage the disappearance. I'd left it in Geoffrey's file at the office, which I'd got back from Jonathan before leaving Brighton for the airport, but the letter had been missing when I'd looked through the file on the flight; however, its absence hadn't concerned me since there was a copy in the file and I'd simply assumed Jonathan had put the original away in the firm's safe-custody cabinet.

The letter was addressed to the trustees of The Greenwood Trust and requested them, in the event of Geoffrey's death or disappearance, to sell the Hall Computers stock, pay all the expenses of the trust, and transfer the entire balance of the trust fund, except for an amount of $100,000, to a company in Panama the name and particulars of which would be supplied by 'my solicitors, Messrs, Brook, Amery and Phillips'. The remaining $100,000 was to be dealt with in accordance with Geoffrey's original letter of wishes.

'Are you telling me that you received the original of this letter?' I asked Jeremy incredulously.

'Yes, I did. From your firm – your partner, Jonathan Amery, to be precise. He came here to give it to me.'

'He came here, to your offices?'

'Yes. When you were – er – having all that trouble, you know.' Jeremy produced another document from his folder. 'He gave it to me with the original of this letter from your firm.'

With growing astonishment and alarm, I read the copy Jeremy now handed me of a letter to Citadel Trustees, dated just about two weeks after I'd been released on bail. It read:

Dear Sirs
The Greenwood Trust
This letter will be delivered by the writer personally to your Mr Lefarge in St Peter Port together with a Letter of Wishes signed by Mr Geoffrey Robert Greenwood a short time before his death.

On the instructions of the late Mr Greenwood, we have to inform you that the company referred to in the Letter of Wishes is Greenwood Enterprises Inc, Edificio Juan Antonio, 59 West Street, Panama City, RDP, Panama.
Yours faithfully
Brook, Amery and Phillips

Jonathan had signed the letter on behalf of the firm.

Horrified, I said, 'You're not telling me you carried out what's in these two letters, Jeremy?'

'Of course we did. What else were we to do?'

'What else were you to do? Check. Verify. Consult me.'

'How could we check or verify anything, Charles? We'd never met Greenwood, remember, and the man was dead by the time we got his letter of wishes. It had been on your say-so that I broke my company's rule against accepting money for a new client I'd never met in person. You assured me it would be OK to do so. We accepted the money on

Greenwood's signature, and we acted on exactly the same authority when we paid it out. And we could hardly have consulted you, could we, seeing you were being prosecuted for the man's murder? We did get our instructions through your firm, you know, and we also had a personal visit from your partner. You talk as if we've done something terrible, Charles. Why is that?'

'What exactly did Jonathan tell you – that is, when he came over?'

'That he'd drawn up the letter of wishes on Greenwood's instructions. That Greenwood had signed it in Jonathan's office. That Greenwood had said he'd come to him because he'd lost faith in you – he claimed you'd been shagging his girlfriend behind his back. That he'd wanted to rearrange everything so that neither you nor she had anything to do with the trust fund in the event of his death. That Greenwood had a connection with this law firm in Panama City and would be setting up a company there, with them. That he'd had dealings with them before – in connection with South African currency controls. And that, although he'd had no problem about the trust fund remaining with us here in Guernsey while he was alive, he'd wanted it locked up there – far away from everyone, if he died.'

'Jonathan told you all this?'

'Yes.'

'Didn't you think to question any of it? How did you know the company wasn't a front for somebody else? It probably had bearer shares and anybody could have given it a name with 'Greenwood' in it, especially in Panama.'

'Such as who?'

'Well, Jonathan.'

Jeremy looked exasperated. 'Charles, Greenwood's letter of wishes said that the company would be named by your firm.'

'But surely you should still have checked it out?'

'Don't you think you should discuss this with your partner Jonathan?'

'I will be doing that, I assure you, Jeremy. But meanwhile please do me the courtesy of answering my question.'

Impatiently Jeremy said, 'Look here, Charles. I can understand your feelings about your client having sidelined you like this, but it was his money, you know, and we were his trustees. I'll recap for you. We took approximately fifteen million dollars in cash and shares into trust here on the signature of a man called Greenwood, vouched for by a reputable legal practitioner well known to us – yourself. The same Greenwood, with the same signature, then asks us, in case of his death, to pay it out to a company to be nominated by his solicitors – your firm. We can't discuss the matter with you because you're facing trial for the murder of your client. Your firm, through a partner not accused of the murder, identifies the company to which the money must be transferred on Greenwood's instructions. The declaration of trust expressly allows us to treat as a beneficiary any company designated by Greenwood. What's wrong with that?'

It was a question with only one possible answer: nothing. This exchange was pointless, I realized. 'I'm sorry, Jeremy, I got carried away. I didn't mean to criticize you. You're right. This is a matter I must discuss with Jonathan.'

'I should think so.'

'Just one more question, Jeremy. Did Jonathan tell you why Greenwood had wanted a hundred thousand dollars left in Guernsey?' When I'd drawn up the letter of wishes, I'd thought of leaving something in Guernsey for Eleanor, but hadn't mentioned her specifically because I wasn't certain yet exactly what financial arrangements I'd be making with her, and that had been the reason for the hundred thousand. It would be interesting to know how Jonathan had explained it.

'Yes. He told me that Greenwood had said he'd had an understanding with you about that, which he was happy to leave you to carry out.'

I wondered what that was supposed to mean. 'What about Eleanor Downing?' I asked Jeremy. 'Surely you should have got in touch with her, the only surviving named beneficiary?' I was clutching at straws; Eleanor was irrelevant; she was only a discretionary beneficiary and had no rights as such. And besides, I had her letter in my briefcase requesting that she be excluded as a beneficiary.

'Well, as I've said, Greenwood had specifically wanted the trust fund put out of her reach as well as yours. And remember, she's not entitled to anything as of right.'

Now there was a long silence, during which I tried – in vain – to think of some legal flaw in the situation.

'Well,' said Jeremy, 'if that's all, I must ask you to excuse me. I'm going away tomorrow and I have a lot to do. Oh, while you're here, Charles, what are we to do with the hundred thousand? That's for you to decide.'

'I'll let you know. Meanwhile, for what it's worth now, here's a letter from Eleanor Downing asking to be removed as a beneficiary.'

'Thanks, but as you say, there's not much point in that now, is there?'

62

All sorts of thoughts ran through my mind on the way home. Could Jonathan simply have decided to act in my interests, so that everything would be in place for me when my ordeal was over? But if so, why hadn't he told me yet? If it wasn't something like that, there could be only one explanation: Jonathan Amery, my friend and partner, had stolen my money – more than $15 million of it. It was unthinkable that he could be such a two-faced, treacherous bastard after all. But wouldn't that explain why he'd been so unselfishly helpful? The thought was chilling. Jonathan – and Barry, who must have been in it too – could have been doing a fifth-column act, expecting me to be convicted. That would certainly have cleared the way for them, though they seemed to have managed pretty well anyhow.

The flight landed at 4.30 and I rang Jonathan on my mobile from the airport. He was out but expected back, so I left a message to say I was on my way to the office and would like to see both Jonathan and Barry on an urgent matter as soon as I arrived.

They were both waiting for me in Jonathan's office and greeted me amicably. Without sitting down, I looked straight at Jonathan and said, 'I've just been to see Jeremy Lefarge, as you know. Please tell me what it's all about.'

Jonathan frowned. 'What's what about, Charles?'

'Surely you know what I mean, Jonathan. You moved fifteen million dollars out of the Greenwood Trust. Why?'

'But Charles,' a very cool Jonathan replied, 'I told you all about it. You couldn't have been paying attention.'

'Precisely what did you tell me, and when?'

'When you came back from Cornwall. I told you all about Green-wood's visit, and what he'd said about you and Eleanor, and the letter of wishes—'

A storm of rage rose up in me. 'You fucking liar!' I yelled, stretching across the desk and reaching for him. Barry tried to restrain me and, as he did so, I turned on him: 'And where are you in all this, Barry? Do you know anything about it?'

'He knows all about it,' said Jonathan. 'Charles, please take control of yourself. I'd hate to see you charged with assault, not after what you've been through. Can we discuss this sanely?'

I was shaking with fury, but I sat down because I didn't trust myself not to have another go at him physically. They've stolen my money, these two bastards, I thought, and they just sit there and lie blatantly about it.

'Charles,' Jonathan continued, 'I can't see why you're so angry. It wasn't your money, remember; it was Greenwood's.'

'Greenwood never existed and you both know it,' I snapped.

'Not that again, Charles,' said Jonathan. 'You tried that one before. It was going to be your defence once, remember, but you had to drop it because it was nonsense and couldn't be proved.' I couldn't believe that he was actually saying these things. 'When Barry and I hadn't yet met the fellow,' he continued, 'we might have believed anything, but he came here, Charles, as I've told you, and we met him in the flesh – both of us. And he told me things and gave me instructions, because he didn't trust you any more – not with fifteen million dollars anyway.'

'What utter crap! He had no flesh, and you know it – both of you. There never was such a person.'

Barry intervened. 'Oh, there certainly was, Charles. I can confirm that. As Jonathan has said, I met him too, and I took quite a liking to the chap.'

I felt like smashing my fist into Barry's lying face, but instead gripped the arms of my chair tightly. I glared at Jonathan. 'Where's the money now?'

'I don't know, Charles. I suppose the guys in Panama had instructions from Greenwood. My impression was that he had other irons in the fire – a girlfriend, or a wife, or someone else somewhere, perhaps even a few kids. He didn't take me into his confidence – nor apparently did you know everything there was to know about the fellow.'

'You've stolen it, you bastards!' I screamed at them. 'You've stolen over fifteen million dollars from me! I want it back, immediately, or I'll—'

'You'll what, Charles?'

It was a good question. What *could* I do? These slimy rats had it all worked out. They'd stolen all that money and there wasn't a thing I could do about it.

'You must please stop this now,' said Jonathan, 'or I'll have to ask you to leave my office.'

Then Barry spoke again. 'Charles, let's talk hypothetically for a moment, just for the sake of argument. Assuming you were right and there never was anyone called Geoffrey Greenwood, you're saying you'd claim that money as your own – all of it? But then you'd have made it while you were a partner of ours, using the firm's resources and facilities, not to mention the firm's time, since your time was the firm's when it came to using your skills as a lawyer. Not so?'

I considered what he was saying. It had never entered my mind that I might be exploiting the partnership in the way Barry was now suggesting. The whole Greenwood thing had emerged from my affair with Lucy and what could have been more personal than that?

Barry went on, 'So, if there had been no Greenwood, that money would have belonged to all three of us, not just to you.'

'And surely,' Jonathan added, 'had you made those gains yourself, you'd not have hidden them from the Revenue, would you?'

How much dirtier could they get, I wondered? I ignored the question. 'The firm was paid fees for my time and services – very handsome fees.'

'Oh, yes,' said Barry, 'it's true we all made handsome fees out of Greenwood, but none of us had any claim to the rest of his money, did we? Oh, except for the hundred thousand dollars he left in the trust – under your control, Charles. He asked us to see that you took that for yourself, for all your extra trouble on his behalf. Why don't you just help yourself to it? We have no objections, do we, Jon?'

'None at all,' declared Jonathan, with a hypocritical grin.

So, I thought, that was their way of justifying what they'd done: I ought to have shared the Greenwood money with them, but seeing I'd done them out of their shares of it, they'd helped themselves to the lot except for $100,000, which I could now have as a kind of sop. But wait, wasn't I missing the subtlety of it all? They were obviously just evading tax by moving the money to Panama and expecting me to realize that without spelling it out. My one-third share must be waiting for me there.

I asked them as much. 'I take it that my one-third share is in Panama?'

Jonathan gave me a tired smile. 'Charles, none of us will be getting anything from Panama. Barry's been talking hypothetically, as he told you. Geoffrey Greenwood did exist, as we all know, and the money's where he wanted it to be.'

63

The meeting broke up pretty quickly after that. I did lose my temper, inevitably, and struck out at Jonathan, missing him but injuring my hand on his desk, at which point Jonathan and Barry got up and walked out, leaving me alone. I sat down again, then got up and went to my own office, where I spent the next hour pacing up and down and shaking with rage, and racking my brain for ways of retrieving the situation and getting back at them. Eventually, in despair, I started rationalizing, trying to convince myself that the situation was, after all, no worse than it would have been had I done as Marion had wanted me to. But that was scant consolation, seeing that the loss of the money wasn't all I'd suffered; what was hurting just as much was my outrage at the abject treachery that had been practised against me and the knowledge that its perpetrators had almost certainly got away with it. Then, utterly dejected and still full of anger, I made my way home, determined never to let the matter rest.

When I walked into the house, Katka was there but Marion wasn't, nor were the children. Katka explained that Emma and Paulie were spending the night at their granny's and that Marion, who was there too, had left me a note in the hallway. I found an envelope there with 'Charles' written on it in Marion's handwriting, took it into the lounge, poured myself a Scotch, sat down on the sofa, and opened the envelope. What it contained was not a note but a fairly long letter from Marion.

Dear Charles,

I promised you I would think about the things we discussed on Sunday night and I've done almost nothing else since. I hope this won't hurt you too much, but I'm afraid our attempt to revive our marriage has failed and I just can't go on. We are both different people now and these two new people are incompatible.

It's not really about the Greenwood money. I've been heading towards this decision for some time now. I kept looking for things that would make it right, but they just weren't there. Had you been willing on Sunday to abandon the money, I'd have taken that as a sign of your commitment and a basis for a renewed commitment by me. But when you refused to do so I cried because I was sad, very sad, for us and for Emma and Paulie, but the new me was actually relieved. Even if you were to tell me now that you had abandoned the money, it would make no difference any more. The moment has passed and I've moved on a step.

Charles, please understand that I don't blame you for anything or think you are a bad person or that I'm a better one than you are. It's just that we see things differently and I cannot, as hard as I have tried, assimilate the whole Greenwood thing, and on reflection I was naïve to think we could simply block it all out. Maybe you can, but I certainly cannot.

I know you will want to talk to me about my decision and try to change it, but whilst I shall never refuse to talk to you, I urge you to accept that you won't get me to change my mind. What we shall need to talk about are all the horrible arrangements, like how we separate and get divorced, and above all the children. As far as they are concerned, I want us to continue sharing them and for there to be as little change as possible in their lives. Some change, I know, will be necessary, but it should be minimized. Knowing you as I do, I am sure you will want me to get my own legal advice. Perhaps you can recommend a solicitor.

For now though, all I ask is that you respect my decision.

If I am not mistaken, you will be reading this on your return from Guernsey tonight, Tuesday. You will know from Katka, who is off duty but at home, that I am at my mother's with the children. I'm sleeping here tonight, too. Please, Charles, I implore you, don't phone or try to see me tonight. It will be better for us both if you wait until tomorrow.

I will always love you, but I can't go on living with you.

Marion

I read the letter through again, and then a third time. Then I sat forward, put my head in my hands, and bellowed with pain.

Epilogue

It's remarkable how we adjust to misfortune. In my case, the double blow I received was something I'd never get over, and even as I write this, I still feel, every day, both the anguish of the loss of Marion and my wrath and bitterness towards my former partners. I've managed somehow to adjust to my huge financial loss – which was, in a sense, not as much a loss as a failure to reap the fortuitous rewards of my own deceptions.

By the time the case against Bill Cooper came to trial, I had joined the small, elite London firm of Storpin and Maze, whose offices faced Lincoln's Inn Fields, and was in the process of exchanging contracts to purchase the flat I was renting in the Barbican. The withdrawn murder charge against me had proved an obstacle to my placement with one or two other law firms, but the partners in Storpin and Maze were happy to disregard the matter once they'd seen my CV and checked out the facts of the case.

Marion had been unbending in her refusal to change her mind or even attempt another reconciliation and I'd eventually had to resign myself to the situation. We'd both been sensible and co-operative about the practical issues and had come to a fair and amicable settlement. We were to have joint custody of the children, who would live with Marion but spend as much time as possible with me. Since I'd be moving up to London, Marion and the children would stay in the house in Hove rent-free until both children had reached majority or left home, unless she and I agreed to sell it and replace it with another home on similar conditions. She would get a part-time job, but I'd supplement her income while she remained unattached. I undertook to provide generously – specific minimum amounts were set – for the maintenance and requirements of the children. It was all very satisfactory – except that for me it was an emotional disaster.

As for the other dissolution, I'd played as little part in it as possible, simply moving out of the offices as soon as I could and leaving the rest to be handled on my behalf by an accountant who specialized in such matters. In that situation too, my determination to undo what had been done proved futile.

I was now just beginning to emerge into the light again – and to think about Eleanor.

At his trial, Bill Cooper admitted killing Geoffrey Greenwood, but under extreme provocation. His defence was that he'd come home unexpectedly and found his wife in bed with a strange man, both of them naked, and that the man had then taunted and insulted him about his inability to satisfy his wife sexually, provoking him to fetch his gun and shoot the fellow dead after following him out of his home and into an adjoining copse. He claimed that the incident had not occurred on the day and at the time alleged by the prosecution, but on the preceding night. His wife, contrite and filled with guilt, had helped him dispose of the body, which he had dumped in the sea from his boat. He had not known the identity of the man he had killed, but conceded, on the strength of all the evidence, that he must have been Geoffrey Greenwood. Eleanor's identification of the body was not disputed. Cooper's counsel argued that the jury should bring in a verdict of manslaughter, not murder.

Apart from the medical and forensic evidence, Jenny and I were the main witnesses for the prosecution. I told the court about my morning excursion with Geoffrey and his disappearance after I'd last seen him swimming in the sea. I was cross-examined aggressively by defence counsel, but stood my ground. I wasn't present when Jenny testified, but Peter Cartwright, who was, told me she'd been shaken by some of the defence questioning but seemed to have impressed the jury as a truthful witness.

Cooper, on the other hand, fared very badly in the witness box. Leading counsel for the prosecution, Aubrey Welles QC, demolished his credibility with some shrewd, skilful cross-examination, playing up his illegal possession of two handguns and the inconsistency of his evidence with mine. What possible reason, Welles asked him, could I have had for concocting a story about a dead man being alive the next morning and then disappearing in the sea? When Cooper replied that he couldn't explain my conduct, Welles put it to him that it was he who had done the concocting, with a view to getting me convicted of a murder he'd already committed. And just as Peter Cartwright had predicted, the witnesses who swore to having seen me alone on the cliffs that morning – a helicopter pilot, his passenger, and a hiker who said he had observed me, unseen, from a vantage point on a higher cliff – admitted, under Welles's questioning, to the possibility of my having been accompanied by someone who was temporarily out of sight when they'd seen me.

The jury didn't take long to find Cooper guilty of murder as charged.

Sentencing him to life imprisonment, the judge said there were no mitigating circumstances. The jury having clearly accepted Jenny's version of events – a decision with which the judge fully agreed – the deceased was killed deliberately under circumstances that did not justify the taking of his life, whatever Cooper might have thought on finding a naked man in his home. He had given the deceased no chance to explain his presence there, but had resorted at once to the use of an illegally possessed handgun in order to threaten, pursue, and kill him in cold blood. His acts were those of a ruthless criminal, not an outraged husband, and the gravity of his crime was aggravated by his conduct in forcing his wife, under threat to her life, to help him get rid of the body, cover up his crime, and later make a false statement to the police about an innocent third party. And in so doing, he had also knowingly subjected me, Charles Brook, a respected member of society and the legal profession, to the ignominious and altogether intolerable ordeal of being wrongly arrested and charged with murder.

That, then, as I reflected on the flight home from Cornwall after the trial, closed the door on what Marion had called my Greenwood experience.

If I remembered correctly, it was Oscar Wilde who wrote, 'The truth is rarely pure – and never simple.' Geoffrey Greenwood was an illusion, yet his life and death had received universal acceptance, so much so that even I, his creator, had been impelled to come to terms with his reality in order to stay out of prison. And could anyone have been convicted of a more bizarre crime than Bill Cooper for the murder of someone who had never existed? And was it really true that I'd been able to amass a fortune in the name of an illusion and then been dispossessed of that fortune by a dastardly hijacking of the illusion?

It is because the truth is neither pure nor simple that the illusion so often prevails, as it did all the way through my Greenwood experience.

But in retrospect, I had enjoyed creating Geoffrey, and being his lawyer – and being Geoffrey himself, and living Geoffrey's kind of life and making wild, passionate love to Eleanor.

And thinking, yet again, of Eleanor, and of truth and illusion, I realized how deluded I'd been to deny to myself the truth of my love for her, and how much I'd been missing her and regretting my own foolish destruction of the wonderful bond I'd had with her. Could that still be retrieved, I wondered? And would she be willing to give it a try?

In the terminal at Gatwick, I took out my mobile and dialled the number of the gallery. Eleanor was there and took the call. She told me how pleased she was to hear from me and we agreed there was a lot we had to talk about and clear up.

My life was on again. But this time it would be entirely my own.